England Is My Village

and The World Owes Me A Living

Other Handheld Classics

Ernest Bramah, *What Might Have Been. The Story of a Social War* (1907)

D K Broster, *From the Abyss. Weird Fiction, 1907–1940*

John Buchan, *The Runagates Club* (1928)

John Buchan, *The Gap in the Curtain* (1932)

Melissa Edmundson (ed.), *Women's Weird. Strange Stories by Women, 1890–1940*

Melissa Edmundson (ed.), *Women's Weird 2. More Strange Stories by Women, 1891–1937*

Zelda Fitzgerald, *Save Me The Waltz* (1932)

Marjorie Grant, *Latchkey Ladies* (1921)

Inez Holden, *Blitz Writing. Night Shift & It Was Different At The Time* (1941 & 1943)

Inez Holden, *There's No Story There. Wartime Writing, 1944–1945*

Margaret Kennedy, *Where Stands A Wingèd Sentry* (1941)

Rose Macaulay, *Non-Combatants and Others. Writings Against War, 1916–1945*

Rose Macaulay, *Personal Pleasures. Essays on Enjoying Life* (1935)

Rose Macaulay, *Potterism. A Tragi-Farcical Tract* (1920)

Rose Macaulay, *What Not. A Prophetic Comedy* (1918)

James Machin (ed.) *British Weird. Selected Short Fiction, 1893–1937*

Vonda N McIntyre, *The Exile Waiting* (1975)

Elinor Mordaunt, *The Villa and The Vortex. Supernatural Stories, 1916–1924*

John Llewelyn Rhys, *The Flying Shadow* (1936)

Malcolm Saville, *Jane's Country Year* (1946)

Helen de Guerry Simpson, *The Outcast and The Rite. Stories of Landscape and Fear, 1925–1938*

Jane Oliver and Ann Stafford, *Business as Usual* (1933)

J Slauerhoff, *Adrift in the Middle Kingdom*, translated by David McKay (1934)

Amara Thornton and Katy Soar (eds), *Strange Relics. Stories of Archaeology and the Supernatural, 1895–1954*

Elizabeth von Arnim, *The Caravaners* (1909)

Sylvia Townsend Warner, *Kingdoms of Elfin* (1977)

Sylvia Townsend Warner, *Of Cats and Elfins. Short Tales and Fantasies* (1927–1976)

England Is My Village

and The World Owes Me A Living

by John Llewelyn Rhys

Handheld Press

Handheld Classic 30

The World Owes Me A Living was first published in 1939, and *England Is My Village* was first published in 1941.

This edition published in 2022 by Handheld Press
72 Warminster Road, Bath BA2 6RU, United Kingdom.
www.handheldpress.co.uk

ISBN 978-1-912766-66-6

1 2 3 4 5 6 7 8 9 0

Series design by Nadja Guggi and typeset in Adobe Caslon Pro and Open Sans.

Printed and bound in Great Britain by Short Run Press, Exeter.

MIX
Paper from
responsible sources
FSC® C014540

Contents

Acknowledgements   vi

Introduction, by Kate Macdonald and Luke Seaber   vii

Note on this edition   xxiv

England Is My Village

  1 England Is My Village   5

  2 The Man Who Was Dead   14

  3 Too Young To Live   21

  4 Return To Life   32

  5 Test Flight   39

  6 Night Exercise   49

  7 You've Got To Be Dumb To Be Happy   59

The World Owes Me A Living   67

Notes on the text, by Kate Macdonald   234

Acknowledgements

David Murdoch, the nephew and literary executor of Jane Oliver, has been a generous and enthusiastic supporter of the project to republish John Llewelyn Rhys's works, and was kind enough to supply information from his own researches into his aunt's life, and his memories of her conversations about her husband. Rees family members James Anderson and Jill Alexander MBE were supportive of the project to bring these novels back into print.

Kate Macdonald is a literary historian and a publisher. She is the author and editor of books on John Buchan and Rose Macaulay, and wrote the Introduction to the Handheld Press edition of *Business as Usual* by Jane Oliver and Ann Stafford, which indirectly led her to the writing of J L Rhys.

Luke Seaber is a Senior Teaching Fellow in Modern European Culture at University College London. He is the author and editor of various works on British literature in the nineteenth and twentieth centuries, including (edited with Michael McCluskey) *Aviation in the Literature and Culture of Interwar Britain* (2020).

Introduction

BY KATE MACDONALD AND LUKE SEABER

John Llewelyn Rees published two novels in his lifetime, both about the danger and poetry of flying in the 1930s. Their excellence shows that his early death was a great loss to the literature of British aviation. In obituaries and reviews his name was repeatedly linked with Antoine de Saint-Exupéry, the legendary French aviator and poet who was an older contemporary. Saint-Exupéry's third novel *Vol de nuit* (1931) had been available in English as *Night Flight* since 1932 and had been filmed in 1933. Yet few people were writing in English like Saint-Exupéry, who wrote about flight as a poet. Rees was working hard to follow Saint-Exupéry's example by lifting the literature of aviation into the realms of art.

Aviation writing in English in the 1930s could be found in newspaper columns, in *Boys' Own*-style adventures by Captain W E Johns, among others, and the terse accounts of long-distance record flights and endurance records written by professional pilots who were concerned with the facts, glossing over the drama of their extraordinary bravery. Aviation in this period was still an exciting novelty, but it was a solid one, a new industry as well as a developing military vehicle, and a new mode of transport that attracted many people, if only at a distance. Flight was also desperately romantic, if a little oily, and it was a profession for which women were as well fitted as men. Flying schools were becoming as common as golf clubs, and flying circuses were not uncommon in the summer months in holiday areas, run by ex-RFC and RAF pilots and their ground engineers from the war. These were the characters and settings for Rees's novels.

Rees was born in Abergavenny on 7 May 1911, the son of a Church of England vicar. He left Hereford Cathedral School in 1929 at the age of eighteen. From a note in an archive of family papers, we know that in the early 1930s he earned his living by writing short stories for English and American papers and magazines, and by driving his father around the parish as a chauffeur. His father tried to dissuade Rees from taking up flying and to concentrate on his writing, for which he had a clear gift, and also tried to steer him towards the ministry. But this, says the note, 'was not according to his inclinations and [Rees] said, "not his job"'. Rees gained his pilot's licence unusually quickly in July 1934 and joined the RAF as a Reservist in 1935. His first novel, *The Flying Shadow*, was published in 1936, under the pen-name J L Rhys; we will use this spelling of his name from here on.

In 1938 he wrote in a letter home, 'There's fog down to the ground today, giving pilots a welcome rest and myself a chance to write ... As you see I'm still up here flying night bombers. One reason for my not writing more often is that I'm slogging away at a book. With night flying every night, time is like gold' (Anderson 2015). His second novel, *The World Owes Me A Living*, about the life of pilots in a flying circus and on a record-breaking flight, was published in 1939 and did well: it was serialized in the *News Chronicle*, and the film rights were sold. It was reviewed in *The Times* as a depiction of 'an isolated and completely unfamiliar way of life' (J S 1939), suggesting that Rhys was clearly exploring new subjects in his fiction, bringing to life the glory and danger of flying in peacetime. But the approach of war intensified his work in the RAF and left him even less time to write.

On 5 August 1940 Rhys was killed in a flying accident, aged 29. Nothing is known about what caused the accident, but the Wellington bomber he was commanding stalled at 14.45 in the afternoon on a training flight at Harwell, north of London. As a flight lieutenant Rhys was the senior officer on board, presumably the flight instructor. He and the two pilot officers in the bomber were killed on impact (Chorley 1992, 24). He was buried by his father, the Reverend Nathaniel Rees, in his parish of Arthog, Llangelynin, in the west of Wales.

When he died John Rhys had been married for fifteenth months, to another pilot who was also an author. In the Preface to his third book, the posthumously published *England Is My Village* (1941) the novelist Jane Oliver describes how in autumn 1936 she had written in admiration to J L Rhys on reading *The Flying Shadow*, so completely had he captured her own experience of flying in his writing. They began to correspond, became friends, and on 25 March 1939 she and Rhys were married. In the Preface she writes movingly of their fifteen months of marriage in the shadow of war. After his death, it fell to her 'to complete the arrangements for this book, to carry out exactly the wishes he had already expressed ... I cannot feel despair that we had so little, but only amazement that we had so much' (Oliver 1941, 14, 15).

Jane Oliver, the pen-name of Helen Rees, née Evans, was an experienced novelist, and seven years older than her husband. Her first novel had been published in 1932, and her first success had been in 1933 with *Business as Usual*, which she had written with the friend and colleague who would become her close writing partner, Ann Stafford (Anne Pedlar). When John Rhys had published his second novel, his wife had published seventeen: she and Ann Stafford would publish at least 92 novels, together and singly, by 1970. When faced with the task of assembling her husband's last book for publication, Jane Oliver had the professional experience to know how to present his short stories to a publisher, armed with evidence of their quality from their earlier publication in magazines. It is likely that she decided on her own initiative to supplement the seven stories he had already selected with three extracts from Rhys's two novels. Without these additions *England Is My Village* – the title comes from one of the stories – would have been an extremely slim volume, probably too short for publication.

It was reviewed well. On the dustjacket of the first edition the *New Statesman* described it as 'Full of the fascination of the air ... an exceptional book'. The *Guardian* said 'his style has integrity and distinction, and in such stories as "Too Young To Live" he shows that he can treat successfully an emotional situation where the slightest mishandling would be disastrous' (E A M 1941). Phillip Jordan, the then features editor of the *News Chronicle*, who had serialized *The Flying Shadow* five years earlier 'because I so admired it', wrote to Rhys's widow that 'nothing is more difficult than to write about flying' and that Rhys 'and Antoine de Saint-Exupéry were the only two literate men who understood how to do it' (Jordan nd). The *New Yorker* said Rhys's writing was 'sensitive, intense, and touched with a poetic mysticism that may remind you of Saint-Exupéry' (Anon 1941).

In 1942, *England Is My Village* brought J L Rhys the posthumous award of the Hawthornden Prize, one of the two oldest literary prizes awarded in Britain. Previous winners of the Prize include Vita Sackville-West's *The Land*, Graham Greene's *The Power and the Glory*, Evelyn Waugh's *Edmund Campion*, Siegfried Sassoon's *Memoirs of a Fox-Hunting Man*, David Jones' *In Parenthesis* and Robert Graves' *I, Claudius*.

In 1942 Jane Oliver and Ann Stafford founded the John Llewelyn Rhys Prize, an annual literary award in Rhys's name, funded by Rhys's royalties as well as Jane's own.

> 'It is not generally known that the idea of founding this Award was Anne's and not mine,' continued Jane, referring to [...] when she and Anne had discussed how best to remember the life of Jane's late husband. 'I shall always be able to picture the exact spot on a Hampshire water meadow when Anne had the idea of founding this prize. I well remember how she suddenly said, "Let's have something for life, not death, something to give young writers the extra chance he didn't get".' (quoted in Anderson 2015)

The John Llewelyn Rhys Prize would be awarded for sixty-eight years. Winners awarded under Jane Oliver and Ann Stafford's leadership of the panel up to 1970 included Elizabeth Jane Howard, V S Naipaul, David Storey, Nell Dunn, Margaret Drabble, and Angela Carter. It only ceased, in 2011, when its funding ended.

As a collection *England Is My Village* is powerful, and the stories are classically simple in construction and narration. They carry the reader back to the late 1930s and early years of the Second World War with a compelling urgency. Above all, they bring to life a culture in which the exhortation 'Be Air-Minded!' was repeatedly given to the British public in the interwar years. Being air-minded was in fashion, but to *be* air-minded was to know about the world of aviation, of flights for pleasure, for war, for business; it was to interest oneself in technology, in celebrity aviators and aviatrices. It was to *fly*, whether this implied learning to pilot an aeroplane with an 'A' (private) or 'B' (commercial) licence; travelling for business or pleasure for a wealthy or fortunate minority; taking 'joyrides' in aeroplanes as one of the attractions of a fairground or other such event for a much greater number. At the very least, it was to take flight vicariously in films, adventure stories, pulp fiction, poetry, posters and paintings, and much more besides. Rarely has a technology that by its nature is not accessible for much of the population become of such cultural importance.

Yet as far as modern awareness goes, this cultural ubiquity did not extend to English literature. English-speaking aviation did not have a narrator like Antoine de Saint-Exupéry whose personal experiences as a pilot were transmuted into novels and other works. Beryl Markham's classic of aviation writing *West With the Night* (1942) was reviewed well on its first publication but sold only modestly. After the book went out of print, Markham was not rediscovered as an author until 1982. The same seems to have happened to Rhys. In 1939 the *Guardian*'s review of *The World Owes Me A Living* explicitly compared Rhys with the master: 'as a writer about flying he is good enough to be compared with Antoine de Saint-Exupéry' (E A M 1941). Rhys's books seemed to have had strong reviews, but his sudden and early death, and enforced wartime paper rationing, ensured that his works too went out of print very quickly. Copies of his books are now vanishingly rare.

The elusive transience of aviation is evident in the fiction of the period, but only as background. Flying creates the sky-writing in Virginia Woolf's *Mrs Dalloway* (1925), 'letting out white smoke from behind, which curled and twisted, actually writing something! making letters in the sky!' (Woolf 1992, 21–2). Lord Peter Wimsey flies back from New York in 1926 in Dorothy L Sayers's *Clouds of Witness* with crucial evidence to save his brother from the gallows. After Aunt Ada flies to Paris to get away from the woodshed, Flora Poste departs from Stella Gibbons's *Cold Comfort Farm* (1932) in a plane piloted by her cousin Charles. Aviation also transports lovers to Paris in Elizabeth Bowen's *To the North* (1933), and they wait by the 'sexagonal seat round the little pharos of clocks' in Croydon Airport (Bowen 2016, 133). This piece of furniture would have been vicariously familiar to thousands, or perhaps tens of thousands, across the British Empire at a time when Croydon connoted the international glamour of modernity. In Dorothy L Sayers's *Murder Must Advertise* (1933), she satirizes the unlikeliness of this fashion for flight with a scheme that encouraged the public to collect cigarette coupons and claim their own airplane and a course of flying lessons, with the inevitable result that quiet suburban areas become cluttered up with private planes that no-one can fly. Freeman Wills Crofts's *The 12.30 from Croydon* (1934) and Agatha Christie's *Death in the Clouds* (1935) have Golden Age murders taking place in the air, two more detective novels in which aviation is not exceptional, but simply another mode of transport. Rose Macaulay wrote her essay 'Flying' in *Personal Pleasures* (1935) as a delicious literary squib designed to entertain, taking for granted that her readers would be intrigued to learn what it was like being up there in the clouds, but also sure that many of them would never do this, and thus could never check the veracity of her descriptions. (It's not even certain that she ever flew herself: Macaulay was imaginatively persuasive.)

Yet, in all of these works those who participate in aviation are merely *passengers*. Their experience of flying is as non-experts for whom the aeroplane holds mysteries, to whom flight is a surrendering of oneself to the expert, to the pilot, to the 'helmeted airman' in W H Auden's poem 'Consider' (1930), a figure that reaches his nightmare apotheosis as the Air Vice-Marshall in Rex Warner's *The Aerodrome* (1941). What is missing is the description of 'the action, the clutter, the machinery, the terminology, the termini of travelling by air', as Valentine Cunningham summarizes it, by someone in the pilot's seat (Cunningham 1988, 167–8).

This is the importance of John Llewelyn Rhys, for he was above all a flier, a pilot. This is not to say that no other pilot in Britain in the interwar years wrote: that great mass of writing now mostly long forgotten does of course include other texts, consisting largely of factual narratives, accounts of new routes and speed records, autobiographies and memoirs. Two important examples show how exceptional Rhys is. Another writer with real expertise both theoretical and practical was C St John Sprigg (better known by the pseudonym that he adopted to write Marxist literary criticism before his death in the Spanish Civil War, Christopher Caudwell). He held a pilot's licence, worked in aviation publishing and was author of *'Let's Learn to Fly!'* (1937) as well as co-author of *Fly with Me: An Elementary Textbook on the Art of Piloting* (1932). He also wrote detective novels, and these two parts of his life combined in *Death of an Airman* (1934), in which the Bishop of Cootamundra solves a murder at the flying school at which he has enrolled. This is an entertaining whodunit, and full of much valuable information on what it was like to fly and learn to fly in those years, but it is not much more than a piece of entertainment to which flying is a backdrop, however unusually expertly drawn. Contrasting with Sprigg's expertise in flight but relative shallowness in literary terms is T H White, best known as the author of the classic fantasy novel *The Sword in the Stone* (1938). In 1936 he published *England Have My Bones*, a country diary of his experiences huntin', shootin' and fishin'

– and flyin'. A significant part of the book is taken up with White's reasonably successful attempt to learn to fly, and it contains some of the best *literary* depictions of flight from the period. But for all White's expertise in literature, he was an amateur pilot at best.

Rhys's combination of a deep knowledge of flying with a commitment to representing that world that he knew so well in literature makes him stand out. We can trace perhaps unexpected commonalities between his work and some of the other texts mentioned, commonalities that shed light on how *different* flying was in the 1930s, how much more an alien world it will be to an early twenty-first-century audience than it might at first appear. In the story that gives *England Is My Village* its title, Robert talks with the Squadron Leader about how he plans to spend his forthcoming leave:

> The leader of the raid looked up, then kicked his heel into the turf. 'Yes: hope this frost holds off. I hope to hunt next week.'
> It was a lot too clear, Robert thought. He hoped there was more cloud over there.
> 'You got some leave, sir?'
> 'Yes, I'm lucky. Six days.'
> 'I'll say you're lucky.' Not too much cloud, he thought, covering the target and only too likely to be full of ice this time of year.
> 'Have you been out with the local pack?' the older man went on. (7)

The strong connection between flying and fox-hunting (found in *England Have My Bones* too) is unexpected to a modern reader, but it is a common 1930s combination. We see it elsewhere in Rhys's work, best expressed perhaps in his first novel, *The Flying Shadow* (1936). Hunting is mentioned various times in that novel (as it is in *England Is My Village* and *The World Owes Me A Living*), but the key to the connection as it was consciously understood comes elsewhere in that book, when the protagonist is talking to a woman who is interested in taking flying lessons:

'You ride?'

'M'm.'

'Are you good?'

'Not bad. I drive a sports car, too, if that's any help.'

'It's not, really. Driving a car hasn't much to do with flying, in the same way that walking hasn't much to do with swimming. I asked about the riding because half the battle in piloting is having firm, sensitive hands.' (32)

We may wonder whether the true connection, so obvious in the 1930s and so invisible now, between hunting and flying is that both were country sports. That is, both were pastimes that needed the space of the countryside and the money to learn to ride or fly, and run a horse or an aeroplane. In other words, the true requirement is not sensitive hands but the social and economic status that allows one to use those hands on reins or a centre stick rather than on work.

But of course, flying may begin as pleasure and become a passion, but for many it may then become work. This is what *The World Owes Me A Living* shows. Doing what you love can lead to an existence that we might perhaps not describe as monotonous – the ever-present threat of death forestalls that – but in which the soaring freedom of flight is in ever sharper contrast with the mundane world of too much to drink, petty rivalries, frustration and financial and social precarity found on the ground. Rhys is very good at showing this world of gin and discomfort, showing the reality behind what the public see (his drinking scenes recall another great forgotten novel of the interwar years, Norah C James's 1929 *Sleeveless Errand*). The key word here is 'public'. The airmen, those figures mythologized by 1930s figures like Auden as helmeted technological demigods are portrayed by Rhys who knew their world intimately as what so often they primarily were: entertainers, and rather downmarket entertainers at that.

This too is an example of something that would have been more obvious to those who read Rhys's work when it was first published than it is to readers now. Flying is much more common now than it had been in the 1930s, when it was regarded as something more rare and exclusive, if we think of flying as something one does to *travel*. As *The World Owes Me A Living* makes very clear, in the 1930s flying for many – indeed, probably most – people – was not about travel. It was a form of entertainment; the joy-rides that Paul and the others spend so much of their working life doing, taking paying customers up for a spin around, giving them their first (and often only) taste of aviation, were extremely common in the period. We no longer think about flying as a form of fairground ride, but in Britain in the 1920s and 1930s it was not the cheapest form of an afternoon's entertainment, but was nonetheless within reach of many people, and certainly more accessible than business or leisure travel by aeroplane. Nevil Shute's 1954 memoir *Slide Rule* describes the air-minded culture of the 1920s and 1930s from the perspective of an aviation engineer trying to sell planes to flying clubs and flying circuses staffed by ex-RFC and RAF pilots.

This was how Evelyn Waugh first flew, in his last term at Oxford with an ex-RAF officer who turned up one day on Port Meadow; it was an experience like this that led to TH White deciding he wanted to fly; it was how W H Auden first flew too, in the summer of 1930 whilst accompanying a school Officer Training Corps camp. Besides such illustrious names, who in different ways contributed much to the air-minded literature of the 1930s, thousands upon thousands of people's true experience of flying was a 'spin'. Despite its worrying military background and exciting technological promise such a flight was not much more than the final incarnation of the Ferris wheel.

All of this background is present in Rhys's fiction but mixed in with it is darker material. The threat and reality of death is always there: sometimes only as ominous undercurrents; sometimes thrusting itself to the foreground. Rhys's fascinating descriptions of the characters' daily lives and his poetic descriptions of the act of flight should be read with this in mind: death is everywhere. It was the airman's most logical end. His short story 'England Is My Village' reminds us of a great piece of British cinema, the opening scenes of Powell and Pressburger's *A Matter of Life and Death* (1946), in which RAF pilot Peter Carter accepts death as his final destination. That acceptance is everywhere in Rhys's work, and on 5 August 1940 the end that he expected caught up with him, and one of the most promising writers of that low dishonest decade died in an RAF training accident.

The World Owes Me A Living was then his most recent novel. It is told in the first person by Paul, a skilled pilot and a good flight engineer, who is scraping a living in a flying circus with his close friend Chuck. Their old flying partner Jack arrives back in Paul's life, with a fiancée whose name makes Paul concentrate hard on not reacting. Eve is Paul's former lover, but Jack doesn't know this, and Eve does not want Paul to enlighten Jack. The novel unfolds with this secret at its heart: not a secret of passion, but of mutual distrust and dislike. The combination of tension in the flying and tension between characters makes this novel a white-knuckle read, with one enhancing the implications of the other. Rhys's management of both elements sets him well apart from writers who can only write people or only write action. He does both superbly well, and apparently instinctively, although we know from Jane Oliver's recollections and his own letters that he worked desperately hard on all aspects of his writing.

Rhys reveals the personalities of the characters by how they treat each other, flying in the shadow of death. These men and women are enthralled by the craft of flying, and with the achievement of managing their planes – boxes made of stiffened cloth and wood and metal strips – thousands of feet up in the air, without killing themselves or each other.

Rhys had written about a pilot's love affair before, set in a flying school in his first novel, *The Flying Shadow*, and his writing there displayed a perceptiveness about women's expectations of men, especially the more taciturn ones. As was standard for 1930s fiction and film, in *The World Owes Me A Living* Paul is world-weary and cynical, but his evident skill and bravery encourage the reader to give him permission to be superior. He is also scrupulously well-mannered, with his class position deriving from a vicar father and a public-school education. His voice and world-view are masculine by default: he singles out women from a crowd as if they do not belong to it.

It's hard to avoid conflating Paul's responses with Rhys's own temperament and personality. He had had less experience in life than his fictional creation but was the same age and from the same background. Rhys introduces women into Paul's narration one at a time, as a series of intrusions in his life. First they are mentioned in passing as part of the mass of stupid spectators. Then they are just girls to be used as advertising bait by being given joy-rides for free by the world-weary pilots in an effort to drum up interest in the flights. This is also a calculated loss-leader approach, enhanced by contemporary social expectations about the sexes: if a young woman takes a ride in a plane, any man she challenges afterwards to do the same risks losing social credit if he refuses.

Next to arrive in the narrative are golden-skinned women to be chatted to in the bar. Drinking at the bar is almost the only relaxation the pilots take, and one of the very few community spaces they can occupy as temporary summer visitors. The sheer volume of drink consumed throughout the novel is alarming, as is the flying and driving done immediately afterwards. This was noted in *The Times*: 'They are bold, loud, hard-drinking, arrogantly "hearty" young men, with a contempt for very nearly everything that is not among their extremely limited interests' (J S 1939). (The reviewer was a little unfair: Paul knows and can whistle his classical music.) In these pub settings the women are nameless and decorative, moving adornments or nuisances, depending on the men's expectations.

Then the first lone wolf appears, a nameless predatory woman in a white dress with whom Paul has an idle conversation while drinking. He accepts her sexualized presence, but he has no interest in forming a stronger connection, abandoning her to another man as soon as Jack appears, his friend and mentor trumping the temporary companionship of a woman. But Paul is to discover that Jack has reversed those values. He tells Paul that he is engaged to be married, which will mean a reorganization in how Jack apportions his time and attention.

This is a perfectly natural state of affairs, and Paul is pleased for his friend, until he learns who the lady is. The arrival of Paul's former lover as Jack's new love could bring about the classic dilemma of a triangular love story. But Paul has no feelings for Eve now except distrust. We learn more about her and their relationship as the novel unfolds, but from the outset Paul's standing in the reader's eyes encourages us to share his view of Eve's character. Eve cannot be sympathized with by a reader who is fully in sympathy with Paul's memories, and Rhys offers no alternative view to give her more than a two-dimensional portrait. Everything Eve does is calculated to throw a poor light on her character.

Paul may be a straight and decent man, but he is not particularly kind. Eve is first depicted in terms of her body and its shape and position. Paul describes seeing her with 'make-up bringing youth back into her face' (79). That harsh observation tells us that Paul prefers women to age naturally, and possibly also that an ageing woman has no place in his company. Her smile leaves 'her eyes unwrinkled' (80), meaning that Eve is superficial, not even skin-deep. She has 'hardness in her features' after she has admitted vulnerability about coming out of rehab (81): this is a real rejection of sympathy from Paul.

But Eve has power. She is the first character to call Paul by his name, to identify him to the reader. This also shows that she knows him well, a position of privilege. During their first meeting it becomes clear that Paul cannot withhold himself from the reader or hide his emotions any longer. It doesn't matter that he is wary of Eve and has no desire for her: it's quite clear that all that is dead. For the sake of his friend he will be studiously polite and neutral: he will not give Eve the satisfaction of showing even the slightest jealousy.

She clearly wants Paul to be jealous, because she interprets his objections to her forthcoming marriage to Jack in terms of Paul's supposed desire for her, but the reader can already see that Paul wants to protect Jack from what he knows about Eve. She is a strong portrait of a manipulative and egotistical character. Paul's resistance to her, and his full awareness of her ways, is his armour.

But Eve is also not allowed to show a more nuanced personality. She is depicted as possessive, and controlling in her reasons for not wanting Jack to fly on a longed-for record-breaking flight, whereas she could have shown her love and concern for him instead. The flight is obviously a very dangerous enterprise, and Eve could be shown to be worried about Jack's safety. Instead Rhys depicts her as wholly egotistical and duplicitous. She is relegated to the role of a bad-girl vamp against whose malevolent energy the pilots' sincerity and bravery and dedication shine all the brighter. She never had a chance to redeem her character, because she was drawn like that.

Paul's cynicism about women he doesn't care about is applied wholesale. Casey's girlfriend is 'a hard-faced blonde who had wept her artificial eyelashes away' (104). That detail, of the woman no longer caring anything for her appearance with weeping, gives her an important touch of humanity. Yet Paul takes even that away by calling her hard-faced and by noting that the lack of her false eyelashes (quite a heavy element of make-up for the period) was visible. This taking and giving away renders secondary characters unexpectedly vivid, because we see them as they are as well as finding out what Paul thinks of them. And he is severe about women whose purpose is limited.

The portrait of Moira Barratt, on the other hand, is all goodness and self-knowledge. She appears first as a ministering angel, and she allows Paul to flirt with her as light relief after the grimness of their hospital visits. She can make a connection with Paul's sincerity because he allows her to, and because she doesn't mess around with games and expectations. She is straightforward, and she has earned his trust by her compassion. Once she has made Paul admit that he wants something, in the first case to take her flying, she doesn't push any further, because she has made him speak the truth, and that is enough. She doesn't seem to be working for victory for its own sake, but her refusal to play mating games makes Paul understand that if he is to have any chance of a relationship with her, he has to drop his affectation of cynicism and behave as honestly to her as she will to him.

Paul's philosophical asides become longer throughout the novel as he responds to the unfamiliar and rather warily greeted sensation of being loved. At the same time Moira grows as a three-dimensional character, in her understanding of Paul's failings as well as of his bravery. His habitual secretiveness may well be natural to his character, but it might also be a closed-off self-protectiveness brought about by the damage caused by his experiences with Eve. Paul grows to care for Moira deeply, but he won't risk his protected core by allowing her in completely.

Theirs is an idealized relationship between equals, between two people who see each other's worth, but Paul has to be persuaded to abandon social bravado to prove his emotional courage. It's interesting that Rhys was able to make this point, that social and emotional courage are as important for masculinity as physical bravery. The interactions between many of the characters in *The World Owes Me A Living* depend on this bravery, or their lack of it. It's possible that as a married man Rhys had been able to reach these insights, whereas at the end of *The Flying Shadow*, his protagonist Robert remains trapped in masculine reticence, unable to tell his father what had happened that summer, and beginning a new job doing the same old thing, unchanged externally, and with unreadable private feelings.

Another point that may explain much of Paul's antipathy to women is that in *The World Owes Me A Living* women hold the financial power. Eve funds the flying circus; Moira funds the record flight attempt; and Mrs Waterman restricts the pilots' access to their market by making sure that they lose their flying field. Rhys writes the latter character as an authoritarian monster by showing that she controls the townspeople's use of their limited leisure time by ensuring that all places of enjoyment are closed on Sundays, in a holiday resort, and at a period when working people routinely worked on Saturday mornings. Was this a metaphor for the iniquity of women controlling men's lives? And why was Rhys indulging himself in such loathing with such concentration?

The last time Rhys's work was revived was in 1945, with the film of *The World Owes Me A Living*. Its screenplay was written by Irwin Reiner and Vernon Sewell, based on Rhys's novel. Jane Oliver's comments to a friend shortly after seeing the film are instructive for showing how the script compared with the novel:

> Of course it wasn't John's best book, and was written and unpicked, so to speak, several times before it finally reached the publishers. I remember so well sitting on the floor beside him with the carpet covered with manuscript and both our hair [sic] standing on end as we wrangled and blue-pencilled! I actually think the film beginning and ending are improvements, which must be a relatively unusual reaction for an author's wife to have! (Oliver 1945).

The film script added a new framing to the novel, setting up the protagonist Paul as a bomber pilot who had lost his memory, which held the details of important military plans. His friends and colleagues set to work to recall his past life as a barnstorming pilot on the joyride circuit, to try to bring his memory back.

It seems a pity that the novel Rhys had 'wrangled' over with his more experienced author wife had to undergo yet more alterations and additions, by other hands, before the public could be deemed to be satisfied. Eighty years later his novels are absorbing, gripping reads, narratives of powerful emotional tension in wholly believable settings with memorable characters delineated with striking economy. Having walked into their lives, we as readers are taken up into the air to see their secret selves and understand the passion for flight that overcomes the inferior passions of the earth. Or, in some cases, it does not. In short, Rhys wrote compellingly about the flying that was the centre of his life. To read his novels, and short stories, is to be plunged into his world. His novels are important reminders that even a short life could produce wonders.

Works referred to

James Anderson, MS of the John Llewellyn Rees memorial speech, 26 July 2015.

Anon, 'Briefly Noted: Fiction', *The New Yorker*, 21 June 1941, 79.

Elizabeth Bowen, *To the North* (1933) (Vintage 2016).

W R Chorley, *Royal Air Force Bomber Command Losses of the Second World War, Volume 1: 1939–1940* (Midland Counties 1992).

Valentine Cunningham, *British Writers of the Thirties* (Oxford University Press, 1988).

Philip Jordan, letter to Helen Rees (Jane Oliver), nd [1941–42], private collection.

E A M, 'Airman as Artist', *The Manchester Guardian*, 25 February 1941, 7.

Jane Oliver, 'Preface' in J L Rhys, *England Is My Village* (1941), 7–15.

—, letter to Mrs Mocatta, 8 January 1945.

J S, 'New Novels', *The Times*, 19 May 1939, 22.

Nevil Shute, *Slide Rule. Autobiography of an Engineer* (William Heinemann, 1954).

Virginia Woolf, *Mrs Dalloway* (1925) (Penguin 1992).

Note on this edition

The original 1941 edition of *England Is My Village* was assembled by the author's widow Helen Rees (the novelist Jane Oliver). After his death she wrote in her Preface to *England Is My Village* that it had been her task to 'complete the arrangements for this book, to carry out exactly the wishes he had already expressed'. The collection consisted of seven short stories, plus three short sections from the author's two earlier novels. These were the opening chapter of *The Flying Shadow* (1936), which was renamed 'Remembered on Waking', and part of Chapter 9 (renamed 'Ice') and the three last chapters (renamed 'Record Flight') from *The World Owes Me A Living* (1939). Those three sections of the novels have been omitted from this edition of *England Is My Village*, as both novels are now available again, one included in this volume.

The texts were non-destructively scanned from the first editions, digitized and then proofread. Obvious typographic and editorial errors have been silently corrected. Some words, such as 'any one', 'to-morrow' and 'some one', and a few others, have been contracted to follow modern style.

England Is My Village

by John Llewelyn Rhys
(Flight Lieutenant J L Rees, RAF)

For My Wife

In his loneliness and fixedness he yearneth towards the journeying Moon, and the stars that still sojourn, yet still move onward; and everywhere the blue sky belongs to them, and is their appointed rest and their native country and their own natural homes, which they enter unannounced, as lords that are certainly expected, and yet there is a silent joy at their arrival.

— Samuel Taylor Coleridge,
   The Rime of the Ancient Mariner

1 England Is My Village

When the old man came into the ante-room the young officers began to rise in their chairs but he waved them back with an impatient gesture. It was warm and comfortable in there and the tenor of idle chatter continued: one could hear the crackle of a newspaper page and the sound of bidding from the four who were playing a Chinese game in the corner, their minds apparently intent on the little walls of white blocks on the table before them.

Beneath the Wing Commander's arm were a number of files. On the outside of the files was a map. Robert recognized its shape and his heart kicked inside him. And now every pilot in the Squadron was watching the Senior Officer, watching him without movement of head, watching him while seeming to read, watching him while crying 'Three Characters'. The Old Man nodded, first at one, then another, and finally at Robert. Silently they rose to their feet, leaving their circle of friends, their reading, their Chinese game, and filed into the neighbouring room. When they had gone the lazy murmur of conversation continued, watchers filled the places at the game, another officer picked up the copy of *The Field* that Robert had been reading.

✳

The Wing Commander stood by the grand piano waiting for them to gather about him. It had been a guest-room before the war but now the fripperies had been removed and the tall windows were stark with gas-proof screens. He looked suddenly older, Robert thought. Now his hair shone with grey, new lines emphasized the hardness of his features. But his voice was unchanged, harsh, imperious.

'Gentlemen! The show's tomorrow.' He paused and looked slowly at the circle of pilots. 'The target you know. Here's the latest from Intelligence and a few other little details I want you to know.'

Robert heard his instructions and memorized them with an ease born of practice, but the words seemed meaningless, rattling like hail on the roof of his mind.

'Any questions?'

But they were all old hands and no naive youngsters among them wanted to make themselves heard.

'Well … good luck! I know you'll put up a good show,' his voice was suddenly shy, 'I wish they'd let me come with you.'

They went back to the ante-room, went on talking, reading, playing the Chinese game. Robert sat down by a friend. They had been together for years but were in different squadrons.

'If anything,' Robert's voice was quiet as he flipped the pages of a magazine, 'if anything were … to slip up … tomorrow, would you attend to the odd detail?'

'Of course, old boy.' The other puffed his pipe alight, swung the match till it was extinguished.

'Tomorrow?'

'Yes.'

'Tough show?'

'Tough enough.'

✖

It was almost day as Robert walked over to Flights with the Squadron Leader, and cold with the half light lying dead on the roofs of the camouflaged hangars and the wind-sock flapping drearily on its pole. The erks were beginning to start up the motors, which clattered protestingly to life, back-firing and juddering on their bearers.

'Looks like a good day, sir?

The leader of the raid looked up, then kicked his heel into the turf. 'Yes: hope this frost holds off. I hope to hunt next week.' It was a lot too clear, Robert thought. He hoped there was more cloud over there.

'You got some leave, sir?'

'Yes, I'm lucky. Six days.'

'I'll say you're lucky.' Not too much cloud, he thought, covering the target and only too likely to be full of ice this time of year.

'Have you been out with the local pack?' the older man went on.

'No, I can't get anyone to mount me.' He wondered if they'd have any of the new twin fighters waiting for them. They hadn't been seen yet, and were supposed to be very fast and to carry cannons.

'That *is* the trouble,' said the Squadron Leader. When Robert got to his machine only the starboard engine had been started. Impatiently he watched the efforts of the crew. If only they'd get that engine running, he thought, if only they'd get it running. If only they'd get it running. He went up to the fitter.

'You haven't over-doped?'

'No, sir. She'll go now.'

Still she refused to start. He climbed up the ladder into the cockpit.

'Got your throttle setting right?'

'Yes, sir,' said the Corporal, 'she'll start in a minute.'

The Second Pilot was inside, busy at the navigator's table.

'All set?' Robert asked.

'Bombs, petrol and everything hunkey dorey, sir,' the Sergeant answered.

If only they'd start that engine, he thought, if only they'd get it going and we could take off.

At last the motor roared to life and he climbed into his seat, ran up the engines, pulled up the ladder and waved away the chocks.

As he waited on the aerodrome, his airscrews throwing long flickering shadows, he kicked the heavy rudder violently from side to side. Where were the others? Where were the others? They would be late off the ground and there'd be a row. Then he glanced at his watch and found to his surprise that it was five minutes to zero hour. Behind him the wireless operator was hidden by his tall set and the gunners were amidships waiting to take up their positions once the machine was airborne. The Second Pilot leaned over the navigating table, setting his maps and charts and instruments.

And now the other machines were taxi-ing towards him, huge heavily laden monoplanes, grim against the dawn, moving fast over the close-cut turf, beating down clean thick lines through the white frost. He glanced down at the controls, felt the various cocks, checked the cylinder-head temperatures, the hydraulic and brake pressures. Then, when all was ready, he pushed open the throttles, the noise increasing till it filled the long narrow compartment, beating mercilessly upon his ears, drowning the scream of the hydraulic gear.

She was heavy with full petrol and a belly full of bombs, but as he felt her becoming airborne he brought the wheel gently back and she bumped up into the air.

They flew in tight formation and far below patches of fog lay pressed into the valleys. The sun threw skinny shadows, exaggerating the place of the leafless trees in the landscape, and blue smoke rose in stiff columns from farm chimneys, a bitter blue against the slight haze. Looking down at this scene of unreal cleanness Robert found it hard to believe it was War. This is an exercise, he thought, Redland against Blueland, and we shall meet the 'enemy' fighter pilots in Mess to-night and have a terrific party.

As they approached the coast he noticed a familiar seaside town to the north. It was lifeless now, the blatant lettering on every house and shop and hoarding screaming to empty streets, to deserted beaches and amusement parks: it was garish in the clear early light, like the face of a prostitute as she slips out in the morning to buy food.

The sea was calm, edged with white froth. The calm was a good thing, he thought, for the rubber dinghy they carried in the wing was not designed to weather a gale.

Always before, the coast had been the meeting-place of land and sea, a convenient opportunity for obtaining a navigational 'fix' or position. But now, as he glanced at the little boats askew on the beaches like burnt matches on a bar floor, he thought, 'This is the edge of England.' Then he looked ahead at the hard cold grey of the North Sea and edged a little closer to the Squadron Leader's aircraft.

From time to time Robert switched on his microphone and spoke to each gunner in his turret. They were alert and cheerful and behind him the Second Pilot worked at his check navigation, taking sights, drifts, bearings, his face expressionless, his movements slow and sure so that he might have been in a classroom.

Sometimes they saw fishing-boats whose crews waved frantically, and tiny minesweepers busy at their deadly task and once a convoy with destroyers like sheepdogs on its flanks. The weather was fine, with high lumps of cumulus, and they began to climb.

In a little while the Second Pilot came forward and held up eight fingers. Robert nodded. Eight minutes. He felt cold inside his guts, his teeth were chattering, he wished they were in the thick of it, and grinned at his companion. The target came into view, a smudge on the horizon. The Leader began to give his orders over the radio and they started a big circle so as to attack from out of the sun. As they came up the sky filled with anti-aircraft fire. The Second Pilot had switched on his microphone and Robert could hear him jeering at the enemy gunners, for the shooting was poor, though some of the bursts were uncomfortably close.

They came over the target and released their bombs. Robert watched the sky unceasingly for enemy fighters, turning a little and holding up his thumb against the sun, squinting round the edge of the glove, wondering if any aircraft were lurking in its glare waiting for the anti-aircraft to cease before diving to the attack.

The Second Pilot was busy with the camera recording the hits far below, whistling as he worked. A burst of Archie off the port wing-tip made the machine rock violently. The Second Pilot kept absolutely motionless for a few seconds. Robert looked out along the wing where little strips of fabric were fluttering back from the leading edge but the machine still flew perfectly and he moved the wheel gingerly, grinning as the ailerons responded. The Second Pilot turned slowly back to his task.

Soon they were out of range of the ground guns and Robert saw one of the other machines break formation and rock its wings. He spoke to the gunners.

'Keep your eyes skinned. There's a fighter about somewhere.' Then he saw it, a lone enemy machine, a single-seat fighter with square wing-tips. It came up quite slowly, lazily, flying on to the tail of one of the bombers. It was so simple a manoeuvre that it might have been a pupil on his circuit at a flying training-school. As it turned off, short jabs of black smoke jerked themselves from the back cockpit of the bomber. The fighter turned slowly on to its side. First smoke, then flames, poured from its engine, splashing down the fuselage. In the bright sunshine, against the blue sea, the flames were orange, and the machine fell slowly, twisting, turning, diving.

'Here they come!' said the Second Pilot, and Robert saw that the sky seemed to be filled with fighters. They broke up and began to attack. Robert watched two circling him from the front. As they turned the flank his rear gunner switched on his microphone and Robert could hear him swearing. He used one obscene word after another. They were meaningless, uttered without expression, repeated over and over again like the rhyme of a child. Tracer from the enemy streamed overhead, curved in graceful trajectory and dropped out of sight. Then the gunner was silent. Robert heard the rattle of his guns and his voice, jubilant.

'Got him, sir.'

'Good. Keep your eyes skinned.'

The middle gunner reported a machine. 'But he's yellow, sir. Keeps out of range.'

'Be patient,' Robert said.

Now a twin-engined aircraft came up on the beam, accompanied by one of the smaller fighters, which attacked from the rear. A burst of fire shattered the roof over the Second Pilot's head. The front gunner coolly brought his guns to bear. The twin was an ugly brute, the first Robert had seen with extended stabilizers on the tail. He was frightened now, his mouth dry, his hands wet inside the silk lining of his gloves.

The gunners reported unceasingly. They were flying at full throttle and Robert looked despairingly ahead for cloud, but the nearest cumulus was miles away. Attack after attack came up, filled the air with tracer, turned lazily away. The middle gunner brought down another fighter before he was hit in the leg. Robert sent the Second Pilot back in his place.

One burst of machine-gun-fire shattered half the instrument panel, sent a shower of broken glass over his knees. Darkness filled his eyes, but in his mind he could still see the face of the enemy gunner, red and foolishly grim as he fired from the rear cockpit of the fighter. The wheel went limp in his hands, the strain of months of war, the nag of responsibility, lifted from his consciousness. This is good, he thought, this is good. To relax, to relax, to relax.

Then his vision cleared and he pulled the aircraft level. To his surprise the fighters had vanished and at his side was the Squadron Leader's machine, which he thought he had seen go down.

The enemy must have run out of ammunition. He began to sing, thumping his hands on the wheel.

✳

They were separated from the others and flew in tight formation, the Squadron Leader turning his head from time to time and grinning and doing a thumbs up. They lost height till they were just above the sea, their patterned shadows sliding effortlessly over mile after mile of watery desolation. On crossing the coast the Senior Officer altered course for base. They flew at a few hundred feet over the sleepy countryside, their shadows now vaulting hedge and haystack, silently, climbing ridge and col, dropping easily into shallow valleys.

The sun was still high in the sky and the country had never been more lovely. Not pretty, Robert thought, in the frills of summer, but beautiful in the starkness of winter. As he looked, first to the north at the black rich earth of the fens, marshalled by dykes, then south to the flatness of Suffolk, woolly with leaf-stripped trees, each feature of the country fitted into its place in his mind, each town he knew, hazy and grey with the mist of a winter's afternoon, each stretch of river, pregnant now with flood, each change of character from county to county. How familiar, he thought. How well I know it all. Truly, England is my village.

✳

Soon the little lake shaped like an elephant's trunk appeared and they dived low over the hangars, then broke away, dropped their wheels and came in to land. There were no other machines about and the camp seemed strangely deserted.

A little later they walked into the Mess. It was warm and comfortable in there and the words and phrases of the many conversations jumbled themselves into a haze of sound. At the table by the fire there was an empty chair at the Chinese game. When Robert saw the other players he stopped in his stride. There was Nails, who got his on the first show, and Dick, who went down in flames, and Thistle his second pilot, and Badger, who was lost in the North Sea in December.

'Come on!' Badger said. "We're waiting for you.'

'But I thought …' Robert said. 'I thought …'

Badger was smiling.

2 The Man who was Dead

Although I was only a child at the time, the memory of him in the picturesque uniform of the Royal Flying Corps has never faded in my mind. My father was the parson and the Vicarage bounded on the Manor, so that we children all played together; games of Indians and Trappers and Explorers and Hunters, playing with that grimness and aggressive self-assertion of childhood that we like to forget when we grow older and become adult in body.

Ray was the eldest of the Squire's scatterbrained family and he used to roar with refreshing unexpectedness into our little world. Sometimes he was in a frail contrivance of silver, brave with Royal Flying Corps markings, that dipped and circled the chimneys, the regular stutter of its motor bringing the villagers out of their cottages, for it was not often that one saw an aircraft in 1917, frightening the stock on the village green, stampeding us children out of nursery or shrubbery into a silent worshipping group on one of the lawns.

At other times he appeared in a stripped racing-car, more than ever a god to us, with jauntily set forage-cap, ragged, oil-stained flying coat over the trim 'maternity jacket' they wore in those days, his fingers yellow with tobacco smoke. (And now, if someone mentions his name, the picture comes swiftly to my mind, the tiny fair moustache, the pink cheeks and curly hair, the regular features still characterless, the speech the platitudes of a schoolboy, clothed in a charming stammer.)

He spoilt us all, remembering our names and fancies, bought us the outrageously expensive sweets and toys and poorly printed books of the time, unashamedly enjoying our excitement. A little while after this he went to France to one of the famous Fighter Squadrons, shooting down several of the enemy before he himself was brought down in flames to spend the rest of the war in hospital.

When he returned they made a fuss of him in the village. There was a reception, I remember, at the parish hall, with a tea thrown in, and my father and the doctor made speeches while he stood, supported by two sticks, on the stage. He made the conventional speech, but his smile had no kindliness in it, his tones were bored and that evening I heard Cook telling my nurse that the Squire's son was drinking 'something awful'. Afterwards I went away to be very unhappy at a public school, and in the holidays when I played with Ray's brothers I understood, from a dropped remark, a sidelong glance, a half-finished sentence, a frown from an elder sister, that there were money troubles and that Ray, who had failed in a garage venture, refused to work, but claimed to be 'looking after the estate' and was running up debts in neighbouring towns and drinking more heavily than ever. He had become such a black sheep that his family were almost proud of him.

Sometimes my father, or a relation, would ask me what I wanted to do in life, and I would always answer without hesitation, 'become an airman'. Then my father would smile and tell me a story of a country boy who went to sea, his imagination fired by a picture at home of a beautiful sailing-ship on a tropic, placid sea. But I used to laugh, being sure with the untried confidence of youth, and felt sorry for my father, who, I felt, knew so little. And as I laughed I thought of a little fighter 'plane, starred with bullet-holes, the tattered fabric fluttering in little streams from the wings as I dived and rolled and looped, seeing my face, framed by a flying helmet and topped by Meyrowitz goggles, mirrored in the air-speed indicator, the earth tilting and swinging below, hearing the cry of the wind in the wires, feeling the slipstream leaning on my face. For I met Ray from time to time and our talk was always of flying.

At first he would be loath to speak, muttering that this shop would bore me, but as I insisted he would begin to talk of the old days, of training in the Flying Corps in England and flying with the legendary heroes in France. And then he would forget himself and there would be light in his eyes again and the words would tumble one on the next as they had used to do, his drawl a thing for- gotten.

⁂

It was dusk as we came back from the raid. We had fought off a series of attacks by enemy fighters and one of my flight had gone down. I felt bad about it in an abstract fashion, for war drives home the place of chance in life, and against my judgement I found myself sentimentalizing about the captain, who was an old friend of mine. I was seeking in my mind for the subject we had been chatting about as we went up to Flights from the operations room that morning, trying to remember what he last did in my presence that I, with the kindness of sentiment, might clothe his last actions in dignity, endow his last speech with wisdom.

The navigator came forward with a map in his hand and peered down into the grey evening. The other member of my show rode at my wing-tip, a big black shape, sinister in the half light, rising and falling as he hit the bumps, but never losing close formation, his red navigation light like an evil eye in the approaching night. Little tongues of flame licked out of his exhaust stubs. I was tired, my clothes were damp with sweat under my Irvin and I could smell the cordite from the gun-turrets that still lingered in the machine. The rotten taste of oxygen was in my mouth.

Soon the navigator put up his thumb and pointed. The aerodrome was on the port bow. I altered course. Switching on my microphone I spoke to the crew. The wireless operator wound in his aerial, the gunners came out of their turrets. One of them was holding his arm, which was bound with bloodstained emergency dressing. When I glanced anxiously at him he grinned and put up his thumb. I would have liked to have shot up the camp, but we had a few holes that might be in stressed parts, so we flew low over the Mess and the groups of troops and workmen and Mess waiters and officers who were awaiting our return, dropped our wheels and flaps and landed.

It was some time before I left the operations room and walked slowly to the Mess with the pilot who had flown by my side for eight hours. He was a young Canadian and excitement and relief had quickened his slow Alberta speech. As we entered the foyer I could hear the sound of a party in the ante-room.

'That'll be the concert bunch,' my companion said. 'It's Thursday. They've been giving the troops a show.'

'Of course," I said. 'It's Thursday.'

For out there is neither day nor night, nor winter nor summer, only light and darkness, heat and cold. One is either alive or dead, filled with hope or despair. One is laughing or crying. Now I was back in the real world of God and right and wrong and patriotism and money.

'Of course,' I said, 'it's Thursday.'

We went in and I sat down in a corner. There was a terrific row going on. The male entertainers wore unbuttoned, double-breasted dinner-jackets, which displayed, usually, a gaudy pullover. The girls had too much make-up on and looked tired and in need of a rest and a good meal. Everyone was making a great deal of noise in their determination to be cheerful. All the guests were drinking Pimms and singing and whistling through their teeth.

Then somebody saw us and in an instant the party was forgotten and we were surrounded. What had happened? Did we get there? What damage did we do? What happened to Jimmy? Was the anti-aircraft bad? Were there many fighters up?'

'We got there,' I said.

'Any luck?'

'Yes. As far as I could see we blew the place to hell.'

'Anti-aircraft?'

'Not bad,' the young Canadian said. "Made the air a bit bumpy at times!'

'And fighters?'

'Not so hot,' I said. 'But one of them got a lucky shot in.'

'Jimmy?'

'Yes.'

'What happened?' The voices were quiet now, almost casual.

'He was flying in tight formation with us for about a minute, with flames coming out of his turrets. Then he went slap into the drink.'

'Anybody get out?'

'No,' I said.

'That's tough. Young Smith was his second dicky, wasn't he?'

'Yes,' I said. I looked round the ante-room. One always found it hard to believe that one had been hundreds of miles over the sea, into an enemy country, fought a battle and returned. One had a feeling of leaving the Mess and then coming back into it again. It was the real and the unreal. 'It's tough,' I said.

'It's tough,' echoed in my mind. It just meant he was dead and wouldn't come into Mess any more. It just meant you lied and told his Missus you thought he was a prisoner of war.

Through it all the familiar ring: *'It can't be so hard … It can't be so hard'*. Suddenly someone began to play the piano, the singing and whistling began again, a drink was pushed into my hand.

I talked to a blonde for a while. Underneath the make-up that deadened her features she had an interesting, intelligent face; but as she spoke she watched one of her companions, a seedy youngster who was tipsy and playing the piano very badly.

In a far corner was a new-comer to the Mess. He was one of the older officers who were taking over the ground jobs, held a very junior rank but had wings above his Pip, Squeak and Wilfred. I watched him for some time before I realized it was Ray, an older, fatter Ray. His neck was very red and bulged over his collar. His eyes were glassy. I waved to him and he came quickly to my side. When we had talked a little he looked shyly at my stripes.

'I suppose I ought to call you "Sir"?'

'Don't be an idiot,' I said.

The drunken pianist began to play a song about hanging washing on the Siegfried Line. A sudden silence fell upon the crowded room, for songs like these are not popular among men who fight. The boy at the piano, oblivious of the faint disapproval about him, played on and on, lifting his hands high above the keys, sometimes striking a wrong note, happy as the central figure in a world of his own imagining.

'You've been on a show to-day?' Ray asked.

'Yes,' I said.

'Hear you lost a machine?'

'Yes,' I said.

He drained his beer at a gulp. 'It's good to be back.'

'Have a drink?'

'Thanks, I will.'

The waiter grinned as I ordered and said he was glad to see

me back. I asked Ray about his people. They were all well, he said. The blonde girl went over to the piano and took the boy away. She began to play herself, some classical stuff. It had a kick in it and she played it well, sitting stiffly, one shoulder a little higher than the other.

'I had a look at one of your machines to-day,' Ray said. 'They're very complicated, aren't they?'

'Not really, just a mass of gadgets you soon get used to.'

'I suppose you're right.' He drank deeply, then looked up at me with eyebrows raised. 'It's a lot different, you know, from my day.'

'I suppose it is.'

'There isn't ... well, it's just different.'

'Yes,' I said.

The Wing Commander came in and talked to me for a while. I introduced him to Ray. Ray began to talk. He called the senior officer 'sir' too often. Kept on referring to the '14–'18 campaign. Then the Old Man drifted away. I took Ray round and introduced him to the Squadron. 'Nice lot of lads,' he'd say as we walked from one group to another. 'Nice lot of lads. We still have the stuff.'

As I stood by the piano roaring out the old songs, I watched him drifting from group to group, talking a little too much, laughing a little too loudly, a little too insistent in his self-deprecation, bragging, exaggerating, so delighted with himself that he had no hesitation in butting into any conversation, so eager to buy a round.

At last, when he had been politely elbowed out of every little clique, he went over to a group of the entertainers and I watched him as he stood in a circle of them. He had bought a round of Pimms and they were all listening eagerly to what he had to say.

3 Too Young to Live

It was some time before the youngster with the broken back realized that he was going to die.

He was placed in the bed next to mine and at first they used to pump him full of dope so that he lay lifeless, body caged in nineteen pounds of plaster, mind smothered with narcotics. We saw but little of him, only a glimpse of a stiff body, even beneath the sheets, and a white face topped with black hair, seen when they moved the screens; or heard a groan or murmur or half-stifled sob in the long bleak night. Truth to tell, I rather think we resented his arrival with something of that umbrage which railway passengers adopt when a late traveller invades their carriage, as if our being together for a little while had given us a peculiar fellowship we were loath to lose.

This was accentuated by the attention he needed, for the ward orderlies watched him constantly, a . Sister looked in every few minutes and Senior Medical officers were often at his bedside.

The mild Spring weather was vile that year, incessant rain beating on the tall ugly windows and low broken cloud drifting swiftly a few hundred feet above. Only occasionally did it clear and the shy sunshine fell in patches on the panorama that stretched out to Oxfordshire, pale and green and lovely with the new crops breaking through the warm earth.

The nights were worse than the days, for in the quiet darkness the huge hospital seemed like a gagged beast and I would lie awake and think of all the mute suffering around me, and steel myself not to look at my watch, and listen to the faraway sound of the rain, and be afraid to die, and wonder how much night flying the boys were doing and whether I should ever fly again.

When Night Sister tiptoed away from the youngster I would sometimes call softly to her and she would come swiftly to my bedside and look sternly at me and ask me why I wasn't asleep, and I would grin and plead for more 'knock-out shot', as we called sleeping draught. But she would smile and switch off my shaded lamp, put away my book, smooth my pillow and tell me to lie quietly and wait for sleep to come. She was graceful and quick, with pain-knowing hands, moving with swish of starched apron, cool and certain in her actions, womanly sympathy ousted by the ability to lessen suffering, an automaton produced by perfect training and experience.

Occasionally, when the dim light of the night bulbs fell kindly on her features, I would catch a glimpse of lost beauty far beyond youthfulness that was shining through the passing of the years and would hold my breath at the thought of it, thinking of her as a girl, mischievous as laughter bubbled on her mouth, forgetting that she was now close-hauled to forty and unpopular with the others, who called her 'the old geyser' and alleged that the decoration ribbon she wore belonged to a Zulu war medal.

Martin was one of the worst offenders in this respect. He too was my neighbour and also suffered from insomnia. We used to smoke a lot in the nights and the tips of our cigarettes would make steady rhythmic arcs in the darkness. He had been brought down by Wogs on the North-West Frontier and was a long time recovering from his injuries. Women, and particularly Night Sister, infuriated him and the orderlies who served under her earned his contempt for obeying her orders. Sometimes we talked quietly, but usually lay silent, for he said but little, living every moment as he came to it, as a good pilot should, remembering little of what had passed, having no dread of the future. His passion was for news, and when the little old newspaperman came round each morning he would buy half a dozen papers, fold them carefully and read each one from cover to cover, an operation which took him most of the day. Yet he would remember little of what he had read and his contributions to heated arguments were conventional to ludicrousness.

The little old newspaperman, whose coming was the brightest event in the morning and who cashed our cheques and ran our errands, made the same joke each morning. 'Better orf in 'ere, gents,' he would say as he shuffled down the ward. 'Better orf in 'ere than outside this weather, gents, you believe me!' But when the youngster had been in a day or two the old man must have realized something of what lay behind those screens, for he joked no more but passed quickly from bed to bed, clinking the shining cylinder of pennies he held in his left hand; a little twisted figure to whom age had brought no dignity, eager to run at the whim of any supercilious whelp with a penny to spend, a man to whom life had brought no more than degradation of caste.

※

After three days the youngster drifted back to life, and when the Medical Officer came round I heard him speak, asking the doctor how bad he was and how long it would take for him to be well and when he would be able to fly again. I was frightened by the elder man's reply as he raised his eyebrows to the Senior Sister, for in those mechanical tones that carried so easily the assurance of early recovery and the explanation of partial paralysis being due to shock, there was, it seemed to me, a hideousness of false hope, a cruelty of misrepresentation that surpassed even the tragedy itself.

Then he asked that the screens should be taken away, and when the doctor had gone one of the orderlies, Hopkins, the good-looking lad who knew all the latest smut and backed horses for us, came and took them away. We watched with interest, Martin and I and the kid who had flown into a hillside, and the Canadian who hit a tree night flying, and the two appendicitis cases, and the Squadron Leader who had broken his arm during a Guest Night. This was something new, an object of interest in our measured day. The other milestones we knew, the early tea, chilled and half in saucer, the washing of patients, the bed making, the floor polishing, the visit of the newspaperman, the flowers brought in, the eagerly awaited meal-times. This was different, an unexpected tit-bit.

He lay very still for a while, blinking in the sunshine, seemingly oblivious of the interest of nine patients. Then in a little while he twisted his head and looked at me. I grinned.

'Good morning,' I said.

'Good morning, sir.'

'You don't call me "Sir" ... How d'you feel, anyhow?'

'I'm ... much better ... thanks.'

'You've come on well ...' I said.

'Yes ... I felt pretty grim at first.'

'You'll soon be all right again now. ...'

'Yes ... I'll soon be ... all right again ... now.'

I had a little mirror mounted on the radiator at my bedside so that I could watch the reflection of aeroplanes passing overhead. Often I would look up from my book and catch a glimpse of aircraft (how easy and simple it seemed and how difficult to imagine the rain prickling one's face and the machines rising and falling on either side as they hit the bumps and one's map sodden on one's knee and low clouds ahead fringed with angry rain). And I would follow the flight unheeding, my mind still busy with my book so that the passage of the machine would be incorporated in some part of it, woven in its essential fabric as a scene sometimes interpolates itself into a conversation, bits of countryside linking themselves illogically to the sequence of the words.

As I idly watched a big bomber moving with stately indifference through the base of the clouds, sometimes growing grey and misty, occasionally disappearing altogether, I heard the youngster's voice.

'Is that a Moose, sir?'

'Yes,' I said, 'it's a Moose.'

'Have you flown them?'

I nodded.

'They must be grand to fly!'

'They're all right,' I said.

'I suppose you've flown a lot of types?'

'Well … I've flown one or two.'

'It must be wonderful … to have flown lots … I mean … and to have done hundreds and hundreds of hours.'

'You get used to it,' I said. 'How much have you done?'

'Seven hours dual and twenty-five minutes solo … it was on my second solo that … it happened.'

'That was hard cheese.'

'Yes, it does … set one back a bit. All the others will leave me far behind now.'

'You'll be fine in a few weeks,' I said, 'and you get the same seniority anyway.'

'It's the flying I want.'

Then I saw it. Flying to him was an adventure. He belonged to the golden age of the Royal Flying Corps, when aviation was the marvel of mankind and the country was fighting for its life, when every flight was an epic, when every pilot flew in the shadow of death, when the silly breath-taking confidence of youth was in its own, when a pair of wings on one's chest meant that one was more than a pain in the neck to a motor insurance company.

When Night Sister came on duty that evening he was writhing in pain and she shot him full of morphia, holding his hand till the drug crept up like a tide and submerged his pain. He smiled up at her, his face stupid with drowsiness.

'Sorry … to make a fuss. Bless you, Sister … bless you … Sister.'

She leaned over him, put his arm beneath the sheets.

'Now you must go to sleep.'

He answered so softly that only I could hear.

'Sister!' his voice was thick with sleep.

'What is it?'

'Sister! what's your name?'

She told him her surname.

'No, not that. That's … what the others call you … what's your real name ?'

'Now you mustn't be silly … you must go to sleep.'

'What's your real name?' He was like a child with its nurse.

'You must go to sleep.' Her voice was quiet, as I'd never heard it before.

'You've been so sweet, Sister … tell me your real name?' She whispered so that I couldn't hear.

'Good night, Catherine,' he said.

The following morning, listening to our conversation, he seemed a little better, more alive. We talked shop, as usual, of men we knew, machines we had flown, stations in which we'd served. We spoke of crashes and tight corners and hair-raising experiences, bragging by understatement, as the English do. He heard, with eyes shining, the famous Service stories of the fitter who took off to Virginia, the pupil who, following a car to Grantham, spun a Snipe into the ground as he waited for the driver at a cross-roads, of the pilots who have flown beneath the Kenkham bridge, and of the deeds of Batchy Lampgroves and other well- known characters. He listened while we compared an Atlas with a Hart, a Gauntlet with a Super Fury, a Spitfire with a Hurricane, adding no word to our conversation, being content to lie speechless.

That afternoon he began to talk to me again, telling me about his people, who were in India, and how they hated him flying and how his mother had prophesied that his career as a pilot would end in disaster.

'She was … sort of fatalistic … about it. But she was wrong. I had a pretty good smack, but not as fatal as she thought.' It seemed they had a place in England, a house in Suffolk, in the lovely wooded country on the Norfolk border. There was a lot of game there and he wanted me to promise to come up for some shooting. It seemed they thatched with reed rather than wheat straw. 'The riding's grand, too; you could have Magpie, and there's bags of hunting and we'd go into market on Wednesday and drink with the farmers and be all friendly with the pubs open all day … you'd love it.'

'I'll come,' I said.

He sighed. 'I like it more than any place in the world.'

'It's grand country,' I said.

'You know it?'

'I've flown over it a lot.' As I spoke I could have kicked myself.

'Of course … you've flown over it.' He was quiet for a little while. Then he said: 'I've never seen it from the air myself … I always meant to go, but I never got the chance. My instructor wouldn't go very far from the aerodrome.'

He could remember every minute of his time in the air, every manoeuvre he had been taught, every mistake he had made, every correction, every rebuke, caution or scrap of praise. He never tired of discussing his experiences, little everyday events for the most part that to him had been adventures, glimpses of a new and promised land. As I listened I was amazed, not that he should seem so naive, but that all I had once felt should now be strange to me, so much enthusiasm be forgotten.

When Night Sister came on duty she went first to the youngster, remarking on the primroses that had just been taken out of the ward.

'They were nice,' he said.

'Yes,' she answered, 'they remind me of home.'

'Where's your home, Sister?'

The orderlies brought the screens around his bed and she began to do his dressing, talking quietly, but with unusual fluency, so that the others laid aside their books and headphones to listen.

'It's a long way from here. In a little village in North Wales. My father's the parson there. It's rather grim till you really know it. A grey village in a valley where the sun hardly shines for eight weeks in the winter. It's got tall, hideous chapels and a village shop that sells everything. The hills are all cut with quarries and the houses look very drab with fences of waste slate. But now there are primroses everywhere; it makes it the loveliest time of the year.'

When she went out, Martin rolled over towards me.

'I didn't know the old girl was so sentimental, did you?'

'I don't know that she was being particularly sentimental,' I said.

'Don't tell me you're getting that way, too!'

'You know me," I said.

※

I was sleeping better now but the slightest sound still broke the net of my dreams and I awoke a few nights later to hear Night Sister whispering to my neighbour.

'Aren't you asleep yet?'

He must have shaken his head for I heard no reply.

'In pain?'

'N'no.'

'Anything you want?'

'Yes … stay and talk to me for a bit.'

'I can't, I've work to do.'

'Oh, Catherine! you're always busy and rushing away … can't you stay just a little while?'

'I've told you, and you mustn't …'

'Call you Catherine? They're all asleep … even he's asleep …' The note of his voice changed as he turned his head towards me.

'Now you must try and sleep yourself.'

'You're awfully sweet to me.'

She said nothing. In a little while he used her Christian name again.

'Yes, what is it?'

'Catherine … you know I'm crazy about you?'

'Don't be a silly boy …'

'But l am … I've always been … since I first came in here.'

'You've talked enough foolish things … be a good patient and lie still.' Her voice was brisk. I heard her pulling his sheets straight. Then she walked past my bed and I watched her as the light caught her face. Her eyes were filled with tears.

✕

The next morning he was much worse and they kept the screens up and told us to be quiet and turned the wireless off and wouldn't let the little old newspaperman sell him a paper. Medical officers came and looked at him every little while and then held long consultations in the Senior Sister's bunk.

It was impossible to understand their mumbled technical jargon, but the orderly who looked after me whispered that the case was quite hopeless.

Then I realized how I hated the place, for suddenly I became aware of the ward, of the sick and smashed men about me, of the smell of ether and floor-polish and radiators and food kept hot in heaters. And more than ever I fretted at the twisted body that held me in bed and wanted to go back to Flights and be with the boys and fly again and get drunk in the nights.

When Night Sister came on duty she stood by his bed for some minutes. Then he recognized her.

'What's ... the matter ... Catherine?'

'Nothing ... we're going to move you into another ward, that's all.'

'A private ward?'

'Yes.'

He didn't say anything for a long while. Then he whispered, 'I guess I had it coming to me.'

'What are you talking about?'

'You know,' he said.

'You mustn't get silly ideas in your head.'

'Catherine?'

'I do love you ... don't cry, lass.'

✗

We never saw him again and the next day a new patient, a young officer injured at rugger, was in his bed. He was very young, very pink-faced, very English, and very dumb, and inside a few hours had begun an argument with the Canadian which went on, with intervals, all the afternoon. When Night Sister came on duty they were practically shouting at one another. She went to each in turn and told them to be quiet as they were disturbing the whole wing.

'Hen-toed, goose-rumped old harpy,' said the young officer when she had gone out, looking about the ward for encouragement. Martin put down his paper.

'You!'

'Yes, sir.'

'Don't you ever make a crack like that again.'

'I'm sorry, sir.'

'You disgusting little twerp.'

'I'm awfully sorry, sir, I had no idea …'

'No idea that she's a fine woman and a good nurse?' He picked up his paper and rolled on to his side.

We grunted our agreement.

4 Return to Life

They had cut away my clothing at the hospital, so I borrowed flying-suit, helmet, and goggles from the locker-room and went out on to the aerodrome. It was a still, warm October day and the intimacy of my surroundings came back to me, the dim clatter of tools echoing through the hangars, the sweet smell of dope, the dust and little bits of grass swirling across the concrete apron as engines were run up, the slow flapping of the wind stocking at the corner of the watch office; these things enveloped my consciousness so that the previous weeks were forgotten and I might never have been away.

'D'you feel all right about it?' asked the Chief Instructor.

'I feel fine,' I said, running the slip-knot of my scarf taut against my throat.

'There's nothing to worry about,' he went on.

'I'm not worrying,' I said.

'There were marks of her heels on the cockpit floor and the under side of the rudder – with the controls jammed like that no one could have got a 'plane out of a spin.'

I nodded, jerked the zip-fastener tabs so that the clumsy flying-suit pulled itself about me, and went out to the aircraft.

'I'll take her round first," he said when I'd plugged the telephone lead home. I grunted, pulling on my harness straps, setting altimeter, petrol cocks and master switches. I did these things unthinkingly, the memory of the crash, revived by the familiarity of my surroundings, hooding my mind.

He taxied out, turned into the wind and took off. As the machine rocked across the aerodrome and then, becoming air-borne, soared smoothly upwards, I found myself following his movements, instinctively checking the synchronizing of bank and rudder as he pulled up into a climbing turn. But the intrinsic understandings of it had gone; I was a passenger, I no longer flew in my own mind.

At six hundred feet he turned again, levelling off, and I looked over the side, remembering the strangeness of the country when first I came to the flying club. How it had gradually etched itself into my mind, the essential shape of it, the pattern of wood and lake, the clear line of canal and railway. And how the time had come when I could dive out of the clouds during instrument flying instruction and, glancing at the ground, tell my pupil to fly on a certain bearing, knowing that, eventually, the untidy aerodrome would come sliding under a wing.

Now there was a light mist on the countryside, light mist on the woods that were touched with winter, on farm and village, stubble and tall trees with their delicate shadows rotting into the quiet fields, on ploughman and turnip-cutter, a light mist as the bloom on a plum that made one rub one's goggles with the back of one's glove.

The Chief Instructor turned once more, and throttling back, glided across wind. Then side-slipping in, landed on the circle.

'Will you take her round?' His voice was casual; too casual, I thought. As I pushed the throttle open I felt my hands and feet harden on the controls. The Chief, wise in twenty years of instruction, sensed it instantly, and as I wrenched the aircraft into the air I saw him look up sharply into the mirror that was mounted on the port centre section strut to enable an instructor to watch his pupil's face.

He began to whistle softly and placed his hands on the sides of the cockpit, as one does to give pupils confidence in themselves. I climbed up steadily until we reached three thousand feet.

'Try a spin, will you?'

Now I hated the casual note in his voice. I was rattled. He knew I was rattled. I turned and glanced downwards. There were no machines about. The haze had thinned with altitude and belonged to the ground. As I looked below I could see only the slabs of lake and pond and the hard lines of the railways glinting in the sunshine.

My hand was shaking as I throttled the engine down. I blasphemed softly, pulled the stick into my stomach, kicked on full rudder. The aircraft lurched into a spin, the horizon heeling upwards. Fear leapt inside me; it might have been my first flight. I set my teeth, hardening my mind against terror, trying to blot out the image of that last spin, my pupil frozen on to the controls, screaming and shouting while I fought to bring the machine out, laughing into the telephones in an effort to ride down her fear.

And now I thought of the ground, losing that map-like appearance imparted by height, twisting upwards and no fear any more but a great interest, observing every detail, thinking again and again: 'It's happened to me – it's happened to me – I'm going to spin in –' Then cutting the switches and pulling the petrol cock shut as we hit.

After that the silence and the smell of petrol and the pain in arm and side as I dragged my pupil clear, the pain making me feel sick, thickening the mist of panic that already threatened to cloud my mind.

And, when I realized that she was dead, the walk to the farm, awed by the silence, seeing nothing moving, no animal or living thing, hearing nothing, wondering if I were dead and this was the terrible loneliness of life after death. Then hope flooding my consciousness as I saw a child moving in the stinking farmyard.

I thought of how I groaned in spirit as I came along the stone walk to the back door, knowing how difficult it would be to make them realize the outline of my story, dreading the re-telling of each detail, trying all the while to build the fabric of my experience in my brain.

They were stupid, too, I crying inside myself for patience, thinking again and again: 'Only a little while now – only a little while now' – speaking slowly, fighting the great fatigue that weighed down my understanding. The pain all this time crusting my body and the sweet taste of blood for ever in my mouth.

When the telephoning was done and I'd told the story for the last time that day, when the sightseers had rushed away to find the wreckage and there was no more noise, they took me to hospital, swinging on an ambulance stretcher, listening to the rattle of the engine (it wanted de-carbonizing) and the water splashing in the tank above the iron-framed washbasin.

As we spun downwards two months later, the tart autumn air sighing in the bracing wires, I could still feel the pain of broken ribs and arm, of dislocated shoulder and crushed hand. I could still hear the flapping of the canvas curtain behind the driver and the driver's voice as he talked to his mate about a dart match he'd played the night before, breaking into long-drawn tactical explanations to ask again and again, 'Are you all right, sir?' until his flaccid voice was inlaid in my consciousness.

When I had brought the Moth out of the spin the Chief Instructor asked me to take her back to the aerodrome and land. I flew badly, skidding on my turns, gliding now too fast, now too slow, my landings wretched, so that I could feel the Chief's hand on the dual control, guiding me. I was frozen on to the control column. After three circuits I began to find difficulty in getting into the aerodrome. He landed her himself.

'What's the trouble?" he asked, leisurely. We were taxi-ing in, and he swung his head from side to side of the cockpit, watching the flying-field on both sides of the engine.

'I don't know,' I said. 'I suppose that pile-up shook me a bit.'

'Nonsense – a show like that does one good. Besides, you've crashed before, haven't you?'

'Yes,' I said, 'I've crashed before.'

'Well, I want you to take her up yourself – fly round a bit and then try some landings. If they get too bad, come in.'

'Right,' I said, watching him getting out of the front cockpit. I felt for the hundredth time the strangeness of seeing someone physically remote climbing out of a cockpit after hearing his voice in one's ears in the clear emptiness of the sky, after checking the movements of his hands and feet on the dual control.

I went up and tried to fly. I was scared stiff, rigid on the controls. My movements were jerky; I was constantly over-correcting, glancing nervously from instrument to instrument. Flying level at two thousand feet, I thought of the hundreds of hours I'd flown subconsciously; how I'd cursed and sworn at pupils because they, petrified with fear, couldn't do what I was trying to do now.

I'd been up for perhaps ten minutes when I suddenly felt that I couldn't land. I thought of the words of an Air Force doctor in the days when I was training in the Service. He was white-haired and quiet, having been much with death, and he told us that every pilot is liable to reach a breaking-point, a time when his flying days are done. We laughed, I remember, being confident with the untried, arrogant confidence of youth.

It seemed that for me, this time had come. That I was finished, destined to crawl about the earth for the remainder of my life.

No more the feel of the engine roaring into life under one's hand, the joy of aerobatics when the horizon dipped and rolled and stick and rudder moved easily, firmly, quickly about the cockpit. No more the rugged comradeship of flying men, but my part to live in the past, glorifying incidents I ought to be surpassing, repeating anecdotes that would become woven into the fabric of my life so that it wasted away till my living was merely a frame for my memories.

No more the pub-crawling; drinking in the happy atmosphere of village bars with flying folk till the world seemed a merry place. No more the aerobatics last thing at night, when the gallery of loungers and gin-sipping women at the clubhouse and the influence of the evening's alcohol brought one too near the ground, the fear of death glowing in one's mind.

I approached the aerodrome. A little group stood on the tarmac. Some of them were men and women I'd taught to fly.

I began to fray my body with my mind. 'Land,' I said. 'Land, blast you!' The first attempt was a failure. I bounced high, put my engine on, fearing for the undercarriage, and went round the aero- drome again. I flew at two hundred feet, so as to leave less time to think as I came in. I turned very gingerly the last time and throttled down to glide. I could feel the sweat cold around my eyes, warm inside my gloves, gathering my shirt about my body. Now! I thought, and brought the stick back … back … back … watching the ground ahead as I'd never watched it since my first solo. When I thought the wheels were two feet above the ground I pulled the tail down, and with body tense and forearm rigid waited for her to stall. I felt the almost imperceptible shudder as she lost flying speed, and then she went down smoothly, softly, a perfect landing with the tail-skid rumbling on the sheep-cropped grass.

I twisted my head sharply to see if there was anyone coming in to land, and then took off again. I felt fine; bugles sang in my mind. I could land, flying was my job again, the future unruffled. I shouldn't have to look for work, for some mundane pen-pushing occupation. I climbed at the stall, rocking the stick to find out when the ailerons should lose control. At two thousand feet I slow-rolled, suddenly loving that feeling of hanging from the shoulder straps as you keep the stick forward to make her climb. Then I spun, stall-turned and half-rolled off a loop, bending my head back to watch the horizon come over. My hands were as smooth as silk. I went in, tail-swishing to drop the 'plane on the concrete apron before the hangars. The Chief Instructor came out. He was smiling, his helmet, which hung from his shoulders by the telephones, swinging as he walked. I could see the red mark beneath his chin left by the strip.

'All right?' he asked.

I grinned.

'All right,' I said.

5 Test Flight

As the test-pilot walked out on to the tarmac he saw that the mechanics had already started the engine with a gas-starter, which two boys were wheeling away on a small trolley. It was difficult walking with a nineteen-pound Irvin parachute on hanging behind one's knees, with fur-lined fug boots and a fleece-and-leather flying-suit that was confoundedly stuffy on a sultry June day. What wind there was flapped the wind-sock about the pole, blew up dust in little spirals from the bare patches where the 'planes were wheeled from the hangars and fluttered the writing-pads that were fi strapped above his knees.

Waiting for the mechanic, who had run up the engine to climb up the step-ladder, he drew on first his dirty silk gloves, then his leather gauntlets, and stooping, pulled in turn each of the parachute straps that hung clinking from the pack hard against the inside of each thigh and clipped them to their appropriate rings on the harness. The metal middle-wing monoplane rocked gently to the rhythm of her engine so that the sun danced in a thousand ever-changing places on her stubby fuselage. She was a new single-seat fighter with flaps, retractable undercarriage and a variable-pitch propeller. On the drawing-board she had been so vastly superior in design, in speed and performance to any fighter in the Service that the chief designer's task in persuading the directors to build her, in the hope of the Government adopting her for general use in the Air Force, had been an easy one. Now, as they stood in a silent, uneasy group in the board-room window, fat, stupid-faced men who were more at home in a golf-club bar, now that the 'plane was completed, they were not so certain.

To be sure, the Government were interested. (An official stood with them. An old pilot, lean and tall with hard blue eyes, wrinkled about by twenty years' flying, and fine square-fingered hands, who listened politely to all they had to say, smiled courteously at their jests, but said little.) But, they thought, Government interest did not justify the spending of £16,000. (Wind-tunnel tests on a model had necessitated expensive last-minute alterations.)

Before one of the hangars stood the score or so picked workmen who had been working on the 'plane for the previous eighteen months behind locked doors. They had watched her grow from finely-drawn plans, from four steel longerons (as the main members of an aircraft are called), with skilled, costly workmanship into the thing of beauty, streamlined to the last rivet-head, that was now to 'go up on first test'. So slowly had she evolved that it seemed to them she was part of the hangar that had seen her birth. A hangar now open to the aerodrome, containing now only tools, packing-cases, trestles, deserted work-benches, oil drums and dozens of rolled-up plans, all numbered and done up with coloured ribbons. And each workman thought of the part he had played, down to the junior who had helped to blow up the tyres, the common pride of workmanship binding them into a comradeship that was above wage disputes, beyond discipline, untouched by personal feeling, so that when the junior, with the eager impetuosity of his age, asked the grim foreman standing next to him, 'D'yer think she'll be OK?' he answered gravely as if speaking to an equal, 'Eh, lad, I hope so … but tha' n'er can tell!' The test-pilot went slowly up the step-ladder, swung his legs into the cockpit, and sliding down, wriggled the pack of his parachute into the bucket seat. A mechanic who had clambered up after him helped with the straps of his aerobatic harness … left arm … right thigh … left thigh … right arm … he strained the narrow bands of webbing over the slotted pin on his chest and pushed home the locking web. As he thrust his toes into the rudder-bar straps, took the stick in his right hand and the throttle in his left, he glanced towards the roadway. He could see roofs of many cars above the hedge and a long white line of faces.

He felt for the pencils that were stuck into the top of his right fug boot, set the altimeter to zero and then, looking upwards (there was a good deal of broken cloud at four thousand) he touched first the magneto switches, then the petrol cock, then the locking web of his aerobatic harness, then the rip-cord ring of his parachute, memorizing their positions.

The cockpit was roughly fitted out, the incredible number of instruments, gun-sights, machine-gun synchronizing gear, bomb toggles, Sutton harness adjustment, flare-release and similar gadgets dear to Service experts were to be fitted later. He felt for the retractable undercarriage release handle and the manually-operated flap gear; both were in easy reach. Twisting his head he brought the stick hard back. Instantly three mechanics threw themselves on the tail. He began to open the throttle, watching the instruments. At fourteen hundred revolutions per minute he switched each magneto on and off in turn, the engine dropping between fifteen and twenty revs. And now he pushed the small steel lever fully forward and the eight hundred horse-power motor roared its pean of power. Slipstream from the propeller beat down the grass in a wide circle, swept bits of loose paper and rag about the hangars, beat the mechanics' overalls fluttering about their bodies. The noise crashed in great waves of sound upon the minds of those nearby. It was demoniac; so far unusual to the sightseers on the road that it brought with it a strange atmosphere of unreality, as in a dream in which the details are familiar but the outline horribly untrue. As they watched, a heavy lorry rumbled past unheard.

The test-pilot, subconsciously listening for any irregularity which might mean trouble, was outwardly unaware of the noise, watching his oil-pressure, his engine revs, his oil temperature. Satisfied, he throttled down again, the roar dying quickly to a rhythmic rattle.

Slowly, he waved his right hand from side to side. The two mechanics who had been waiting with the ropes in their hands jerked the wheel-chocks away, the port wing man saluting and pointing to a Gipsy Moth, belonging to the flying club who shared the aerodrome, which was coming in to land. As he turned downwind (turning on the ground was easy with wheel brakes) and instinctively eased the stick right forward so that the breeze blowing on the down-turned elevators would keep the tail down, he thought how good the mechanics were. But they were specially picked and subjected to long and arduous training. The average human being didn't take kindly to discipline and quick thinking.

The monoplane picked her way fastidiously to the far end of the flying-field and as the pilot turned slowly into the wind his eyes once more searched the sky. But the Gipsy Moth had landed, bumping her way across the aerodrome and the sky was empty. He wound the tail-incidence forward, pulled down the old Meyrowitz goggles, rusted about the rims, that were suspended about his shabby helmet by two lengths of parachute-pack elastic, set the variable-pitch to 'climb', held the stick hard back and pushed the throttle wide open. As she gathered speed he put the stick forward to bring the tail up, and then eased it back to central and waited for her to fly herself off. Just before the wheels lifted she swerved to port, her opposite rudder hardly checking the yawing movement, so that she took off slightly out of the wind. He took a quick glance at the Air Speed Indicator, then pulled up in a steep climb, rocking the stick from side to side so that he should learn when the ailerons lost control and could therefore put the nose down some time before a wing would stall. Keeping an eye on the slots he pulled up the undercarriage and set himself to find the best climbing angle.

✕

Ten minutes later he was flying level at nine thousand feet, and one of the writing-pads was covered with sprawling figures. He had found the stalling speed, the climbing and gliding angles, had flick-rolled and dived with throttle closed until the revs screamed up from seven hundred to two thousand three hundred (the needle against the little red danger pointer, the earth, mist-ridden and unreal, swooping up to meet him, the stick hard in his hand as he stroked it back the sixteenth of an inch at a time).

'Now,' he muttered, 'a slow roll.' He pulled the aircraft round in a tight circle, looking above and below. Then opening the throttle he pulled the nose above the horizon (the earth had no significance save as a checking medium) and put on full bank to the right, counteracting aileron drag by a touch of bottom rudder. He closed the throttle as he reached the vertical and, grunting as the 'plane went on to her back, pushed the stick forward to keep the nose up. He was now off the seat, hanging by the aerobatic harness. As he came up the other side the nose began to drop. He put on full right rudder, gave the engine a burst to get some slipstream on his tailplane, getting the stick a back hard as the wing came up. But it was a dirty finish, the nose was down and forty degrees off the little cloud he had picked as a mark going in.

That must have looked rotten from the ground, he thought, glancing at each slot in turn to see if one were stuck open. But they were both closed. He was certainly impressing the Government bloke the wrong way; it was probably the rudder, the damn thing had looked too small anyhow. A spin would tell. He climbed to twelve thousand. One never knew what was going to happen in the first spin in a new type, especially when one was worried over the control in the yawing 'plane.

He flew level once more, made a note of the slow roll, looked below him and touched the rip-cord ring of his parachute. This sort of life was dangerous, there was no doubt of that. And yet, he reflected, closing the throttle and easing the nose up, that was how he liked it. When aviation became just another form of transport, when 'planes came to be universally fitted with compression-ignition engines, thereby eliminating the bogy of fire after a crash, when they could get down safely in any sort of field, when a simple and foolproof method of landing in a fog had been devised and every town had its airport ... then he'd quit flying, and so would other pilots ... who were flying now. He flew because it was risky, because it was exhilarating, because it called for the confidence that is born in the conquest of fear, for skill and coolness in danger.

The broken clouds were far below, white and hard, framing patches of the dim landscape that was studded with woods, laced by glittering bands of stee] that he knew were railways, dappled by huge drifting pools of sunlight. He could just see the aerodrome with its regular boundaries, its marshalled hangars, its white landing-circle.

Queer to think he'd be having a drink down there in five minutes ... if all went well. He was level with another layer of cloud, grey drifting cloud that hung in long drifting tendrils, obscuring the horizon. And now the airspeed had dropped to sixty-eight, the stick moved loosely in his hand. He kicked on full right rudder. Instantly the right wing went down. He pulled the stick right back. The nose dropped and the monoplane began to spin. The lower, whiter clouds came up to meet him, the horizon out of sight above, whirling about him. He watched the round shadow of his head flash over the instruments, counting the number of times he was turning.

On the third turn the 'plane kicked and was forced into a spiral nose-dive by the slots. He went round once more and then put on top rudder and pushing the stick central (it had been forced to the right by autorotation) thrust it some six inches forward.

The monoplane spun as before. Fear rolled upwards in a great wave in his stomach.

'You bastard,' he yelled and his voice was thin and ridiculous amidst the rushing wind.

'Come out, God rot you!'

He rocked the stick full forward, kicking on full top rudder to no effect, the earth rolling upwards. He held the stick full forward and opposite rudder hard over, giving the engine burst after burst of full throttle, but it was of no avail.

He was very frightened, very cool, very certain of what he was going to do.

He pulled his feet from the rudder-straps, cut his magneto switches, pulled back the petrol cock, jerked the locking web out of the pin, thrusting his shoulders upwards so that the straps flew off.

It seemed that time had no reality, that he was living through an age of experience that could neither be measured by days nor years. The force of the spin threw him about the cockpit. He remembered being told that one had to get out on the inside as the centrifugal force of the spin would push one back if one attempted to climb over the outside. The clouds were very near now, he must have gone round at least nine times. If he didn't hurry he'd experience 'black-out', which usually came after ten times round. ('Black-out' is the draining of the blood from the head by terrific centrifugal force, causing temporary blindness.)

He grabbed the cockpit side and stood on the seat with knees bent. Every action seemed to take an eternity, there was no contact with everyday living. To die, he thought, must be like this. Clutching his rip-cord ring he hurled himself head downwards over the side, feeling a sharp stab of pain as a wing-tip caught his leg a glancing blow, slitting the leather 'fug' boot.

Now he was falling. It was terrible. He was so frightened that he found something akin to ecstasy in his fear, and above all a great familiarity as if he had been through all this before, had subconsciously known it was to happen, had lived his whole life for this one second. He waited till he should be well clear of the aircraft before cracking his 'chute. The spinning 'plane seemed to be shooting upwards. Vaguely he wondered if he would drift into its path.

He tore at the rip-cord, which came cleanly from its protective cable. Thank God, the pins weren't bent. He'd never put on a 'chute again without looking at the pins which held the pack closed. Fool … the 'chute hasn't opened yet … something may go wrong … it may have been badly packed … I may fall into it … the shroud lines may be twisted.

Came a jerk that wrenched him into a sitting position. He swung gently in a great arc, looking upwards at a blessed white canopy that seemed to lean away as the clouds passed over it. As he passed through a hole in the clouds the monoplane shot by with the nose right down, spinning wildly. He watched it go down. It was hard to tell how high it was, aircraft a long way below one always seemed to be going into the deck. He hoped to hell it didn't fall on houses, on children, on the high road, anywhere where it would cause unhappiness … there was enough of that in the world. Would his switching off and closing the petrol-cock prevent fire? Probably not.

Perhaps he ought to have stayed in, tried some more to have got her out, people might say he was parachute-conscious and that wouldn't help a test-pilot. Besides there was a lot of money, work, ambition in that beautiful 'plane that no power on earth could now save from crashing into useless débris.

The silence was new to him. Never in seven years' flying had he experienced anything like it. He could hear the soporific clatter of a train, the rattle of the fire-bell at the aerodrome and a tiny blob of sound that he knew was a motor-horn. It seemed he was hardly moving. Now surely the 'plane must crash. As the thought moulded itself in his mind he saw the monoplane crumple into the middle of a ploughed field, saw pieces of the cowling glint in the sun as they flew upwards. In a fraction of time it had lost its form and grace and become a blazing wreck, for as he watched, flames shot upwards and a tower of black smoke climbed lazily into the sky. In a few seconds he heard the roar of a crash and then there was silence again.

As he came near the ground he saw that the wind had risen since he had taken off. Just his luck. He would be dragged by the canopy. He didn't want to be dragged. Not with a leg that was dead below the knee.

The delusion that he was suspended in mid-air had altogether disappeared, the ground came steadily upwards, drifting slowly by. The crowd who had lined the flying-field hedge were running up the road. Well, they were having their cheap thrill this time.

He landed heavily on his toes, falling forward, his injured leg crumpling under him and was dragged nearly the whole length of the field before the canopy flapped into a lifeless carpet of silk.

He got uncertainly to his feet, stripped off his harness and gathered the canopy in his arms. The first of the sightseers approached, a thin, round-shouldered, spectacled man, his wan face flushed with the effort of running.

'Are you all right?' he panted, and his obvious anxiety robbed his words of their inherent absurdity. 'Are you all right?' The pilot, who had been arranging in his mind the details of having the parachute repacked, of what he would

say to the directors, of making his reports, of seeing that the
a burnt-out débris was collected and carted back to the works
as soon as it cooled, of going up again immediately to restore
his shaken nerve, looked up smiling.

'Yes,' he said, 'I'm all right, it's just my leg. If you'd be so
good as to help me across to the aerodrome?'

'Why, of course. Put your arm on my shoulder.'

The test-pilot thanked him and smiled again, this time at
the other's eagerness, thinking how this was an adventure
for him, the making of a tale that he would often 'remember
with advantages', a story that would bring him silence among
his fellow clerks as he related how he had been, for a few
glorious moments, a man in a world of men.

6 Night Exercise

It was getting dark as he left the Mess, the western sky stained with a perfect sunset and a light easterly wind blowing coldly off the aerodrome, so that he turned up his great-coat collar and clapped his gloved hands together, thinking with faint longing of the warm ante-room and the circle of chairs about the large brick fireplace.

The sentry outside the guard-room slapped his rifle-butt smartly. Automatically he returned the salute, then gazed upwards, wondering if the wind would remain constant and the weather hold throughout the night. It was peaceful as he walked through the windswept camp, and heard the thin tinkle of radio sets in the barrack blocks cutting through the clatter of a slowly running motor on the tarmac. The hangars, silhouetted big and gaunt against the bleak aerodrome and coloured sky, poured solid light through huge open doors so that the mighty night-bombers, crawling with maintenance crews, threw long straggling shadows on to the concrete aprons.

His own machine was being towed out by a tractor, the tractor-driver swinging his head over each shoulder in turn, watching the mechanics who walked, one beneath each wing, with arms extended to show that the tips were clear of obstructions. He walked quickly through the hangar, his hollow footsteps flung back by the tall roof; ducked beneath the bellies of aircraft on inspections and overhaul; then, with a mechanical salute entered the Flight Commander's office.

A junior officer sat by the telephone engrossed in a thriller. He was young, with smooth, characterless features, absurdly handsome with forage-cap set well over one ear. At his side was a sextant, a pile of maps, logs, parallel rulers and navigational instruments. He looked up as the other entered.

'Hullo, Jimmy!'

'Hullo, old boy.'

'I've worked out all the tracks, distances and times. Here's the weather – seems all right.'

He nodded as he took the flimsy sheet, then crossed the room to a large map of the British Isles and began to study it, his forehead creased over one eyebrow. At the side of the map were little flags, each marked with a letter and the number of an aircraft. Absently he pulled out one marked 'X' and stuck it in at the home aerodrome. Then he walked back to the table and picked up the telephone.

'Langdon here.' The voice of his Squadron Leader was crisp and imperious with twenty years of command.

'Brown here, sir. Due off on the first show at eighteen-thirty. Have you seen the weather?'

'Yes – seems good. Got all your instructions?'

'Yes, sir.'

'Right. Off you go.'

He hung up the receiver and turned to his companion. "We're off. Get your gubbins aboard.'

He went up to the locker-room and began to dress. Sheepskin-lined knee-boots, flying-suit, two pairs of silk gloves, helmet with earphones and microphone attached, sharp pencils and a couple of small flashlamps from his overcoat completed his preparations, together with the parachute he slung over his shoulder.

Crossing to the open window, he peered out the waiting monoplanes. Grim they seemed, he thought, their broad wings like arms crucified against the dying day. Precise machines, designed, built and flown to one end, to bring destruction to every part of the inhabited globe. Pray God, he'd never have to fly one, with tons of death in its belly, over some darkened town while old men and women and children grovelled in trench and cellar far below.

'Smithers!' his voice went ringing over the tarmac.

'Sir!' came the far-away reply from somewhere in the twilight.

'Spin 'em up!'

'Very good, sir.'

※

As he walked towards the door he could hear his fitter's instructions, followed by 'Contact starboard', and the thousand horse-power motor stuttered into life, rocking and twisting on its bearers till the cylinders fired evenly. Then it was joined by its fellow, the fitter throttling down till they ran over quietly, little tongues of flame flickering out of the exhausts.

Even now the slipstream was sufficient to blow his sidcot hard on to his limbs as he walked round the tail, and to send his scarf streaming out beneath his chin. A waiting mechanic wrenched open the door and pulled down the ladder. He climbed inside, buckled on his parachute and then went forward, stooping beneath the cross members and worming his way in the darkness past the navigator's table and tall wireless apparatus, where an operator tapped out morse, watching a jittering needle.

The fitter slipped out of the pilot's seat and held the wheel central as the Captain slid in. He settled himself comfortably, adjusted the rudder pedals, pulled up the seat, set the gyro and plugged in his telephones. Then he started to run up the engines, watching a bewildering mass of instruments. As he checked revolutions, temperatures and boost pressures the noise became a solid block of sound that shut out the world, absorbing all sound, blocking his ears. He listened for any irregularity, switching off each circuit of the dual ignition system in turn. His mind was blank, he was part of a machine, working with unthinking efficiency. Finally satisfied, he nodded to the fitter, who ran nimbly aft and banged the door behind him.

He pulled up his microphone, switching it on.

'Pilot calling navigator!'

'OK, Skipper. First course one eight two magnetic.'

'One eight two magnetic. Thank you. Wireless operator?'

'OK, sir.'

When the front and rear gunners had answered he gave the time, telling the crew to synchronise their watches, then turned off the lights. An answering flicker from below told him that the chocks were away and he let off the brakes and opened the throttles. Ten tons of aeroplane began to move slowly out into the darkness.

✳

Out on the aerodrome a flare path, paraffin flares set at regular intervals, stretched out into the wind. As he taxied he began to signal with his identification light, sending out his letter 'X'.

Instantly it was answered in green from the first flare, where a group of men huddled about a brazier like gipsies about a camp fire. He rounded the bottom of the path, pumped on flap, felt his brake handle and variable pitch levers (to check that the airscrews were in line), pulled back the override and began to open the throttles.

Slowly the huge machine began to move, the flares sliding by, flashing yellow light through the windscreen that caught his tense features, expressionless with concentration, as he pushed the heavy wheel forward to bring the tail up. She was accelerating now, the last flare rushing towards him. Judging by the feel that she was almost airborne, he eased the wheel towards him. She bumped twice and began to climb into the darkness.

He bent his head backwards and looked up at the stars, glancing quickly at engine revolutions and airspeed, estimating by these means that the machine was climbing straight and level. As he climbed he pumped off flap, throttled down, slapped the airscrews into coarse; then, turning on a dash light, caught the navigator's eye, putting up his thumb and making a circular movement with his hand. The other repeated the signal to the wireless operator, who nodded and let out a hundred and fifty feet of trailing aerial.

At two thousand feet he began to turn on to his first course. It was exactly half-past six as he crossed the aerodrome and he held up his thumb to the navigator, who set a stop-watch and departed aft to his maps and instruments.

Now, as they left the little cluster of lights that meant the aerodrome and its attendant village, and set off, climbing into the night, the stars, distinct above, seemed more real than the hazy mounds of reflected light that represented distant towns, and the cabin, cramped with the complicated paraphernalia of modern war, became a cosy little room, a tiny world in the dark emptiness of the sky.

Soon they passed over a seaport. He knew it well. By day it sprawled in untidy squalor, its extensive smoke-slurred slums scummed by docks. There seemed no pattern, no attempt at planning; it appeared, as indeed it was, a festering sore on the face of the countryside. But as they slid over it in the darkness, the chains of street lights linked up evenly below, with arteries of brighter blue and green bisecting a beautiful pattern. It was huge and clear-cut and still, the lights ending abruptly at the docks, gleaming on the black hard surface of the water.

The steady roar of the motors became a background of noise of which he was only subconsciously aware. Every few seconds his eye swept his instruments, seeing that each flickering, luminous needle was in its place, while his feet held the bomber steady on her course. Sometimes a little group of lights that was a village or little town came back out of the darkness to slide beneath a wing, as drifting seaweed seen from the deck of a steamer. The shop lights would fall harshly into the streets, framed in tiny oblong shadows like a strip of film.

An hour and a half later they were fifteen thousand feet above the English Channel. Far below the English coast stretched before them, its line marked by blobs of lights that were coastal in towns, lights that reached eastward like a chain of buoys. Somewhere below, too, the Navy were busy and searchlight beams swung in jerky arcs beneath. The Captain turned on to a new course, then signalled to the navigator to take over the controls. When he saw the junior settled on his course, Brown went aft. He bent over the wireless operator's shoulder and read his log, a large book neatly filled with times and hieroglyphics and groups of letters. Then he tapped the Corporal on the shoulder so that the latter looked up quickly, his fingers leaving the key and pulling back his helmet from his ear.

'Take five minutes off ... got any tea?'

'No, sir.'

'Help yourself to mine.'

'Thank you, sir.'

He walked down the fuselage, feeling his way in the darkness. Amidships, the front gunner, who was also a fitter, stood by the petrol gauges, filling in a large chart pinned on a board. The Captain took it from him and studied the figures, then nodded and handed it back. Now he went into the tail, treading the narrow catwalk gingerly, stooping lower and lower, conscious of a feeling of claustrophobia as he approached the little cabin behind the rudder and elevators. The rear gunner was working on a reconnaissance report with a stub of pencil. The Captain read it carefully.

'Have you been asleep?'

'No, sir.'

'Well, make a more detailed report from now on ... there's much more activity than you've reported.'

'I've been doing my best, sir.'

'I'm afraid your best isn't quite good enough. Try and improve it.'

※

Walking forward again he thought that the pilot up in the front seemed very far away and remote at the end of a long tunnel, the soft reddish dash lamp picking out the brighter parts of the intricate machinery which lined the aircraft. There was no sound-proofing and the fuselage was filled with noise, while each part of the structure quivered with the energy of two thousand horse-power.

He looked through a tiny porthole at a town to the north, a skeleton of lights picked clean like the bones of a herring. Somewhere in one of those blocks of darkness was his home, and near his home lived a girl named Hazel. Standing with shoulders hunched, weight supported by elbows that leaned on vibrating longeron, he thought of her, building her semblance in his mind. One day he hoped to marry her, but he was due for discharge from the Air Force in twelve months' time. Perhaps he'd be lucky and land a civil flying job. He sighed. It seemed a pity to be forced to leave the Service which he loved so well, but a Short Service Commission was a Short Service Commission and that was all there was to it.

Suddenly he thought it strange that there should be living people in the tangle of lights below, that it should represent a settled orderly world with Hazel reading or sewing, her feet twisted up on the sofa beside her, her kitten sleeping with its head in her lap.

The navigator's table, lit by a shaded lamp, was covered with maps and a seeming jungle of instruments topped by a log sheet. This was kept in pencil, lines of closely written figures and abbreviations. He picked it up and read it slowly, his mind, familiar with its involved system, absorbing each detail in sequence, seeking for errors, which he failed to find. Standing by the pilot once more he stooped and read the bombing thermometer. It was twenty degrees below zero Centigrade.

The pilot kicked him gently and pointed ahead. Before them rose a tremendous mass of white cloud, hard and real, towering into heaven. It was almost frightening in its cold, still purity, with the lonely mysticism of its deep valleys enhanced by the moonlight that cast long shadows, lending contrast to the tall face that now blocked their way.

He plugged in his telephone lead and switched on his microphone.

'Go through … chance to practise a drop of blind flying.'

※

Swiftly the storm approached and suddenly the aircraft began to pitch and roll, bumping violently as they flew through the rising currents. Then cloud was all about them, wiping away all distance and altitude, deadening the windows, emphasizing the little interior; and the pilot wriggled in his seat, cut off the cold air carburettor supply, leant slightly forward and concentrated on the miniature aircraft belonging to the artificial horizon. It began to snow, flakes drifting in through the cracks of the windows and powdering the instrument panel. Next, ice crept over the windscreen, first a thin film like the covering of a newly-washed doorstep on a winter's morning, then building rapidly, thickening with astonishing quickness on all leading sections of the machine. The Pitot head became a lump of ice, the airspeed needle flickering and then sagging to zero.

The Captain touched his companion's shoulder and jerked his head, taking the controls again as the other slipped out. He pushed the throttles wide open and began to climb. A few minutes later the bomber was droning through clear sky again, high above jagged peaks of cloud, its wings and fuselage heavy with ice, gleaming white in the moonlight. The Captain called up the navigator as he worked at his table

'I'm going to stay above this stuff ... you'll have to get the sextant out and shoot the odd star.'

'OK, old boy.'

Six and a half hours after taking-off they were approaching the home aerodrome again. All the village lights were extinguished now and they could see only the camp lights and the hangars blaring light through their open doors and the crucifix of the flare path standing out in the haze that had made the base difficult to find.

The Captain circled the station till his eyes became accustomed to flying at a low altitude, then sent out 'X' on his identification lights. He saw a tiny patch of light on the ground as the signaller tested his lamp; then a green winked up at them. He sighed thankfully, switched on lights, adjusted mixture controls and throttled down his motors. The navigator came forward, intimated that the aerial had been wound in, and stood at the pilot's side, one arm resting on the window ledge.

Now the silence was strange to them, the steady pounding of the engines still sounding in their ears so that it was some seconds before they heard the familiar gliding sounds, the wind swishing in the open windows, crying in the undercarriage bracing wires, driving the airscrews so that the motors muttered and popped back in rebellion. He turned in to land, trained fingers slipping the airscrews into fine, cutting off the supply of cool air to the oil systems. At a steady eighty miles an hour he skimmed the trees and bumped the machine down at the first flare for a perfect landing.

'That all for me, cock?' asked the navigator as he climbed out on to the tarmac.

'Yes. Don't hog all the sandwiches before I get up.'

A few minutes later he left the locker-room, set forage cap over one eye and walked quickly to the Squadron Leader's office. The latter looked up on quickly from a little pile of wireless messages as he saluted.

'All right?'

'Yes, sir. Cissie trip.'

The older man smiled. 'Your bombing results weren't too good, and you seemed to have a spot of bother finding this place!'

'It's a bit thick, sir.'

'Shouldn't have bothered you if you were dead on your track. How's that navigator of yours shaping?'

'He's going to be good, sir.'

'That's fine,' said the senior officer and lapsed into silence.

'Will that be all, sir?'

'That'll be all, old boy. Good night!'

'Good night, sir."

He saluted and went out into the brilliant lighting of the hangar. There was no-one about. He could hear a mechanic whistling and the rhythmic thud of a refuelling unit. He hurried towards the Mess. He was cold. He was tired. He was twenty-two years old.

7 You've Got to be Dumb
to be Happy

The second winter on that station was harder. It was a bleak part of East Anglia, beet and corn-growing country with only trees to break the incessant gales from the North Sea that tore the brittle leaves from their branches in early September, found every crevice in our smoky huts and billowed the carpet on the ante-room floor in the temporary Mess.

The contractors were still busy. There were piles of bricks and steel window-frames and tiles by the concrete roads, and great pools of half-mixed plaster. Lorries cut smooth-edged wounds into the mud beneath the wet grass and the half-finished buildings were fringed with steel scaffolding that seemed like a three days' growth on a tramp's chin when we looked down from the air. Only the hangars were finished, but they had no heating and we crouched about the oil-stoves when mist deadened the countryside, burning the soles off our expensive shoes.

Half the aerodrome was waterlogged and there was mud everywhere and nothing to do after dinner, if there was no night flying, except play bridge or sit over the fire in one's room. Usually we changed out of dinner-jackets and drove out of the camp, past the half-frozen sentry and the whores who waited for the troops at the corner of the wood, into rural Suffolk, between the dead fields, the grey leafless trees, the pale cottages neatly thatched with Norfolk reed.

It was a relief to leave the camp and see ordinary life again and drink with strangers and watch the children playing about the lighted shops stuffed with Christmas rubbish. For when one flies the landscape has no reality but is only a flat far-away vista, a panorama with elusive landmarks to be recognized or high ground to be avoided. (A village with a thousand years of tradition only a few untidy cottages washed up about a church, a great industrial area but a glowing mound of light in the darkness.)

Some of the officers went down to the coast, to the empty seaside resorts with deserted promenades and huge faded tattered posters, or inland to the market towns where the old-fashioned shops had steps and small-paned windows. There they looked for women, driving many times through the streets, scanning the walkers till they saw a likely couple, then, running the car into the gutter, the driver would touch the horn lightly, till the girls came sliding towards them, their smiles and clothes masked by the dusk, stinking of cheap scent, not unattractive so long as they remained silent.

Every other week we flew at nights. Sometimes it was fine and we were high above the sleeping world with the stars real above and the rhythm of the motors sweet in one's ears and the little clusters of lights that were towns floating back till they disappeared beneath one's wing like drifting seaweed. But sometimes the weather was bad and the rain would beat into the open cockpit and we would fly in cloud for hours, the huge night-bombers rocking in the bumps and ice forming on leading edges and on the interplane struts and on the airscrews and we would be lost and frightened 1H in the storm-filled night.

The camp grew, but not in our eyes. Several officers were posted. Johnson finished his time and went into Dominion Airways. A new pilot was burned to death following a night-flying crash. The Mess Committee put a penny on beer and Wally was placed under close arrest for bouncing another cheque. The police raided Dawn's flat where we used to go after they closed, alleging it was being used for immoral purposes.

The Spring was sad with rain; but occasionally the weather lifted and the shy sunshine fell in moving patches on the country that stretched out to Cambridgeshire, pale and green and lovely, with the new crops breaking through the warm earth.

Dick was a good leader. Time after time he had brought the formation faultlessly over the far hedge with twenty feet to spare, so that we landed well down the aerodrome and the wheels had stopped turning before we reached the circle. Later in the morning we took off on engine test, climbing towards the ceiling of grey clouds that here and there showed a lighter pattern where the sun strove to break through. Below, visibility was bad, the familiar landmarks falsified by light mist, the very shape of the landscape camouflaged by the rain that slid in big tears down the surfaces of our goggles and drove in tiny pricks against our faces.

I put George (as we called the automatic pilot) into operation and we sat silently behind the dual wheels that moved now a little one way, now a little the other, now slightly backwards, now slightly forwards, holding the aircraft in a steady climb with uncanny precision. Dick looked down and I followed his glance. A number of Harts moved swiftly beneath us, locked in squadron formation. The grey light, gleaming on their wet silver wings, accentuated their effortless progress over the dim land beneath. It was impossible to estimate their height, difficult to judge their speed, hard to imagine that each unit was a separate machine, flown by a man who sat immobile, strapped in his narrow cockpit, his eyes, hard and alive behind his rain-coated goggles, fixed on his inside neighbour. My companion switched on his microphone.

'Cissy work!' He jerked his head sideways.

I nodded and glanced once more at the array of instruments before me, instinctively checking the oil pressures and temperatures of one engine against the other.

Now we were nearing the base of the clouds. As I looked up, wondering how thick they were, I felt a vague apprehension, a faint distaste for climbing into their cold, rainful interior that was stifled with a shrug of the shoulders. It was as if I feared the very obscurity of them, the sense of losing oneself in an unknown world. It was as a child lying awake, afraid to allow itself to sleep. For sleep it imagines clearly, not as a relief or rest from toil but as a surrender of the body, a twisting and blinding of the understanding, akin to death.

Suddenly the clouds were about us, shutting out all movement, all distance, blowing damp and cold against our faces. Minutes passed with only the rhythmic roar of the unsupercharged motors in our ears and the airscrews behind us cutting spinning circles of light in the haziness. Dick sat a little forward, the mist condensing on his helmet and eyebrows and fair moustache.

When we came out there was no sunshine, only a space with another layer of cloud above. It was a lost empty place with no living or moving thing, stretching to a far horizon in every direction, lit by an unseen sun. I took over the controls and flew with the wheels cutting the misty floor so that even the old-fashioned bomber seemed to be travelling fast. Then my companion nudged me in the ribs and pointed to the time. I held her on her course, crossing a silent white valley, then smashing through the opposite hill of cloud. It seemed that this was where the aeroplane really belonged, where the height and depth were in the scene about one, out of sight of the drabness, glittershot, so far below.

Dick nudged me in the ribs again and I closed the throttle and let the machine drop into the clouds, the wind crying in the wires, the big wooden airscrews whistling as they overran the motors. I began to sing a dirty song, moving the wheel from side to side to hold the wings level.

We came out south of the aerodrome, easily distinguishable by the glint of the wet tarmac, the gaunt hangars, the even expanse of greener grass.

I throttled down and turned in to land, finding a certain satisfaction in the purely mechanical actions of controlling the aircraft, in trying to fly well with even rates of turn, steady airspeed, good hold-off in a sure approach, sighing with contentment and pushing up my goggles as she dropped lightly on to the wheels and came to rest a few yards from the circle.

A little later I was standing outside the Flight Commander's office. From inside the hangar came the rattle of a drill, the clatter of tool on metal, the voices of the fitters and riggers as they sang and talked and swore. Outside they were filling the aircraft tanks with the rhythmic chugging of refuelling unit pumps. I could hear the flap of the wind stocking above me and the wind moaning and whimpering in the wires of the aircraft on the tarmac. There was the smell of petrol and dope and a flight droned overhead, sliding easily across the cloudy sky.

Dick, who had been up again in another aircraft, came in to land. He glided in, held off, then let her go down smoothly. I thought how easy it seemed and how one forgot the sweat of learning to fly, the fears never realized, the ambitions never achieved. Now the machine taxied towards me with Dick sitting very straight, swinging his head from side to side, keeping the aircraft moving with bursts of either engine, distinct twists of the throttle grip that made an airscrew sing in a halo of light and the engine snarl, then lapse to a mutter again.

As the four wheels of the undercarriage rolled on to the tarmac and the machine turned into the wind, the motors sobbed into silence, the airscrews jerked to rest, I watched him, silhouetted against the grey light above the cut-away edge of the cockpit, his strong familiar features framed by shabby leather helmet, topped by rusty goggles. Sometimes, the sight of some intimate scene, villages sprawling like puppies in the sun, rain-smoothed pavements inlaid with the lights of shops, of pub doorways, strangers lost in work, children in the grim world of their play, seem to hold more than the lingering picture thrown on to the screen of the mind. It is as if they mock the introspective glance, taunt the jaded passer-by with elusive, evasive promise.

So, watching Dick, for a flash it seemed that he symbolized youth; youth glorious in untried confidence, unconquerable in hardly-used courage, in its disinclination to profit by the experience of others. Then it was gone, the magic of it a thing shattered so that his image no longer brought a lump to my throat. It was only my friend, a hard-drinking flying-man who was ragged in Mess for his good looks.

It was a supper night, so after tea I changed into flannels and strolled down the corridor past the open door of Dick's room. He was brushing his hair and grinned at my reflection in the mirror.

'Shocking hair oil, this stuff of yours!'

I went in and sat on his bed. There was hardly room for the tin washbasin, chest of drawers, wardrobe, table and bookcase, while an iron stove pipe ran through the ceiling. The window gave an interrupted view of the next hut a few yards away and an oblong strip of sky. On the wall over the bed were several drawings of naked women, a large photograph of a very pretty girl and a placard from a dance-hall proclaiming that 'No Dressing or Undressing was allowed in these Lavatories'.

'Don't tell my mother I'm in the Air Force,' screamed another notice; 'she still thinks I'm playing a piano in a brothel.' The bookshelves contained several German beer mugs and some Service publications with the uninserted amendments neatly stacked at the side. In common with other rooms in the hut, a wireless played at full volume. One had to shout to make oneself heard.

'What are we doing to-night?' Dick said.

'Oh, I don't know, we might go down to the Bear for a quiet drink.'

'Euh! Euh! Not me, I'm economizing.'

'So that's why you sent your batman round to borrow my soap?'

'Surely. I've got to economize this month. My Mess bill's fifteen quid already,' he laughed. 'I don't know how I'm going to find the cash, especially as my tailors get a fiver on a banker's order.'

'You'll manage,' I said.

One of the sister squadron's aircraft flew over on a night flying test, a sudden roar of sound, a shadow flickering across the window.

'We might go to the movies,' Dick said.

It was getting dark when we arrived at the Bear. The cobbled yard was full of cars and through the open windows of the bar I could see that there were many of my brother officers inside, and women too, brave with make-up, their charming inane chatter glittering in the pattern of sound. In the bar we were immediately surrounded, drinks were pushed into our hands. Dick's, as usual, was neat Scotch.

Someone told the story of the bomber captain who handed over to his second pilot at twenty-five feet. The second pilot's name was Newton. I went over to a man who sat in the corner. He had recently been discharged from hospital after a crash.

'I thought you were on sick leave?'

'I am.'

'But you live …?'

'In Scotland. I went home for a month. But after a few days, well …'

'You don't fit any more.'

But most of the talk was of shop, of the recent exercises, happenings on various stations and when we were to get the new monoplanes. It was all easy now with the bright lights gleaming on tankard and bottle and a pretty girl at one's side. One was a night-bomber pilot, courageous and confident, there was nothing in the game, it was pansy.

Only occasionally, as the door opened to admit someone with the rain sliding from the edge of his hat, shaking himself like an indignant dog, one was reminded of the darkness outside which waited for us, patient and quiet, because there was no need for haste.

The World Owes Me A Living

I went hunting wild
After the wildest beauty in the world,
Which lies not calm in eyes, or braided hair,
But mocks the steady running of the hour…

— Wilfred Owen

Chapter 1

At the beginning of the summer I got a flying job again.

It was with a circus that travelled to a new town each day and gave joy rides and exhibitions of aerobatic piloting. We worked right through the sun-filled days, for it was a fine season, the long hours and responsibility offset by our ever-changing surroundings.

Every morning we waited on the temporary aerodrome for the Chief Pilot who led the formation from town to town. Our mouths dry with the previous evening's drinking we would grumble softly at the delay as we watched the last of the ground equipment being loaded into lorries. It would still be early, a little after sunrise with the dew-coated grass holding our footprints, only the clatter of tools or the rattle of an engine running up, etching into the stillness, the air tinged with the bitter smell of burnt oil or the sweet scent of dope. And the slipstream of each aircraft would flatten a fantail of grass, beat cold and damp against our faces, shape our flying suits about our legs.

Then, when the lorry convoy had departed, we would take off and formate on Chuck who would lead us with quiet confidence over the pale countryside to the next town. We usually flew at eight hundred feet or so for advertising purposes, the brightly doped aircraft as a string of coloured beads against the grey English weather.

If the visibility was very bad, for we were compelled to fly whenever it was possible to get off the ground, I would edge up inside Chuck's wing-tip and he would turn in the open cockpit of the giant air liner, doing a thumbs-up as he raised his hand to wipe away the rain from his goggles.

Often I would glance from the sodden map on my knee to the rain-grey ground, uncertain of our exact position. But

Chuck, although a Canadian, seldom erred, for six years of Service flying had given him an intimate knowledge of the essential shape of England so that presently a familiar piece of country would slide back under my wing, each copse and road junction, each curve of railway, known to me, the pattern of it engraved in my mind. Then memory would trap my understanding and the sequence of time would be broken and I would again be stationed at some neighbouring aerodrome.

When we arrived we would find the advance party busy marking out the field, setting up the wire rope to hold back the crowd and wiring up the loud-speaker system. After a shoot-up of the town, over which we flew as low as previous experience of the police told us was unlikely to result in trouble, the first of the spectators would be buying tickets at the gate.

There would be small boys, often armed with model aircraft and a surfeit of technical knowledge who tampered with the machines if they were given the slightest opportunity. Giggling girls too, bold-eyed and hare-brained, strolled in couples, flaunting what beauty youth had given them. If takings were low they were sometimes given free flights.

Now the loud-speakers would begin to play dance music and the mellow inane rhythm would sweep the bare field, ripple against cars filled with picnickers and journey outwards losing itself in the placid countryside.

Occasionally some man, middle-aged and neat in shabby suit, would approach and mention diffidently that he too had once been a pilot, in the German War of 1914-18, and would ask to be taken up 'for the first time in years'. He was generally very frightened, the flight serving to resurrect long-forgotten memories, to breathe life into fears dead these years. And then it was difficult to reconcile him with the saga of the Royal Flying Corps, to imagine him slim and arrogant in youth, clad in bearskin flying coat with nervous tobacco-stained fingers, to believe that he had lived and flown in an earlier age of aviation.

Before the programme began Cookson, our announcer, would commence his sales talk interspersed with flippances that went on over the speakers all the afternoon. 'We are not here to- day and gone tomorrow,' the confident impersonal voice would blare above the multifarious noises of the flying field. 'We're here to-day and gone to-night if we can get the money.' With the true showman's contempt for the mentality of his audience he would sell flights by shrewd understanding of their fear, pride, and ignorance, the upper-class accent and affected casualness of his trade serving to gloss the insidious genre of his patter.

Operating from small aerodromes, or more often fields, demanded skill above the ordinary, but we were all experienced and knew each others' habits in every item of the show. We did as much joy-riding as possible and by cutting down the circuit to an absolute minimum could take a customer up for a flight of three minutes.

I used to look up at my passenger's face in the tiny mirror that was mounted on the centre section strut. The majority of them had never flown before and fear was usually stamped on their features. But sometimes there was wonder and awe in a face taut against the slipstream and one could sense the sudden appreciation of flight, understand the magic of first entrance into a new world. On these occasions I would look backwards in my mind, wishing that I was beginning again, memory throwing a kindly light upon the drudgery and more unpleasant details of my learning to fly.

As the crowd's interest began to flag and the queues wilted away from the ticket kiosks some item of aerobatics would be announced by Cookson or some sponsored competition quickly organized.

Now and again, always when least expected, a machine would crash, the melodramatic unreality of it ploughing into the tenor of our flying, the placid tones of the announcer as he calmed the crowd at variance with our feelings as we each gauged the extent of the damage to aircraft and personnel, drawing for this purpose upon experience that was only too sound and mature.

Knowing the pilot intimately we would, illogically, match our skill against his, wondering as usual at the strangeness of fortune, reassuring ourselves that he at any rate had been the victim of bad luck 'the only luck in flying' or that he had taken a chance once too often.

And the pilot's joining of that throng of good fellows one had known who had climbed into a cockpit for the last time brought the familiar thought, forgotten in an hour, the wonder that one should still be alive. In Mess and Pilots' Room that night the genteel voice of a radio announcer would freeze all interest, still every movement, command silence till someone, glass half raised, murmured 'Christ' very softly, adding in thoughtful tones some guarded praise of the deceased couched in flying slang.

※

Autumn came early that year and the trees were filmed with brown as we flew back to winter quarters. The clouds were low and we flew beneath them since none of the aircraft had blind-flying equipment. It was bumpy and I followed the stick about, bending my head against the prickling rain.

Before doing this circus work I had never really understood how much there is of England, how many lazy villages and prim market towns, how much pasture and ploughland set with neat farms, how much fen and bog and moor, how many great houses still standing in the quiet of their deer-flecked parks. I had never previously realized how the great industrial towns, palled by smoke, scabbed the green countryside, and how much wildness still lingers in mountainous country, away from the Scottish lowlands, the Sabbatical Welsh slate villages, or the clean red roofs of Yorkshire hamlets.

As we flew, banks of hanging cloud would drift towards us, grey and angry, weighing on our shoulders as they crushed us earthwards. Then we would forget the rain-dimmed earth and concentrate even more closely upon each others' wing-tips till we came into a clear patch and flew once more in freedom.

It took us two and a half hours to cover the hundred and ninety miles to the farm where the flying headquarters were and we scraped over the last range of low hills with two hundred feet to spare. One by one the pilots went in and touched down, seemingly careless as they swish-tailed over the fence for a perfect landing.

I rolled on to my back and pulled over the cock of the inverted petrol system. As I hung on my straps looking down at the sky it suddenly angered me that I should be flying this specially built aerobatic machine for the last time. In many hours flying I had never strained a wire and it now seemed to have become part of me, the control surfaces extensions to my body.

When I landed some minutes later the secretary of the circus was waiting on the tarmac. Tall and bald with much jaw he was unpopular with the pilots. As I swung into wind with a burst of throttle he walked up and waited for me to get out. I switched off, pushed up my goggles and got out slowly noticing once more the strange feeling of being in a familiar world after the deadness of it seen from above, a thing apart and map-like.

'Was that necessary?" he spoke with the confidence of authority.

'What?' I said.

'That last ten minutes of aerobatic flying!'

'Are you trying to give me a raspberry?' I could see Chuck grinning as he leaned against the hangar door.

'It was definitely dangerous. You're not paid for that sort of thing except as part of the display.'

'Talking of pay,' I said, 'you owe me forty-five quid for the last few weeks as it is.'

'That'll be attended to.'

'When?'

'To-night. The Owner's paying out at the Black Boy.'

I said I was glad to hear it. As I walked away I could hear him whimpering at a mechanic. I got into Chuck's car which had been driven down by one of the ground engineers.

'Hear they're paying out,' Chuck said pressing the starter. I nodded and took the proffered chewing gum.

'We'll have a couple of beers on that.'

'You bet," Chuck said. He put his hand out- side the windscreen and played with the wiper till it began to work. 'You've heard that this show's bankrupt?'

'It's a fact, is it?'

'It's a fact all right.'

'You won't see another good circus in this country.'

'It's about the end of the racket,' Chuck said. 'It's been good fun.'

We began to climb and he changed into third holding the knob forward to prevent her slipping out of gear. 'What are you going to do this winter?' he went on.

'Now that I've got the odd ticket I'm hoping for an air-line job,' I said.

'Muck that 'bus driving.'

'It's better than washing cars in a garage. I did that two winters ago.'

'Remember the old advertising game? Flying banners? If I can't get into ice hockey this winter I guess I'll be trying

Charlie to take me on again.'

'Muck that, too,' I said, 'nice pre-war kites with a ceiling of minus two hundred feet.'

Chuck laughed. 'I hear Jack's coming down to the Black Boy to-night.'

'Good Lord! What's he doing now?'

'Well, you remember him piling up on that long-distance record?'

'Yes, I remember.'

'That put him down the pan financially, but I think he's all set again now. He's been joy-riding for the Owner of this outfit all the summer … down in some God damn East Coast seaside town. Doing his own maintenance too, I believe.'

'Did the Owner back that record bid?'

'I guess that's about the size of it,' Chuck said.

⚹

By seven o'clock we had been paid off and were seated down the cocktail bar of the Black Boy. As usual the conversation began desultorily with mundane things but quickly became an eager discussion of flying laced with the jargon of our trade.

Several of the pilots were already chatting to golden-skinned women who perched gracefully on high stools sipping their cocktails. After several drinks a blonde, hitherto unattached, began to smile at me. She had a well-made body, its slim lines aggravated by a tight white dance frock of dull material. Her hands were small and capable with pointed fingers and when she smiled her cruel little mouth showed tiny perfect teeth. She came over to my neighbour, whom she knew, and skilfully included me in the conversation. We were introduced and she finished her Pimms and toyed with the empty tankard. I bought her another and we talked politely of the weather.

She told me she was a member of the local repertory company, which was a lie, then steered me on to flying. I began to brag by understatement in the English manner. She told me the joke about the Jew and the fishing-rod and I replied with the story of the Zoo keeper and the porcupines. Suddenly I saw Jack through the glass door and pushed myself away from the counter.

'Hey!' said my neighbour, 'where are you going to?'

'To purchase a horse.'

'What! already!'

'Buy the blue-eyed popsy a drink. I'll be back in a minute.' I chased Jack through the foyer. He turned quickly as I touched his shoulder then smiled and grabbed my hand. He had grown a moustache to cover the scar on his upper lip.

'Hullo,' I said.

'Well, I'll be ...'

'You're looking fit,' I said. 'They made a good job on that face of yours.'

'Haven't I seen you since then?'

'Not since the start ...'

'I went partially through the dashboard,' he said, 'but luckily it was my face.'

A middle-aged couple in evening dress passed into the dining-room viewing our flannel trousers with distaste.

'We must have a drink on this,' I said.

'Several drinks, old boy,' he lit a cigarette. 'Oh! By the way, I've a surprise for you ... I'm going to be married!'

I expressed the correct amount of surprise and I congratulated him.

'I think you know her ...'

'That's hardly likely,' I said, 'who is she?'

'Her name's Eve ... Eve Heathly!'

I searched for matches and he lit my cigarette.

'Yes,' I said. 'I know her.' I hoped my voice sounded normal.

'She's here to-night. I want you to …' An effeminate waiter slithered up and said that Captain Graves's trunk call was through.

'She's in the lounge. Will you go along. I'll be up in a minute and remember you're feeding with us.'

I found her seated on the arm of a huge armchair by the fireplace, a familiar pose with one foot twisted about the other ankle, her skirt as she leaned backwards drawn above her smooth knees. In the diffused light with make-up bringing youth back into her face and the clean lines of her features drawn against the funereal setting of the lounge, with the firelight playing wet on her silk stockings, I caught a glimpse of her as I first remembered her. (As a scholar, some phrase of a dead tongue lighting his mind, transiently sees and knows a world long forgotten, understands men rotten these thousand years.)

'Hullo, Eve!' I said.

She looked up and greeted me saying that Jack had told her to expect me. I went over and sat down.

'Cigarette?'

'Thanks.'

The fire burned brightly with a thin brittle sound. A telephone bell rang and I heard the laminated rattle of voices in the bar as the porter opened the door, a sudden hush falling as he called a name.

'So you know Jack?' I said.

'I'm engaged to him.' She twisted the ring on her slim finger.

'So I understand.'

'Any objections?'

'Yes.' As I spoke I heard her suck her breath through her teeth.

'I never remember you wanting to marry me!'

I made no answer and she went on: 'So now you're going to butt in and save your friend's soul?'

'No,' I said. 'I don't think I am.'

'Thank you, Paul.' She flashed me a smile that left her eyes unwrinkled. 'It would hurt him terribly if … if you told him things. He's terribly in love with me; and I with him.'

'You always are.'

'You may feel virtuous,' she said, 'but there's no need to behave like a swine.'

'You're not doing so badly,' I said, 'Jack's a good type.'

'And why shouldn't I make him happy?'

'You never stuck to one man that long. Why d'you want to marry him anyway?'

A waitress came in and asked if we wanted dinner. Eve ordered for the three of us and I told her to bring drinks.

'You wouldn't understand,' she said when the room was quiet again.

'Have you stopped drugging yourself?' I asked. She was making up her mouth and tilted her head bird-wise, watching her reflection in a tiny vanity mirror before she answered.

'What are you talking about?' her voice was too sharp.

'You know what I mean. Cocaine. Snow. Call it what you like.'

'Yes. I've stopped.'

'When?'

'Three … three months ago.'

'I didn't know you had it in you!'

'I went to a home … a terrible place … you can't imagine what it was like.' She got up and smoothed down her skirt. 'Give me another cigarette.' Puffing it nervously alight she moved across to the fireplace and leaned against the mantelshelf.

'Paul!'

'Yes.'

'I think it would break him if … if he knew what you know.'

'What do I say?' I said.

She ignored me and went on: 'He idolizes me, Paul. You've got no idea … it … it frightens me sometimes.'

'Well?'

'What are you going to do?'

'I'm keeping quiet,' I said.

'Thank you, Paul.'

'I'm not doing it for you,' I said. The waitress brought in the drinks. 'I hope you'll play the game by him.' We sat silently for some seconds. She went across to the grand piano and began to play Chopin's Twentieth Prelude. She sat very still, the firelight now lambent on her hair, an expression of concentration bringing out the hardness in her features.

'Stop that,' I said.

'But you …'

'That's all dead,' I said. 'Leave it that way.'

A few minutes later Jack returned and the three of us went down to dinner. Over the meal we discussed the future.

'You're lucky to have your licences,' Jack said, 'Chuck's well away too.'

'What are your plans?' I asked.

'We're getting married soon,' he said, "then taking a flat in Town and I'm going to work for my Second Class Navigator's Ticket.'

I looked across at Eve.

He'll be working at Martin's Navigation School in Notting Hill Gate, I thought, as I was when I first met you. It was summer then, the girls pink-faced under their face powder, the beer warm in the pubs and the flower sellers standing in the shade and sprinkling their wares. The pavements were fervent to one's feet and the hot air lay thick in the streets.

In the nights the light mists held the glare of London so that the sky was domed with bronze. Only down by the river was it cool and we used to wander there stepping lightly along the dirty pavements while the black water slid by; blind to the newspaper-clad sleepers and the bright-eyed whores who peddled love in the dingy streets running up to the Strand.

As we lay in bed in the mornings it was so quiet that it might have been the country except for the somnolent mumbling of the traffic. Then the clatter of hooves and the thin rattling of milk bottles, sometimes the swish of tyres, the distorted cries of street vendors, the mellow tinkle of a barrel organ.

'Have you got DTs?' Jack said. 'Sink that drink.'

Later in the evening we went back to the bar. One of the other pilots had got my blonde.

It was just before closing time that Chuck thought of his great idea. He was leaning heavily against the bar but only his eyes showed that he was drunk.

'We'll form a joy-riding company,' he said, touching my arm, 'you and I and Jack and keep the old spirit going.'

'Not in the winter surely?'

'Next summer.'

A Dachshund bitch belonging to a woman in the corner waddled across and began to beg. I fed it on almonds and potato crisps.

'It's not a bad idea actually.' Jack took a long pull at his beer.

Eve, who was laughing and gay with men about her, took sudden interest. Chuck explained the project. She rushed to him and caught his hands.

'My dear, I think it's a lovely idea, absolutely wizard. We could get down South somewhere, perhaps Bournemouth way. God, how I hated the peoples' accents in the North this summer.'

'What about the cash?' I said.

'Paul's going up-stage,' Chuck murmured gently.

'It's all right for you, Paul,' Jack said. 'With your tickets you can get a job any time wiping lavatory seats on Dominion Airways.'

'To hell with Dominions,' I said. 'I'd have to go to their school and then be second pilot to some bog rat. I'd rather come in with you boys next summer. I'll get work with a lesser Air Line for the winter.'

'It's kind of awkward about the dough,' Chuck said suddenly. "But I should be in the money this fall on the ice hockey racket and if you boys live chaste lives you ought to be able to save something.'

'I'll back you,' Eve said.

'Then it's settled,' cried Chuck.

The more we discussed the matter the more we liked it. Alcohol had warmed our minds, every trouble was dismissed, every difficulty shelved as unimportant. Tomorrow, I thought, we will each of us wake, sober and mindful into a real world. And then this idea, flaccid and impracticable when seen in perspective, will blur into the memory of another party when comradeship and sincerity and a meaning to life brimmed every tankard.

※

Jack and Eve were married late that autumn. The bride was held up on her way to church by a funeral which foretold bad luck, ill wishers said. It was a cold unkind day with the wind insistent in the telegraph wires.

Chapter 2

I sat back in the cockpit, the spring sunshine warm on my face. To the east the snow had robbed the landscape of its character, only the yellow faces of the houses, the keen line of railway and road standing out in the quietness. But westwards there were great patches of countryside mournful with winter, the rotting snow edging the wan fields, lying in crutch of tree, drifted in sunless corners.

The second pilot, who was flying the machine, glanced sideways and grinned, jerking his thumb first at the clock and then downwards to signify that we were on our track and on time. It was an easy route, crossing featured country and beaconed for night runs. The youngster had been flying with me for some months, and at first a sharp inquiry as to our position or the estimated time of our arrival would bring no specific answer and I would look up from my log to find him several degrees off his course.

But, gradually, flying the same route in all kinds of weather, he became accustomed to the rhythm of it, the details of the run clear in his mind. Soon I would vouch for his ability to the Chief Pilot who would await a favourable day and then pack him off alone, proud and confident, with a load of freight.

Whenever I was able I went to one of the ice rinks to watch Chuck playing ice hockey.

As I sat there, huddled in my greatcoat against the cold air that drifted off the arena, as I heard through the ragged roar of the crowd the crack of the puck against the boards, the hiss of skates cutting ice, the clatter of sticks, the sharp commands of the players, there was something familiar in the solemn concentration on Chuck's face, in his certainty, his quick deliberate movements. I had seen all this before in aircraft dodging through thick weather, or building up ice in stifling cloud, or lost at night when the petrol gauges had a new fascination.

One evening late in the season Chuck was cut in the face by the puck and I went round to the dressing-room to see him. I found him standing in the corner arguing some technical point with another player who had been hit on the head and smelt of chloroform.

Waiting for them to finish, the steam and smell of sweat and embrocation, the ribald conversation, brought back memories of rugger, of draughty stone-floored school dressing-rooms when a place in a boys' team represented the consummation of ambition. And later in London when meetings at Waterloo and a scrappy game in the suburbs followed by an evening's pub-crawling brought action and friendship into a grim existence, provided an escape from dismal lodgings and a fear-ridden office.

'That's a fairly useful-sized cut,' I said.

'You ought to see what the puck can do back home,' Chuck said, "when you're playing some place way up in the sticks on an open rink and the damn thing's frozen!'

I lit the Camel he offered. 'How's things?' he asked.

'They're all right,' I said. 'And you?'

'This racket finishes in another fortnight.'

'And then?'

He got to his feet and began to pace the changing-room.

'I'm still thinking about this joy-riding show.'

'Good Lord,' I said. 'I never thought you were serious about that.'

'You bet I'm serious. Jack's keen too … you know he pipped his navigator's ticket?'

'I didn't see his name in the pass list in *The Times*.'

'He failed the DR paper and something else. It's getting tougher all the time I believe. You know they're both back in Town?'

'I hadn't heard.'

'They've been expecting you.'

'I haven't had much time lately. How are they getting along?'

'Swell as far as I can see. Anyhow, what about this joy-riding business?'

I thought for a minute.

'I'm in,' I said.

'We're both keen for you to come in but we don't want you to throw up a good job.'

'It's not a particularly good job and I'm browned off with 'bus driving in any case. What's the jen on your idea?'

'Eve's putting up the money … can you manage a couple of hundred quid?'

'I might scrape about a hundred and forty!'

'That's grand.'

'What about kites?'

'We've practically got 'em. Two old '504's and 'EN' your old aerobatic ship in the circus. It's been in the market since.'

'Don't I know it.'

'I also think we've got the right joint … Swanmouth on the South Coast. I don't think there's ever been a joy-riding concern there except for barnstormers … and it's no jerkwater town either.'

'What about a field?"

Chuck grinned. 'I flew down there the other afternoon and photographed the outskirts of the town. There's one ideal site. I went along afterwards and saw it from the deck. About two miles from the town with an old hay shed we could use for a hangar and the local hard by. The field's been used for grazing.'

'Sounds too good to be true. Did you try the owner?'

'No. Thought maybe it would rocket the price.'

'What about maintenance?'

'There's Matthews who was with the circus … a damn good

ground engineer … he's all set to muck in. He'd want a boy to help him and you could do a spot with the daily inspections?'

'Fair enough. It all seems to be working out beautifully. When do we get going?'

'About the end of May.'

The trainer came up and swore at Chuck telling him to get changed as the Doctor wanted to see him. Chuck cursed him back automatically and paid no attention. When he spoke his voice was suddenly thoughtful.

'It's going to be fun, Paul … the three of us together again. We don't belong to this modern flying, they like little pansies who have dozens of tickets and fly by clocks and gadgets and radio. There's nothing left in it. We were born a damn sight too late.'

'It takes a crack in the face to make you sentimental,' I said. 'Get changed and see the Doc and we'll trickle down to the local for the odd noggin.'

※

Suddenly, through the haze, I caught sight of it, the shapelessness of the town with the smoke from the chimneys piling up thickly down wind. I turned over my map and oriented the photograph pinned on the back, turning the aircraft steeply so as to look down sun.

I soon found the field, much smaller than it had been in my imagination, with the two Avros lined up before the hay shed. I pushed my map into my pocket and dived towards them. The airspeed needle climbed steadily, the controls grew stiff beneath my hands and feet. As the pasture that was to be our aerodrome grew clearer, more earth-like, till it seemed that I was flying into the trees at the north end, I pulled back sharply on the stick relying on the specially strengthened structure to bear the strain.

And now, stone-like and immobile, I was pressed hard into

the seat. As every rivet, strut, spar, and longeron took the strain it seemed that my body joined the protest screamed by the interplace bracing wires, the anguish expressed by airscrew thrash and the rattle of the engine.

The horizon came up to meet me, the sky rolling itself away as a blind. I eased the stick forward and the strain was lifted from me. Putting on full bank I rolled off my back into normal flying position again, keeping up the nose with top rudder while the engine fought for revolutions and the airspeed needle dropped off the clock.

Looping and rolling and spinning for the first time for months, the outline of each manoeuvre clear in my mind, I felt suddenly happy in the insecurity of it, the quick certain movements, the latent fear that braced the mind. Again it occurred to me that flying was the only reality: that as every action of life is but relative to the act of being alive, so every aspect of consciousness was, to me, subordinate to the mere piloting of an aircraft.

Chuck and Jack were standing by the Avros when I landed and ran across to help me turn into wind.

'Nice drop of aerobatics,' Chuck said. 'How was the weather?'

'Trifle on the thick side,' I said. 'Circled some town for a long time, couldn't recognize it till I saw a girl I knew coming out of a chemist's.'

'That line will cost you a round,' Jack said. 'Anyhow, you're a lucky lad to have missed all the donkey work.'

'I realize that.'

'We certainly had some fun, what with gas supply, getting posters out and fixing up this field,' Chuck said.

'Was there bother over that?' I asked.

'Not really. It belonged to the local minister – '

'Parson,' Jack said. 'Cut out that bum American talk.'

'I'm a Canadian.'

'It's the same thing – '

'What d'yar mean, the same thing?'

'Pipe down you bastards,' I said, 'what about the field?'

'It's glebe,' Jack explained.

'Was the Holy Man any trouble?'

'No, he was all right. He's got a couple of queer sons though. One's ill or something and the other hasn't worked since he was cracked up in the War. He's been shooting down Germans in bars ever since.'

'That's where all the best flying's done,' I said. 'Are there many visitors in Swanmouth yet?'

'Not many, but the locals say they should start rolling in next week.'

'I see Matthews is here?' I said.

'He's actually in Town at the moment,' Jack said.

'I saw his goats as I came in to land.'

'Of all the hobbies …' Jack said. 'But if we had him at all, it had to be goats and all.' He scratched his jaw. 'I must remember to tell Eve to be careful how she mentions them. I believe he's rather touchy on the point?'

'Touchy?' Chuck said. 'Remember the time, Paul, when someone in the circus made a crack about him taking them around in his car?'

I nodded and the others gave me a hand at pushing 'EN' into line with the Avros. There they stood, the three aircraft with whose aid and our own skill and a little luck we could hope to wrest a living for some months to come. We stood there silently, looking at them, the gaunt Avros with many years' flying to their credit, their broad wings swaying in the breeze, and my machine neatly dwarfed beside them, rocking gently on its wide undercarriage.

Now that we had committed ourselves and the undertaking was about to begin we all felt a sense of awe tinged with foreboding. Jack voiced the general feeling when he said: 'If we crash one of 'em, my lads, we're certainly ditched.'

'We'll be OK,' Chuck said. 'Anyhow, we're wasting time, Eve's waiting for us at the Blue Boar. There's an excuse for a rye or two to-night.'

'How is she?' I asked as we walked across the field.

'She's grand,' Jack answered, 'and very excited about this show. She's quite sure it's going to be an enormous success.'

She was ever that way, I thought, eternally hopeful for the future. No disappointment could dull the keenness of her anticipation, no painful experience convince her that the future did not hold the secret of happiness and peace of mind. Greedily she went forward, blindly confident as an animal. And animal-like only old age could disillusion her, only death be her defeat. It would take the withering of her body and the fading of her beauty to kill this meretricious faith.

※

As Chuck drove out of the field I noticed a poster advertising the flying stuck on the gate- post.

'What's all this ace aerobatic pilot stuff?' I asked.

'That's you,' Chuck said. 'It's all for advertising purposes so there's no need to be modest.'

Chapter 3

By the end of the week we were working hard.

I would drive out each morning before breakfast to help Matthews with inspections. It was peaceful out there in the clear freshness, the gaudy posters, the tattered wind stocking, the cigarette packets and sodden cellophane, belonging to a sleeping world.

Matthews whistled as he worked, occasionally pausing to talk in guttural tones of the work in hand or of animals which were his main interest in life.

Often it was cold, the tools clumsy in our hands and on some mornings rain drifted into the open-sided hay shed, soaking us as we checked each detail of engine and airframe.

One of the engines caused us a lot of trouble as the aircraft had previously belonged to a concern whose custom it was to fit a serviceable engine for the few days covering the annual inspection and then having obtained a year's Certificate of Airworthiness, replace the original power unit, which would have been immediately condemned. It then only remained for them to forge the necessary details.

The foibles of civil aviation was one of the ground engineer's special subjects and many a story of shady undertakings or inside information concerning famous flights was woven into the pattern of our early morning work.

After breakfast we tested the machines over the town, flying in tight formation and breaking up over the promenade for aerobatics. Then the long day began. The morning was usually quiet and when customers were few we sat around in deck-chairs reading and listening to the radio. The greater part of the afternoon was spent in the cockpit given good weather, passenger after passenger being provided with some of the thrills of flying for a few shillings.

First they were shown how to step into the cockpit without putting a foot through the wing fabric and then how to do up the safety belt. Then the engine roared and we bumped off on another trip, the front seat occupant's hands grabbing nervously at the frail cockpit doors. A few moments later we landed again, I having earned a little money and my passenger having been given a transient topic of conversation.

Through the day I would watch the progress of farm workers, of roadmen ditching and hedging, follow carts or the trend of a golf match, watch the high diving at the open air baths or scan the yard of the Blue Boar for strange cars. Now and again I did longer flights up and down the coast, or among the clouds, tearing through virgin valleys, climbing lonely slopes, crashing into dazzling hillsides that came wet and grey into one's face, till sunshine was reached once more.

Some of the customers were almost permanent, mostly girls Chuck had picked up in local cocktail bars. Spectators too would gather on the road or sit inside the hedge and watch the flying. If business was bad they could sometimes be persuaded to pay for a flight.

The evenings, with the hazy rays of the sinking sun picking out the hedges and so emphasizing the pastoral pattern of the neighbouring country were the busiest of the day. We worked steadily now, taking off across wind to save taxying, till darkness smoothed the colour from the land and stars netted the sky.

The last flight completed and the crowds shooed away by the boy who helped Matthews, we gathered in the bell tent we called 'Head- quarters' and lay back, happily exhausted with the day's work, drinking some of the bottled beer that was stacked in crates at the back of the tent.

Chuck would often play on what he called his 'gee-tar', singing softly in clear tenor, sometimes songs of his own composing, sometimes flying, ditties to which we roared the ribald ending to each verse and sometimes his favourites, songs of 'the boys back home', 'He was coming down the grade', 'Sweet Emalina', and 'The Tattooed Lady'.

Jack would sit still and silent except for joining in a chorus. If he ever spoke it was to phrase some experience in stereotyped expressions or to couch some hard-thought conclusion in evasive flying slang. Often he left as flying finished for Eve would be waiting for him with the car, impatient for an evening's drinking in the more fashionable bars in the town itself.

After the first few days we expected one or other of the parson's sons for a drink or a chat. The elder, whose name was Jerry, was small and finely made, his features deriving a certain passive arrogance from the scars of a war-time crash. He came in quickly, silently, almost sullen, seemingly ashamed of his inability to earn a living, quick to resent any remark which he could twist into a reflection upon his character.

We offered him beer, saying little, and once alcohol had dulled the sting of pride he would quickly become talkative, bragging till Chuck winked at us to cover his embarrassment. And finding, with intoxication, a glorious justification of himself in half-forgotten deeds, recalling the German War now triumphant with twenty years of peace, he would become ridiculous as, flushed and glassy-eyed, he swaggered till one of us took him down the dust-soft lane to the Rectory, oblivious to the surroundings that were rich with summer.

His brother Brian was of different calibre. He was big and good-looking, his cheeks and eyes aflame with the hectic colour and life of phthisis, his mind sharp with that filthy disease. A small disability pension, for he too had suffered in war, satisfied his few needs and he was able to give some of it to his brother. He drank necessarily very sparingly and was unusually quiet and eager to repay any small kindness by helping with the books or getting goods we wanted from Swanmouth.

They shared a hobby which consisted of the most careful perusal of the *London Gazette* through which they followed with some avidity the Service careers of those who had been equivalent or junior to them in rank as comrades in arms.

One day early in June we were asked to join in a pageant at a town some miles along the coast. I was to give a demonstration of aerobatics and crazy flying and the others would be giving joy-rides on a percentage basis. We worked late the previous evening, completing fuelling and inspections by car headlights and took off at dawn with Eve and Matthews as passengers in the Avros.

An early-morning mist, as the bloom on a plum, took life from the earth, lay in the hollows of the hills to the north as milk in a saucer. We flew in tight formation, often grinning at one another in exultation at a perfect day. Chuck, who had been to a party the previous evening and was suffering from the after effects, had a flagon of beer with him out of which he drank from time to time, holding the stick with his knees as he did so.

I looked at my companions occasionally as we moved across the sky, wing tip to wing tip, the machines gently rising and falling as a line of buoys in a swell. The precision of their piloting represented years of training under stringent discipline; each manoeuvre showed a polish gained through hundreds of hours in the air, every decision resulted from the devotion of a life to a trade.

And glancing at my map and pushing it back into my pocket, I thought of the pilots I should meet that day, many of them old friends. On the journey westwards with the little shadows of the clouds puddling the calm sea I considered, not for the first time, the satisfaction I should have in their company, in the realization that being one of them somehow gave a meaning to my own existence. Shabbily dressed, with motor salesmens' accents, usually trained on short service commissions in the Royal Air Force, taught to drink and live above their incomes while still in their teens, turned out to look for work in their middle twenties, they cared for no one, drifting from job to job, nearly always in flying, till it killed them or broke their health so that they failed a medical examination.

✳

All was in readiness when we arrived and the pilots had already gathered in a special beer tent at the rear of one of the hangars. By eleven o'clock crowds were thronging the enclosures and flying began. Cookson was announcing, his well-known voice bringing back a nostalgia for the days of the travelling circus.

I took ten people up before the luncheon interval and then adjourned to the beer tent. A pilot I had known in the Service was telling a story of a passenger of his that morning who had implied that his part in the German War as an aviator had been no mean one and had gone on to ask to what pressure were the wings inflated these days. We talked on, mostly of crashes and escapes from sudden death, each incident being greeted with general laughter and Rabelaisian comment.

A tall diffident man approached and asked if I remembered him. I said I didn't, though I thought I'd seen him somewhere.

'I was in your flight once for a few days. M'name's Casey.' We shook hands and I bought him a drink.

'You're running a joy-ride show, aren't you?' he asked. I nodded and he went on to ask how we were doing.

'Quite nicely,' I said.

'You wouldn't be wanting another pilot, I suppose?'

It was something in the way he looked at me as he spoke that jogged my memory. Then I remembered him, and the scandal that he had never lived down for abandoning a light bomber by parachute, leaving a young gunner to be burnt to death. And after that several dubious crashes in civil flying till the aviation insurance companies had put up his premium to a prohibitive figure and so ruined him. I told him that we were full and he sighed and swallowed his drink in silence.

'What are you doing now?'

'I've struck rather a bad patch lately, but hope things will look up soon. It's all these youngsters who've been trained at Kemble and never seen the Service. They snap up the jobs because they're lousy with money and have a couple of tickets.'

'Are you flying here?' I asked when he had brought the beers.

'Yes, Got a temporary berth for the day. Taking up five at a time in a single-engined kite. Talk about being browned off!'

'I'm sorry I can't help – '

'That's all right, but this sort of thing does get one down. Of course, you heard about me crashing?'

'No,' I said. 'I haven't heard anything.'

'I've had bad luck,' he went on. 'Got a bastard against me when I was in Cambrian Coast Airways. When I came out of hospital last time he put the ruddy insurance wallah against me. Now I'm bloody well mucked. No one can say that I can't cope … I can fly as well as the best of 'em.' He rubbed his jaw nervously with the back of his hand. 'Some of the boys say that I've got the jitters. I've heard them. But I'm OK. If I wasn't all right I wouldn't be able to pass the Medical Board … would I?'

'No,' I said. 'I don't suppose you would.'

'You haven't heard them talking about me?'

'No,' I lied.

Far away I could hear my engine being started.

'Have another drink?'

'Not for me – '

'Why not? Have one for the road?'

'I'm doing aerobatics in a moment.'

'A couple will set you up. Don't tell me you've never flown when you're half shut?'

'I've flown when I've been gassed all right,' I said, 'but there's too much courage in that stuff for this job.'

'As you like, old boy.'

'Chin, chin,' I said, 'I must go and juggle with death.'

✖

The strong sunlight splashed into my eyes as I came out on to the aerodrome. Soon I was in the cockpit again with the straps hard on my shoulders.

Doing my demonstration, hearing the roar of the crowd who swung their white blobs of faces to follow me as standing corn swayed by wind, sensing their inarticulate lust for the blinding novelty of a crash, seeing the ground horribly near, stick and rudder moving quickly and easily through full range of movement, feeling ever subconsciously attentive for the slightest irregularity of engine note, the combination of these things suddenly pleased me, driving the normal apprehension from my mind.

I turned at low altitude over a solitary farm worker who was etching the symmetrical pattern of his ploughing into the surface of the field bordering upon the aerodrome. He paused to watch me, red face stupid with amazement, a symbol of enduring things set against the craziest facet of man's inventive genius.

Flying a few feet above the crowd I was glad to be alone again, thinking how once beauty had been all but tangible, a thing known to me, often identified with some transitory mundane loveliness but a step beyond my reach; whereas it was now associated in my mind with contempt for danger, the artificiality of drink and a certain sense of technical superiority.

When I landed a few minutes later, face flushed with the rush of blood to my head through flying inverted, eyes sore through eye- lashes blown back by the slipstream, Cookson was announcing that the next passenger flight piloted by Casey would be the last item before a demonstration by the Royal Air Force.

I taxied into line, switched off and swung on to the edge of the cockpit, idly watching Casey taking off. He opened his throttle and ran a long way across the aerodrome, finally bouncing the aircraft off. Immediately he was airborne he began a steep climb, pulling the machine higher and higher till it seemed to be standing on its tail. For a fraction of a second the aeroplane was pinned on to the sky, still against the cloud-hazy horizon.

I felt my heart leap and fear quiver in my belly. Every pilot and mechanic was struck into immobility, instantly silenced, their thoughts hammered into a common mould.

Then the machine dived earthwards and I braced myself for the terrible crash of impact which, when it came, seemed to bridge the sky and beat down upon the quiet multitude. Women began to scream, the shouts of men forming a background to their high-pitched hysteria.

I ran across and jumped on to the running hoard of the fire tender which was bumping over to the crash. The plane had fallen just inside the aerodrome boundary and, torn to pieces, was spread about a radius of some fifteen yards. The first thing I saw was a girl who had broken her back and was writhing and screaming. Three of the others were obviously dead while Casey, still in what remained of the pilot's seat, was badly injured. I pulled off his belt. His face was green and his broken body oozed dark blood.

'Hullo," he said, 'what happened?'

'Hullo, you old souster,' I said.

'Jesus Christ,' he was talking through his teeth. 'I've bought it this time. I think my pin's gone.'

'You'll be all right.'

'What about the kite?'

'The kite's fine,' I said.

'You're … you're … sure?'

'I'm sure.'

'What about the passengers … what about … what about … what about … 'bout passengers?'

'They're OK, too,' I said, 'there's nothing for you to worry about.'

Royal Air Force personnel gathered round and kept the crowd back. The girl was still screaming. A tall red-haired young woman pushed her way past a policeman and, kneeling down, took the girl's head in her lap. It grew quieter now except for the moaning of the injured and Cookson's cool measured tones as he reassured the mob and called for a doctor. I could hear the red-haired woman repeating comforting gibberish, gaining the injured girl's attention through the curtain of pain that had fallen over her mind, calming her so that her screaming subsided and she reached up and caught the hand of her comforter.

A man came out of the crowd. He was crying, waving a ticket, shouting that his small son should have been in the machine but all seats having been sold he had been refused at the last moment and told to get a refund at the kiosk. He knelt down, his son standing embarrassed at his side, and began to pray.

'We thank thee, O Lord, that thou hast seen fit in thy boundless mercy to spare the life of this thy little servant. For as Isaac the son of Abraham of old was saved by a ram caught in the thicket by his horns, so hast a similar miracle preserved the life of this Thy humble servant's son.'

The strangeness of it, the sudden melodrama that had ripped, in a second, into an ordinary afternoon, had hooded the crowd with silence. The little boy, now crimson-faced, plucked at his father's sleeve, but ridiculous the latter's sob-crusted quivering voice persisted, repeating phrases edgeless with repetition, while his squat figure rocked to and fro in ecstatic relief.

Chapter 4

After the ambulance left, the crowd withered away for the remainder of the display had been cancelled. A burst tyre on one of the aircraft forced us to stay the night and we began to picket down the machines to leeward of the hangar. I was scrounging for rope when I noticed the red-haired girl sitting on the running board of a car. Her face was deadly white against the lovely colour of her hair and she leaned against the door, the back of her hand pressed to her forehead.

'Are you feeling … all right?' I said.

She nodded.

'What about the girl?'

'She's very bad.'

'That was a brave show you did." I pulled a small flask from the breast pocket of my flying suit. 'Try some of this!'

'It's …?'

'Brandy!'

'No. I don't think I – '

'Come on …'

She looked at it dubiously and then sipped, her head bent back on her smooth neck, the fierce spirit almost choking her and thrusting colour back into her cheeks. She handed back the flask and sat still, looking out against the sun at the far end of the aerodrome.

All pilots, I thought as I followed her glance, were eager for experience and out there on the level turf was the greatest experience of all, in twisted longeron, earth-tipped, in crumpled tail unit held together by flapping fabric, in windshield starred with cracks, in eyeless instruments and bits of cotton wool and bandage lying on the grass,

'Are you one of the pilots?'

'Yes.'

'Was … was he a friend of yours?'

'Hardly … I knew him.'

'He's pretty bad isn't he?'

'Yes.'

I screwed down the top of the flask.

'Why did he crash?'

'Error of judgement.'

'What does that mean?'

'Almost anything.'

Chuck called from the tarmac. I asked to be excused. She thanked me for the drink. I walked across.

'I've bin looking for you,' Chuck said.

'I was getting some rope.'

'So I noticed. Where did you pick it up?'

'You've got a low mind,' I said. 'What's the trouble?'

'Eve's getting up stage.'

'Why?'

'She wants to go home to-night.'

'What the hell!' I said.

'Some party or other.'

'Where's Jack?'

'Oh, he's mucked off somewhere.'

'I'll go and talk to her.'

'I wish you would.'

I found her sitting in a tea-room in the town reading a magazine. She smiled at me as I ordered tea and then went on reading again. The tables were occupied by a school outing, pink-faced girls in ugly frocks, straw hats, and black stockings who either whispered and giggled over tremendously important trifles or were nervously silent as frightened ponies. The whole place was stuffy and stale with the smell of fly-blown food, hot with the sunshine that poured on to the cracked linoleum.

'It's a pity we can't get back,' I said.

'You're sure we can't?'

'It would be pretty awkward,' I said.

She lit the cigarette I gave her.

'I want to go,' she said.

'Is it important?'

'It is actually.'

'A party?'

'So you've been discussing my affairs?'

'It is a party, isn't it?'

'I know,' I said. 'Plenty to drink and a row between the girls because they don't mix socially.'

'Cynical … aren't you?'

'I'm afraid we can't go, for all that.'

She twisted her head to watch a man who had just entered, then suddenly turned towards me again.

'I get a rotten sort of life just now,' she said. 'You're all away all day and most of the evenings and when I want a small thing it's too much trouble. Let me remind you that it's my money that's running this show. To-night I ask a small favour and you sit there like the Saviour.'

I said nothing, but smiled at the red-haired girl who had just come in.

'Oh, don't be so bloody superior.'

'I'm not having a row to-day,' I said. The last one (and how well I remembered it) was in the New Forest. It was autumn then with the smell everywhere of slow-burning garden fires and the leaves were crisp underfoot and small white clouds were still in a clear blue sky.

We had been smouldering all the way down from London, becoming increasingly conscious that our mutual terms of endearment were but tricks of speech.

It started over a thermos flask mug (which I said was unwashed) and went on through the whole gamut of human quarrelling. Neurotic and drug-ridden, her mind quick with anger, her reason blind with hatred, she brought up incidents I had long forgotten, quoted trivial inane phrases uttered in the heat of temper. And I, becoming less and less reasonable, gradually reached a similar pitch till we shouted at each other at the tops of our voices and passers-by stopped to watch our slowly moving car.

'How are you proposing to spend the evening?' Eve went on.

'Oh, I don't know. Have a quiet beer and perhaps go up to the hospital to see how Casey is.'

'He's going to get better, isn't he?'

'I hope so,' I said.

Jack came in. He was tired and red marks on his cheeks showed the shape of his goggles.

'Oh, hullo Paul. I've just been telling Chuck that I'm flying the Missus back to-night. You can both come along in the morning.'

'What about inspections?'

'That's all right. It only means losing a couple of hours tomorrow. The weather'll probably be duff.'

'Paul doesn't want me to go,' Eve said.

'Don't be silly,' I said. 'I'm frightfully keen.'

※

Casey died early that same evening and it was dusk when we came out of the hospital, Chuck and I and Casey's girl friend, a hard-faced blonde who had wept her artificial eyelashes away.

We walked down to the main road seeing through the trees the town stretched before us with line of roof and street merging in the twilight and smoke standing in columns on the chimney pots. The rays of the setting sun caught the underside of the clouds, hardening them till they formed a copper roof to the world. In the next field they were carting hay with jingle of harness, sloven word of command, thud of

Shire hoof and the slow creaking of the wagon.

The girl paid no attention to these things, talking incessantly of Casey who was already canonized in her mind.

I felt browned off, thinking of death in hospital wards, of east winds in mean streets, of slum children playing round dirty doorways, of Sunday afternoons in cathedral cities. 'What we want now is a lift,' Chuck said and proceeded to stop the next vehicle passing in the right direction which was an immense lorry.

'Going into town, pal?' he asked the driver. The latter replied that he was and the three of us climbed into the cab.

'Nice weather,' he suggested genially as he let off his vacuum brakes.

'Yes, grand,' I said.

'On holiday here?' he continued.

'Kind of,' Chuck said.

Our way was past the aerodrome and as we went by the girl turned her face into Chuck's sleeve and began to cry softly and hopelessly, the sound absorbed by the compression ignition engine which sent waves of hot fumes back into the cabin.

'Shockin' business here to-day,' the driver said, indicating the flying field by a sideways and upwards movement of his head.

'Yes,' Chuck said.

'I 'eard the pilot was drunk,' the other went on. Chuck leaned over and talked quietly for a few seconds.

'I'm sorry, sir,' the driver said. He rubbed his nose with the back of his hand and sniffed. 'I'd got no idea.'

'That's all right,' Chuck said.

The driver switched on his lights and I was trying to understand his switchboard when he spoke again asking if we were pilots.

'Yes,' Chuck replied, 'we're pilots.'

'I wouldn't go up, not for a thousand quid I wouldn't.'

'You've sure got it wrong,' Chuck said.

'Anyone 'oo flies is a brave man,' the driver insisted,

'You've got that wrong too,' I said, 'you just get tough to it.'

'What about when you begin – ' the driver was interrupted,

'For Christ's sake can't you stop talking about flying, just for once?' the girl's voice was hysterical. 'You're all the same, nothing else in life matters, nothing else in your narrow lives. Even when ... when someone ... goes ... you must still talk about it. I hope ... I hope I never see a bloody aeroplane again in my life.'

We were all quiet, watching the road ahead. Cars filled with foolishly dressed holiday makers passed us with mannerless driving, with shouts and the tinkling of car radios. Soon we reached the outskirts of the town, saw brown-backed girls graceful in beach costumes and tired children hugging brightly painted toy buckets or dragging little tin spades on the pavements.

Postcards and magazines and coloured rock and shrimping nets filled the shop windows, boards before the garages announced trips to every corner of the West Country. From upstairs windows shapeless bathing things hung to dry.

Seeing a large hotel of the road-house type Chuck told the driver to stop. As he pulled up the Canadian went on: 'Cut your motor, you're coming in with us for a drink.'

'I can't, sir, unless it's in the bar. It's a posh place, a proper toffs' joint.'

Chuck turned and looked at me.

'I know,' I said. 'It's this country; and it's not only the way we eat boiled eggs that makes you sick.'

The lounge was decorated after the style of an empty swimming bath. The majority of the customers were English bourgeoisie engaged in their favourite sport of pretending that they were further up the social scale than was actually the case. 'They stopped talking as we came in, sizing is up with a peevish interest. A cash register sang out in the silence and Casey's girl friend slumped into a chair.

I went across and ordered drinks. The barman was large and assertive with drink-coarsened features. He pulled the beers slowly looking up at the girl from under his eyelids.

'What about the gin and lime?' I said.

'For that lady?' he jerked his head towards her

'Yes,' I said.

'I can't serve 'er.'

'Why not?'

'Not in that state.'

'She's stone-cold sober.'

'Looks it.'

'OK.' Chuck said. He was standing behind me now and talking between his teeth. 'What's the trouble?' he said to the barman.

'I don't serve drunks. That's the trouble.'

'You be careful what you say,' Chuck said.

'I'm going to put her out,' the barman's face was purple, 'and all of you with her if you don't shut up. My Gawd, I'm having some trouble to-night.'

'I've warned you,' Chuck's voice was soft. I was conscious that he was thoroughly enjoying himself. So quiet was the bar now that the ticking of a clock became audible and little noises, hitherto unheard, grew out of the stillness. Chuck slipped behind the counter. The barman led with his right. A woman screamed. When he levered himself out of the empty-bottle basket he was bleeding from the mouth.

'I'll have the police on you.'

'Crawl back under your wet stone,' Chuck said, 'or I'll hit you again.' He turned to us: 'Let's get the hell out of here!'

We came out into the car park. The garish arc lights beat down on to the orderly rows of cars that formed a gloomy foreground to the road-house itself. I could hear the faint beat of a dance band and the unreal fabric of far-away conversation, see couples slide past the big windows as they danced. Children were shut up in some of the cars and one little girl was crying bitterly, beating her hands against the windscreen.

When we had taken the girl home we went from bar to bar till finally the lorry driver announced that he must be on his way and departed Londonwards, both of us watching until the lumbering monster dissolved into a tail light that slowly curved its way up the hill.

In one of the bars I met Cookson.

'What the hell! I've been combing the town for you. You're wanted!'

'Not me,' I said. 'I've finished for the day.'

'You've got to go up to the hospital again. Some technicality to do with Casey.'

'You can't find me,' I said. 'I've been there enough to-day and besides I've got no car.'

'Take mine.'

'Oh, all right. Many thanks. Where do I leave it?'

'In the yard of the Aviating Gee-gee.'

'The what?'

'The Flying Horse. You're staying there, aren't you?'

'I hadn't thought much about it.'

'It's where the boys all go. I'll tell 'em to keep you a room.' I thanked him and went out to get the car. It was an Italian racing model of ancient vintage and possessed awkward gears.

As I drove through the town I noticed that the visitors had drained away from the less fashionable quarter and looking at the workless fishermen who hung about shop doorways or stood to leeward of street corners I wondered how they felt with no drink inside them, how they went on in hopelessness, unemployed, enduring long dismal days, losing all the joy of life through poverty, suffering as slaves of a great civilization have always suffered.

But again, I thought, they must pass beyond any but the harshest feelings. If they know not women's favours and a measure of security and full bellies, they knew little of fear chilling the understanding or the lonely nagging of responsibility.

Theirs was a negative state; they were the unburied dead.

✕

By day the hospital was almost hidden by a fringe of trees, but now with hundreds of uncurtained windows blazing into the darkness it towered up into the night, gaunt above the fanciful lights that followed the main sweep of the promenade.

As I came out a quarter of an hour later I saw the red-haired girl again. She was standing at the hall-porter's desk asking the times of the buses. I went over and asked if I might give her a lift. She looked at me for a little while without answering. I wondered if she could smell the alcohol on my breath and marvelled at the clear beauty of her skin, noticed how the symmetry of her features belied the character that was latent in mouth, in eyes, in line of chin.

'Thank you … my car's broken down.'

When we got outside I walked round the Alfa Romeo to open the door.

'Too bad about that girl,' I said.

'It's too bad about them all,' she said.

'She'd have been crippled anyway?'

'And you all fear that?'

'Yes,' I said.

We swung out on to the main road with a merry clatter of empty bottles rolling about on the floor at the back.

'This is a nice car!'

I murmured an affirmative, adding that I had raced this type. I was too much of a snob to admit that the car wasn't mine or that the race was a novices' handicap. She crouched out of the wind that tore over the narrow racing wind-shield.

'I suppose you get used … to scenes like this afternoon?'

'Yes,' I said.

I stopped the car at a bend in the road, put my arm around her shoulders and kissed her on the mouth. She sat very still.

'What do I say?'

'I'm sorry,' I said. 'I suppose I'm a little crazy about you.' It was a game. The rules were simple.

'There's no need for that part too,' she said. 'You're a little drunk, aren't you?'

'Yes, but you've got the wrong idea about me.' I kissed her again and she smiled up at me.

'Tell me about yourself … do you work here?'

'No … I'm in a joy-riding concern along the coast.'

'You like flying?'

'It's all the world to me.'

'Don't you get bored sometimes?'

'If you get bored … you soon get frightened.'

'And?'

'Oh, there's more …'

'What?'

I considered how sometimes when hard work and bad weather held one to the ground one grumbled feeling a sense of ennui, thought kindly of commonplace ground jobs. And how on other occasions, when it killed a friend or acquaintance, one suddenly hated aviation, hated the sound of an engine or the sight of an aircraft riding upwards towards the clouds. But it always came back, the faint thrill at the smell of a cockpit, a sense of satisfaction in manoeuvres correctly carried out, one's mind sharp with detail, with constant watching of the weather, one's individuality realized by the remoteness of the world beneath.

'I don't know,' I said, 'it's difficult to explain.'

She twisted herself upright.

'Why did you pick me up?'

'I don't know.'

'It's very silly.'

'Why try to justify everything?'

'You're very conceited, aren't you?'

'No … no I don't think I am.'

'Then you're very sure of yourself?'

'Yes.'

'And you haven't much respect for women?'

'I behave myself.'

'That's not the point.'

'It seems very much the point, if you ask me,' I said.

She touched my sleeve with a brittle hand. 'Will you drive me home now, please?'

We went through the sad slum streets where the fishermen lived.

'You've catechized me,' I said, 'now it's my turn.'

'Well?'

'Will you come along and fly with me?'

'Where?'

'At our place in Swanmouth?'

'I might do … love flying,' she said quietly.

'Have you done much?'

'A little … I had great ambitions once.'

'You don't have to be ambitious to fly with me … Ill ring you up in the morning.'

'You'll be sober then.'

'I'll ring up just the same.'

The hotel was large and respectable with an over-fed look, white in the moonlight, its windows staring as blind eyes.

'What's your name?'

'Moira … Moira Barratt.'

I kissed her once more and she went up the steps. Like hell I'd ring her up, I thought. A commissionaire, who had been a little too disinterested in our farewell, pushed the revolving door and she disappeared, the rotating glass panels flashing in the street lighting.

※

When I got back to The Flying Horse I could hear the row from outside and they unlocked the door to let me in as it was after closing time. A voice roared in the lounge: 'So when we asked him about his car he sobered up and said he'd hit a policeman or a tree in Bournemouth or Southampton.'

Shouts greeted my entrance and a pint was pushed into my hand.

'You look smug,' Chuck shouted, 'where have you been?'

'Out in my sex wagon,' Cookson said.

'Euh! Euh!' Chuck cried.

'You've got a mind like a drain,' I said. 'But don't let me interrupt. Surely you were telling the boys about the first moose you shot!'

'Is he still telling that?' Cookson asked, 'all about it being a cow moose and his having to bury the head?'

'I'm having that animal stuffed and sent over,' Chuck said, 'just to convince you boys.'

Someone told the inside story of a record flight to the continent by a pupil with only a few hours in the air to his credit; how he'd been led there by an autogiro and even then had managed to miss his way.

'Talkin' of gettin' lost,' Chuck said, 'did you boys ever hear of a pilot back home who went up late one fall to rescue a fan dancer who was kinda stuck at some place up in the sticks.'

'No … what happened?' someone asked.

'Nothin' except that he got lost for three days flying back on a route he knew.'

'By the way,' Cookson said, 'where's Jack?'

I said 'He's flown his missus back to our base.'

'Of course, I'd forgotten he was married … his wife's a bit of a high stepper isn't she?'

'I think they're quite happy.'

'Well, holy matrimony hasn't blinded her to the outside world from what I've heard.'

'What have you heard?'

'Oh, just idle talk … nothing really.' He picked up his glass, looked at it thoughtfully and drank the half pint off in one gulp. 'Do you think she'd mind him doing another record bid … with another woman?'

'With another woman … yes.'

He clicked his teeth and grunted introspectively. 'That's very awkward.'

'Why?'

'I met a society woman a few days ago who's the answer to a pilot's prayer. She's young, good-looking, fairly immoral, crazy on flying and keen to make a record bid. I promised to find her a pilot who'd get her there … thinking of Jack.'

'Well, you could go yourself … or there are plenty who would.'

'I start a test pilot's job next week and the firm won't give me the time off. Besides there's nothing left in the game now; it's just getting more dangerous and more difficult. But in any case she could come down and talk to Jack about it, couldn't she?'

'Yes and he'll probably go too.'

'I'd like to see him make it, he's a cracking chap.'

'It's funny how these rich people hang about flying!'

'Isn't it!' He fetched our drinks from the counter. The others were quieter now, the soft thud of a dart preceding a burst of ribaldry. 'If had a lot of money would I fly? Would I go over Niagara Falls in a barrel? I'd sod off and do something worthwhile … marry and have a place in the country and stop drinking and have kids and – '

'Don't cry in my beer,' I said, 'it's diluted enough already. And don't try to shoot a line. You know you'd be hanging about aerodromes just the same. It's in your blood.'

He grinned looking down into his beer and said that I was probably right.

Chapter 5

Rain thudded on the tent wall, dripped in the open door, lay grey across the flying-field. I lay back in a deck-chair, tired after a long day with a stubborn engine, reading a novel by one of our leading women writers. It concerned fornication, adultery, and the intellectual superiority of the writing classes; love, one gathered, was a most important part of life.

I heard the swish of footsteps in wet grass and Brian, the younger of the parson's sons, came in and looked around the empty tent.

'Has my brother been here?'

'I haven't seen him,' I said.

'That's queer … I can't find him anywhere and the governor wants him for something.'

'Come in and have a drink!'

'Not a drink thanks … but I'll come in for a bit if I may and I'm not disturbing you.'

'I'm glad to see you … just waiting for a chance to test a machine.'

He sat down in a deck-chair and rubbed his knees with the palms of his hands. He was a little puffed and breathed through his mouth with a slight rasp.

'You read much?' he asked after a pause.

'A little.'

'I'm rather keen actually … when I was in the sanatorium there wasn't anything else to do except play cards and one soon got tired of that.'

'I should imagine one would.'

'I still read a good deal and potter about the garden.'

'I've often noticed you as I fly over … you've got the place looking very nice.'

He looked up with sudden interest. 'My brother does most

of it … he's very keen on that kind of thing. He's been hoping for some time to get a job as an estate agent or something, but luck seems to be against him.'

'That's too bad,' I said, 'pity he couldn't have stuck to flying!'

He nodded. 'But then you remember how things were at the end of the War … but then of course you don't … you were only a kid. Oh, incidentally, speaking of flying, I'm afraid there's some trouble brewing.'

'What's the matter?'

'It's about Sunday flying.'

'Yes.'

'Several influential people in the town don't like it and they're bringing pressure to bear on my governor to stop you by threatening to turn you out of this field.'

'I thought things were going rather too well.'

'Perhaps if things were arranged, about flying during church service times I mean … it might be all right.'

'I'll have a chat with the others about it,' I went out and looked up at the weather which was improving, 'thanks very much for tipping us off.'

'You won't tell my governor that I told you?'

'Certainly not … if you'd rather it that way.'

'I would really … he's a grand old boy but he's got some funny ideas.'

'I'm just going to fly,' I said, 'like a flip?'

'N'no thanks … my health's not frightfully good you know.'

'Well, hang about,' I said, 'I'll be down again in a moment.'

It cleared up as I walked over to the hay shed and the field was fresh with a smell of wet grass and sodden earth, the hedgerows drooping with heavy load of raindrops. I took off and climbed to find the cloud base at five hundred feet, dirty grey and shapeless, occasionally engulfing me blowing wet and cold in my face.

I tried the engine on both magnetos at various throttle openings, looking down at the streets and roots of the town, polished with rain, watching the mackintosh-clad visitors who dawdled about the shops and turned white specks of faces upwards as they twisted their heads to follow me.

Summer waves lazily crinkled the edge of the sea and I did a stall turn over the promenade, wondering whether any customers would turn up at the flying-field during the hour of daylight that remained.

Turning I flew inland, dodging low clumps of cloud, singing softly, all cares forgotten now, feeling proud of the sweet note of the engine I had worked on all day.

A few miles north of the flying-field there was a pub to which we sometimes went to play darts with the villagers. I soon picked it up and, throttling back, glided down on the leeward side. When I had sunk below the level of the eaves I pushed the throttle wide open and brought the stick gently back into my stomach. The roof slid from under me and twisting my head into the slipstream I watched the crowd pour into the yard from the bar.

I came back and did a slow roll, throttling back as I came out and raised my hand to the landlord's wife who was frantically waving a tablecloth, being under the common delusion that all pilots are practically blind.

There was a car parked in a lane to the rear of the hotel and as I flew over I recognized it as belonging to Jack. The drop head was down and Eve was in the driver's seat with a man's head on her shoulder. He was big and wore a grey sports jacket.

I flew homewards, skimming clumps of trees and sending flocks of birds tumbling into the sky.

Chuck was sitting in the tent door when I landed, strumming on his guitar, while Jack stood behind talking to Brian.

'You've heard about this Sunday flying business?' Jack asked. 'The point is, what are we going to do about it?'

'Go and see the minister,' Chuck said. He looked upwards and began to sing softly in mellow tenor.

'I'm very much afraid that's not much good. You see my father's hands are tied almost as much as yours are.'

'How come?' Chuck broke in.

'Well, he's beholden to influential people in case they stop their subscriptions and also to the rest in case they stop coming to church.'

'Kind of makes things simple.'

'Who started it all?' Jack asked.

'A Mrs Waterman who lives in Swanmouth,' Brian said, 'she's a wealthy widow.'

'I know 'em,' Chuck said, 'flat heels, dogs, a god damn English accent and a face like a can of worms.'

'Pipe down you wog,' Jack knocked his pipe against the tent pole, 'she must have a lot of influence,' he added in a pensive tone.

'What! … her?' Chuck said.

'Enough to take people's jobs away,' Brian said.

'For Pete's sake,' Chuck said, 'we're doing no harm. We never fly over the town on Sundays. We're only trying to make a living.'

'That's not the point,' I said. 'To her there are three classes of society. The one she belongs to which has God Almighty as a kind of house captain, the working classes whom she regards as domestic animals and treats as such when she can, and ourselves, the outcasts. She probably thinks she's doing us a good turn.'

'Let me go and take a gander at her,' Chuck said.

'That', Jack's voice was patient, 'would just finish everything. I think Paul ought to go,' he grinned at me, 'he's the sort of Cissy that would make a hit there.'

'You rat,' I said, 'why don't you go and shoot your special line of bull?'

'Kidding apart I think Paul ought to go,' Chuck said.

'All right,' I said, 'I'll try and see what I can do.' Hearing a horn I turned and saw Jack's car lumbering towards us. Eve was wearing a handkerchief over her head and Jerry, the elder parson's son who had on a brown sports jacket, was sitting up very straight at her side.

She slipped gracefully out of the car and came towards Chuck and myself, smiling and holding out both hands.

'How are you, my dears?'

'Grand,' I said, 'and you?'

'Feeling much better.' She turned, ducked through the door and kissed her husband.

'How are you darling?'

'A little bored with being on the ground,' Jack said. 'Had a busy day?'

'Not very ... went to a mannequin show ... did some shopping ... just found Jerry here,' she indicated him, self-conscious in the background, 'walking up the road, so I brought him along with me.'

'Have a beer, old boy?' Jack pulled a couple of bottles out of the crate.

'Well, I don't mind if I do!'

'The Governor wants you,' Brian said.

'What for?'

'I don't know.'

'Surely it's not important!'

'I think you'd better go.'

'Surely there's time for a drink,' snapped the other. 'He's got me at beck and call all day.'

'Well, you know how he is about alcohol and if he smells ...'

'Oh, shut up,' Jerry's voice was agitated, 'shut up just for once.'

Chuck began to sing again, starting with the chorus from 'The Tattooed Lady':

Shame on the man who pursued her,
The villain who viciously wooed her,
She fell in a faint,
So he pulled out his paint –
And the first thing she knew he'd tattooed her.

We sat without speaking while he played on. The light drained away and summer darkness flooded the world. At the end of a song he would pause till someone hummed a few bars or suggested a chorus. Then, shifting his instrument, he would glance down at the fingers of his left hand and begin, leading the singing, swaying to the rhythm as he sat cross-legged before us. Occasionally a shouted line of a familiar ribald song would bring a smile and a signal, his hand being shielded by his body, calling repeated attention to Eve's presence.

Peace began to build itself in my mind, as at night, not when one wakens to whine in spirit at the transiency of life, but lying contented knowing that sleep will come, adding story after story to the edifice till the urge of time is forgotten and beauty, tangible, and long known, is within a step.

Without warning Jerry got to his feet, murmured thanks and went out into the cool night. Chuck stopped playing and the spell was broken. I began to talk to Jack of the record attempt Cookson had mentioned, telling him of his his opportunity. He did not answer for some seconds and then Eve broke in.

'No, no, he mustn't go … he promised that before we were married … didn't you darling … you promised not to go?'

'Yes," Jack said, 'I promised.'

'And you'll keep it?'

'I'll keep it.'

'Well,' I went on, 'Cookson asked if you'd see her. Sort of tip her the odd wrinkle?'

'Why should he do that?' Eve asked. 'Why should he give her the benefit of his experience? I suppose she's just a cheap little adventuress like all the others!'

'What is she like?' Jack asked. I've never seen her. She must be dumb and pretty from what Cookson says.'

'Done any flying?' '"A"' licence on a Moth.'

'That all?'

'That's all.'

'It's going to be a tough trip for someone, just how tough she's no idea.'

'I bet she hasn't.'

'But what an opportunity.' He brushed his hand over his face. 'Now I've been thinking. Given a kite with sufficient fuel load and full modern blind-flying equipment you could easily knock a couple of hours off the Australia run if –'

'Darling!' Eve broke in. 'You know that's all over and done with now!'

'I know ... but before we were married – '

'That's all I hear ... before we were married ... before we were married . . . one would think you'd gone into jail on the day you married me ... what the hell did you do before we were married?'

'Wasn't half as happy as l am now,' Jack said smiling and put his arm about her.

'I see there were three bumped off in the Service today,' Chuck said. I asked if we knew any of them.

'Slim Martin was one,' my companion replied, 'did you know him, any of you?' We all shook our heads.

'He certainly was one of the boys ... split-arse like all these fighter kings. We were at FTS together ... he was the guy that went up before the AOC for pinching a steam roller ...

he certainly put up some blacks in his time … yes sir.'

'I heard about him,' I said. 'The best blokes always seem to go.'

'You've been flying quite a long time, haven't you?' said Chuck.

'So have you, you ham-handed monkey,' I said and threw him a bottle of beer.

'Doesn't it worry you … when … when fellows you know go like that?' Brian asked.

'You get used to it,' Jack said.

'I envy you people,' Brian continued. He stared out into the gloom as he spoke. I could hear the faint rasping of his breath. 'Most folks' lives to-day seem to be ruled by fear. They're afraid of losing their jobs, they're afraid of death, of disease, of war, of the future and of the past: they're afraid of men set over them or afraid of responsibility. They're so frightened that they don't dare to think but have to keep themselves occupied.

'But you don't care for anything in the world, you're not scared of anyone dead or living, of anything that might happen to you, you're some of the very few people in the world that're really free. As I said just now, I envy you.'

In a little while he took his leave and we climbed into the coupé and drove back to the Blue Boar for supper.

'Quite a nice chap,' Jack said as he turned into the main road, 'that Brian. I suppose it's being ill that makes him talk such tripe occasionally.'

Chapter 6

Later that evening I left the bar of the Blue Boar and telephoned to Moira Barratt's hotel. A supercilious voice replied asking me to wait and I stood, receiver at ear, listening to faint whisperings, far-away snatches of conversation, flashes of other lives threaded on to a string of dance music.

A young man came into the hall opposite me nervously twisting a loose overcoat button that goggled on a length of thread. Several times he went up to one or other of the doors then turned swiftly away, fluttering fingers touching table, wall or chair. He looked at me as I leaned against the panelling with eyelids drooping, and flushed with embarrassment, turned away and repeated his former movements.

The pitiful lack of confidence, the shyness that racked his existence, his obvious unrealized desire to merge into ordinary life, these found an echo in my mind; and by my indifference as I stood there with silent contempt I wilfully accentuated his discomfort, deriving pleasure from something I had driven from my own understanding, finding a passive satisfaction in another human being's pain.

'Hullo!' a woman's voice, low and cool, on the telephone.

'Can I speak to Miss Barratt?'

'Miss Barratt speaking.'

'This is the roughneck who gave you a lift home last night.'

'Yes.'

'What about that flight with me?'

'I didn't think you'd phone.'

'I know.'

'Is that why you did?'

'No'

'Why do you want to take me up?'

'I promised to.'

'Is that the only reason?'

'No … I just thought … well I just thought that I'd like to … that's all.'

'I'd love to come.'

'What day?'

'Thursday suit?'

'Certainly … any time. You can't miss the place, it's on the main road into Swanmouth.'

'I won't forget. Thanks so much. I must rush now … there's a dance here and my partner's waiting. Good-bye.'

'Good-bye,' I said and hung up. I thought of her partner, probably slick and gutless, dancing beautifully with five degrees of bank on, talking charmingly to women of the burden of his existence.

✕

Mrs Waterman's drawing-room was well stuffed with useless furniture. Four clocks kept different time noisily and one of them was a quaint affair with revolving gold balls under glass. There were appalling religious pictures and a family photographic gallery showing each member to his or her best social advantage.

Each chair was provided with an antimacassar and each small table with a frilled mat. A red cloth ending in fluffy tassels hung from the mantelshelf while above and around the aspidistra were framed addresses to Mrs Waterman's father, loud in their acclamation of his every quality both as a wool merchant and a Nonconformist lay preacher. Bric-à-brac relics of Cook's tours filled a china cabinet while paintings of Continental towns on plates hung on the walls.

In a little while an old woman came in. She walked gracelessly with a creaking of stays. Rings and bracelets were embedded in the puffy flesh of her fingers and wrists. Her face was horse-like and expressionless, baggy beneath the eyes, heavily powdered; her hair which showed signs of dye, was carefully piled on the top of her head.

She apologized for keeping me waiting, explaining that she had been busy with some accounts. I bowed and assured her that it hadn't mattered, knowing well that she had been disturbed from an afternoon in bed.

We talked for some ten minutes of the weather and kindred subjects. I was careful in my recital of trivialities for I knew that this woman, seemingly devoid of intellect and incapable of useful action possessed one talent, peculiar to upper-class Englishwomen, the ability of being able to pin anyone into their exact social position after about ten minutes of apparently aimless conversation. And I realized that should I fail this initial test, all my subsequent pleadings would but aggravate the situation.

'I've come to see you about this Sunday flying business,' I said. 'I've heard that some of you influential people are … well … opposed to us and I thought I'd come along and see you about it.' She sat without speaking. 'I wondered if something might be done that would satisfy both sides … this does mean rather a lot to us.'

'We've managed up till now,' she answered, and her voice was prideful, 'to preserve this town … to keep the peaceful English Sunday here. We've tried so hard to make it a real day of rest.' She got to her feet and rested one arm on the mantelshelf; her lorgnette swung before her corseted waist. 'We've had a fight … I'm proud to say it … a fight to keep the cinemas, the shops and even the dance halls closed.'

I nodded thinking of how one had to queue up for a drink in any bar in the town on Sunday evenings.

'So you see young man that your flying business hasn't exactly helped us.'

It was as boxing, I reflected, where at all costs one keeps one's temper, where one's feelings are far away, being subordinate to purpose, where a stinging blow brings a smile, where the race is to the swift and the battle to the strong.

'I quite realize that,' I said, 'but our livelihood's in this job and most of our capital. We have to work hard for long hours and Sunday's our best day. Now we never fly over the town on that day and we could easily arrange not to fly during church service times.'

'I'm afraid you don't understand ... it's a question of principle ... of the observance of the Lord's Day.'

'But couldn't you possibly make an exception. I don't think we'd affect the residents and after all we shall only be here for a few months.'

'I'm very sorry but when I feel that a matter is my duty ... nothing will move me.'

'I'm sorry too,' I said, 'because this means that we shall have to move to another field. However, we'll fly on Sundays all right. Good-bye Mrs Waterman and perhaps I shall be able to do you a dirty turn myself some day.'

Flying had finished when I got back. Matthews had found a dog wandering with an injured paw and was rendering first aid in the headlights of the coupé.

'Well?' Jack said.

'No good,' said I.

'What do we do?' Eve asked.

'Stay here till we're told to quit,' Chuck said.

'And then?'

'Move some place else, I guess.'

'What about the aircraft?' Eve's voice was petulant.

'Picket 'em down.'

'More work,' Matthews looked up as he spoke.

'It won't kill us,' I said.

'Let me go and see that dame,' Chuck argued, 'she lives on the main drag don't she?'

'That would be the end,' Jack said.

'You're always saying that, what's the matter with me?'

'You should know,' I said.

A long sports car pivoted itself through the gate, picked us up with its lights and grunted across in low gear. In the driving seat was Cookson who switched off and came to rest beside us.

'Jack there?'

'I'm here yes …'

'I've brought Miss Barratt down to see you. I think Paul will have told you about it?'

'Oh, the record show?' Jack said, 'yes, of course, old boy!'

Introductions followed. Moira peered hard at me in the twilight.

'So it's you,' she said. 'I thought it might be when I discovered our destination.'

'And you're the record-breaking woman?'

'I want to be.'

'Hey,' Chuck said, 'where have you two met before?'

'He picked me up,' Moira explained, "and very nicely too.'

'He's had a lot of experience,' Eve said.

✳

Supper was the usual affair of ham and eggs and Moira sat next to Jack, lips parted, eyes shining as she listened. Eve and Cookson were getting on well together, talking quietly and bursting into laughter at regular intervals.

The evening was gracious to us, I thought, with the sweet-scented air rustling the heavy-leaved trees outside and the mellow lamplight (not too exacting for Eve's beauty) bringing the long table and ourselves into actuality in that dim room. I was tired with the peaceful tiredness of a day's hard work done and the voices of the others merged, were a pattern inlaid in the darkness. Then gradually I became aware of the content of Jack's conversation.

'Have you done any long flights?'

'No,' the other answered. 'I did one of two and a half hours, once.'

'I'm afraid you'll find this trip rather different ... you'll be in the cockpit for three days or so.'

'Still ... I suppose Blasket will be doing most of it ... if I can get him to come.'

'I've promised to get him,' Jack said, 'he'll come all right.'

'He must be a wonderful man.'

'Have you ever met him?'

'N'no ... I saw him at a party once.'

'He drinks like a fish ... he may be whistled for part of your trip. He's a real roughneck and there'll probably be some language coming over the phones at times, but he'll get you there if any man in this world will. He's guts all the way through.'

'He's done pretty well already, hasn't he?'

'Yes, he holds, or has held, as many records as anyone alive at the moment,' Jack's voice became pensive. 'I was in Basra when he landed there on his last attempt. There were three empty brandy bottles rolling about on the floor and he'd been sick over the dashboard.'

'But I thought – '

'I know what you think about record-breaking,' Jack said. 'Everyone thinks the same way until they try it. It's an overrated pastime.' He poured himself a pint from the large jug of beer that stood on the table. 'For the first time in your life', he went on, 'you'll be tired. And when I say tired, I use the word because we haven't got another. You'll get cramped and sore and a pain in your back, you'll fight sleep till it seems you never went to bed, fatigue till you have to shake your head to clear it before reading the instruments because they're all double. Just before dawn is the worst, although you're awake you dream, imagining friends in the cockpit with you, seeing mirages of storms and obstacles ahead. Sometimes you can't remember where you're heading for and seconds pass when all you can do is to hold her on her course and try to concentrate.

'All you'll have to do is to keep the gyro on 'O' and the artificial horizon in place, but you'll find that quite enough. Blasket will do all the take-offs, trimming, navigation and landings. Sometimes you'll think you're lost at night and then you'll find and recognize a town. And as you set off again into the darkness, it will take all the drive in you to go off God knows where. You'll never believe how friendly those lights are, or how it bucks you up to find 'em.

'Again there's fear. A master at school used to quote some wog or other, a Greek I think, who said something about there being no limit to human experience. Well, record bids will teach you that. Maybe there's no limit to endurance either. You'll be afraid when you ice up at night and the ASI flickers and drops to zero, when you can't get a fix and the petrol's running low, when you're hundreds of miles out at sea and you start bothering about your compass, thinking of the errors it might have developed.

'Then there's listening to the engines. God! How you listen! Many times you'll think you hear a knock or a misfire and occasionally one will jib a bit and you fly on with your face red and your chin on one shoulder watching it.'

No one else was speaking now for none of us had ever heard Jack talk for long before. I wondered if the reason for this sudden outburst of eloquence was nostalgic and looked across at Eve who was playing with a little heap of salt on the tablecloth and gave no sign of interest.

'You think a lot when you're over the sea or above clouds,' Jack went on, 'and there's nothing to do for hour after hour. You remember things you thought as a kid and silly things you did at school, women you've known and friends you haven't seen for years. You bawl out poetry, sing and worry about dying. And towards the end of the run when you're in a sort of stupor, there's the hell of a temptation to throw it up, and when fitters take a quick look at your engine, something inside you prays that they'll find a major defect, tho' if they did it would be the disappointment of your career.'

'And yet … you like it? And if you could you'd go like a shot?' Moira suggested.

He smiled and nodded, saying that things evened out and that it was a grand experience; worth anything one went through to gain.

※

Jack was interrupted by the barman who said that one of the gentlemen was wanted on the telephone. "That'll be for me,' Cookson said and left us. When he returned he walked to his place and sat down without speaking.

'What's the matter?' Moira asked.

'It was a call from the Service 'drome near here. They've lost a night bomber locally and want to know if we've seen anything of it.'

'What d'you think's happened?'

'Oh, they've crashed, I suppose.'

'It won't be a crash,' Eve said, "there wouldn't be anything as thrilling as that tonight.'

Out in a near-by field, I thought, the wreckage would be lying, the torn remains of a giant night bomber. And the wind would be sighing through the broken members, swaying the hanging fabric, blowing listlessly over odd boots, burst gut-fouled parachutes, over all the broken intricate machinery, over untidy bloody heaps of what so recently had been men.

It would be not in the least thrilling, no bravery there, no indication of steadfast courage, only a shapeless earthy mess in a field, only death to men who had wanted to live and the waste of an aircraft … the essential uselessness of it nauseating.

And perhaps one of the crew with broken body dragging himself over the plough by his hands, face comic with blood, screaming at the car lights that go blithely by.

When morning comes they will find them, with medical orderlies standing on them to straighten them for the stretchers.

Chapter 7

'Did you see Cookson when you got back last night?' I asked Chuck at breakfast.

'No, but I hear he wanted to see me.'

'He certainly did.'

'What was the trouble?' Eve looked up from her *Daily Mirror*.

'Cookson, Paul, and I were doing some quiet drinking –'

'I heard you,' Eve interrupted her husband.

'And when Cookson wanted to take the fair Miss Barratt back to her hotel we found that Chuck had whistled off with the new barmaid in their car.'

'We were going to look for the crash.' Chuck helped himself to marmalade.

'Yimkin,' I said.

'Disgusting,' Eve muttered. 'I mean there are social limits, even for Colonials.'

'I see they found 'em,' Jack said folding his paper.

'And? …' Chuck asked quietly.

'Five … all stiff.'

'What time did you get in?' Eve inquired.

'I don't know exactly,' Chuck said, 'but I remember that the birds were singing.'

Jack was looking through the mail.

'Any of you lads like to make good money in your spare time?'

'Lead me to it,' Chuck said, 'what do I have to do? Sell my body?'

'I said "good money" … searchlight flying around midnight from the local Service 'drome … Ted Bond's crowd. They want a few extra pilots. It's just a couple of hours a night.'

'I'm on,' I said.

'Me too,' Chuck added, 'what about you, Jack?'

The latter tapped his fingers on the cloth. 'Not for me. I don't see much of the missus as it is … besides I loathe night flying.'

'Don't shoot an imperial line," I said, 'you're just lazy.'

'What type are they using?' Chuck went on.

'Whippets, I believe,' Jack said.

'Paul's flown them,' Chuck turned to me. 'What are they like?'

'They're all right," I said. 'Glide's a bit flat. Thank the Lord they're twins.'

'Amen, Chuck murmured.

※

When Moira Barratt drove into the flying-field I was giving ten shilling's worth of flying to a curate in one of the Avros. On the ground he had been a very muscular Christian with the superciliousness of his calling, but now he clung to the cockpit side as we came over the top of a loop, teeth set, breath held hard, face a little green.

As I came in to land I kicked the machine into a vertical sideslip, the wind protesting in the wires, the horizon bisecting the centre section, the aircraft dropping like a bat out of hell. At twenty feet I ruddered hard into it and levelled up, determined to make an especially good landing to impress the girl now waiting by the booking tent. But as I touched down I hit a ridge we always avoided and the machine bounced so that I had to let her down with a burst of engine.

I taxied over to the tent past Chuck who was refuelling his aircraft.

'Nice landing,' he shouted, 'why don't you learn to fly the thing?'

I put two fingers up and, when the wheels stopped turning,

helped the curate to the ground, talked with him for a few seconds and then went across to Moira, conscious of my grubby overalls.

'So you came!' I said.

'Yes.' She looked round at the Avros. 'Are these your aircraft?'

'They are,' I said.

'They're not quite this year's models … are they?'

'They're all right,' I said. 'What have you flown?'

'I've done about forty hours on Klem Swallows and Leopard Moths.'

'I see … well, if you'd like to fly in something else there's my kite in the hay shed … the little red one.'

'Yes … I'd like a flip in that.'

We walked over and I helped Matthews to run it out, sending the boy over to borrow Chuck's new flying helmet as he had just taken off.

'Are you a good pilot?' she asked as we waited for 'EN' to warm up.

'You ought to hear me brag when I'm screwed.'

'I'm almost certain I have.'

'Like to try a drop of aerobatics?'

'Why not?'

'Why not indeed!'

I helped her into the front cockpit, did up her harness and plugged in her Gosport tubes. Then I ran up, waved away the chocks and took off. For the first time for years I really wanted to fly well and the aircraft came off easily, the stick light in my fingers.

I climbed steadily rocking the stick laterally to gauge my maximum climb. A light easterly wind pushed little white clouds across the sky high above us and the sea was calm with summer while here and there a ship slowly towed a tiny patch of wake.

I did a vertical turn, hearing my passenger whistling through her teeth, then dived and did a slow roll, seeing her crouch as her weight came on to the straps.

'Let yourself go with the machine!'

I climbed through a cloud on the new blind-flying instruments I had installed, then lost height by putting the stick forward coming out of a slow half-roll. We were above a slight haze and could see for miles along the coast, while to the north the land was coloured with crops, gay with vivid pasture, with half-cut hay, spring corn and maize. It was nearly midday and the trees were standing in their shadows as cattle in pools, while the sunlight followed the cruel lines of the railways into the mist and picked out the little round ponds in the fields.

I looped, stall turned, flew inverted, flick rolled and spun. The controls were smooth to my hands and feet and my movements were automatic as I watched the ground to judge my height and scanned the sky for other aircraft.

'Like it?'

'Yes … it's lovely … but rather frightening.'

'You should fly some more', I said, 'and you'll get used to being chucked about.'

We went low over the conglomerated slums, the narrow twisted streets that were so picturesque from above, and around the west of the town, the church towers standing out of a blue-slated expanse. Then I flew out to sea, coming down to within a few feet of the water and dropping a wing tip to disturb the gulls who were sitting in great flocks outside the little waves that pulled themselves lazily out of the depths.

Returning to the field I saw a machine skid-slipping in to land and smiled, recognizing Chuck's sure approach. I flew very low now so that the ground was familiar, giving one an unusual impression of speed.

The field swung into view under a wing and I went over into a vertical slip, then pulled out and did one the other way, whistling contentedly as 'EN' went down for a smooth three-point landing, the skid grunting on the grass.

'Does it still thrill you to fly?'

'It's hardly a thrill,' I said, 'but it certainly pleases me.' As I helped her out she asked how much she owed.

'You were invited,' I said, 'it's on the house.'

'But – '

'Please?'

'Thank you,' she smiled, 'it was lovely and now I must be on my way.'

'When do I see you again?' I asked. This interview was taking me back ten years.

'Some evening perhaps.'

We walked across to her car.

'Where's Captain Graves?'

'He's flown up to Heston for spares.'

'And the Canadian?'

'Oh, Chuck … he's flying now.'

'Do you have to fly in a concern like this?'

'What are you trying to do? Fire me with ambition?'

'No … I just wondered.'

'I don't really,' I said feeling virtuous, 'but it suits me.' She gave me back the helmet and goggles, thanked me again and drove off.

I stood for a few seconds watching her car, noticed a graceful movement of her head as she shook back her hair. It suddenly occurred to me that I knew nothing about her.

※

'Any time you'd like to borrow a helmet', Chuck said with hyperbolical politeness as I came into the tent, 'just come in and help yourself.'

'Oh, I couldn't do that without your permission.'

'You rat!' he said and then added thoughtfully, 'you seem to be ringing the bell with that bit of frippet ... how d'you do it?'

'You wouldn't know ... she's not your class!' I caught the book he threw and grinned at his language.

※

I came back early from lunch to help the ground engineer to change an Avro tyre. He was unusually tacit and after a few moments I laughed, asking what was the trouble.

'That ruddy 'unt's been round again to-day,' he said.

'What hunt?'

'Otter.'

'Oh!' I said.

He devoted a succinct and obscene sentence to hunting people in general and followers of otter hounds in particular.

'Come! Come!' I said. 'They're not all that bad.'

'It's not the way they dress,' he answered, 'and it's not the way they talk, tho' Gawd knows those things are bad enough. And it's not the way they walk through this field as if the ground 'ad been fouled, it's the principle of the thing if you follows me, the runnin' of an 'armless animal to death.'

'Most hunting people are very nice,' I said.

'You're dodging the issue,' Matthews went on, 'and besides, you like every one.'

'I like to be friendly and drink beer with people and laugh. If they want to be up-stage I'm quite willing to slap 'em one.'

'That's not the point ...' Matthews put down a spanner very deliberately and I knew that he was ready to run out a stock argument.

'Good afternoon!' Brian stood behind us, a book beneath his arm. He was very pale and carried a stick.

'Oh, hullo,' I said, 'where have you been for the last few days?'

'In bed I'm afraid.'

'I'm sorry,' I said, 'are you feeling better?'

'Thanks yes, I'm fine again.' He looked at Matthews: 'Can I speak to you for a moment?'

'You push off sir,' the ground engineer said to me, 'I'll soon finish this now.'

'That's grand.' I turned to my companion: 'Come over to the tent and tell me all about your sex life.'

He opened his book as we strolled over and gave me an envelope.

'Here it is … the notice to evacuate this field I mean.'

'It saves us having to have the grass cut anyhow,' I said.

'Have you got another place?'

'Yes … Jack's fixed up a meadow about a mile from here but it's not nearly so convenient. We shan't get anything like the crowds.'

'I'm sorry about all this,' he said. 'I wish I could have done something to stop it.'

'That's all right. It's nothing to do with you.'

He lowered himself carefully into a deck-chair and put his stick between his knees. 'By the by, has my brother been here in the evenings lately?'

'No,' I said, 'now that I come to think about it, he hasn't.'

'Well, he's going out a lot and getting a good deal to drink somewhere.'

'It's not here … not lately anyway.'

'Jim must be down,' the other said. 'He's an old pal of Jerry's. They were together in the war. Jim's very high up in the Service now … a Wing Commander. He comes down every summer and takes Jerry about. My brother lives for it.'

'Nice for him,' I said and got myself a bottle of beer.

'It's not really,' Brian said.

'A drink?'

'Thanks, no.' He leaned over and caught the side of the door, staring out at Matthews. 'God! It's a rotten life we live; the two of us.'

'It's not your fault,' I said.

'I'd be all right for a job … if I wasn't ill.' He turned his head quickly. 'I don't suppose you can understand how I despise myself for being ill. I would have a hopeless and incurable disease … it's like beating against prison bars. My brother can work … but now he's lost faith in himself, he's getting afraid of meeting strangers. He's terrified that someone who doesn't know him will ask him what he does.' He stopped for a few seconds, looked out at the flying-field again and said: 'I don't know why I'm telling you all this!'

I knocked the cap off my bottle on the edge of the crate. 'People often talk to me,' I replied, 'it's my face or something.'

'The only thing I could do would be to write,' Brian continued, "but I've tried that and it's not much good. First of all,' he talked very slowly and softly now, 'first of all I wanted to be an author because I thought I had a message or something. I thought I could write a great book. I was day-dreaming all the while in a sanatorium. But I soon found that you can't put dreams on to paper. Even a genius can only create a poor illusion of them. Nothing I wrote was any good, everything I submitted was rejected. I used to rile against editors, but I knew that actually it was my stuff that was to blame. My governor once, behind my back, sent fees to some correspondence college who teach people to write by post. The idea was to train you to flog newspaper articles.

'I realized after a bit that I hadn't got the craftsmanship, let alone the ability. And even if I got the first by hard slogging, I'd still be at the mercy of the second.

'I finished a book a few months ago and it's just come back from the third publisher. I knew it was no good. I didn't even hope it would be; but it's a bit of a knock all the same. The days when I felt in the early mornings what a shame it would be if I were to die and no one would ever know of the book that was running round in my head … they're gone. But I did want it published … I wanted to justify our lives that much … throw it in the teeth of those who criticize us so much.' He began to prod the earth before him savagely.

I got lazily to my feet. 'You'll excuse me, I see customers. Stick around a bit if you feel like it … the others will be down soon.'

But my companion made no reply, continuing to stare across the field.

Chapter 8

The fourteen forgotten days went quickly by, for there was a lot of work to be done over moving to the new field. The Rector's solicitors made themselves unpleasant over patches of turf that had been ruined by petrol and oil and also claimed damages for the fence which had been partly eaten away by Matthews' goats.

We hired a lorry to transport the ground equipment and I was loading up a tool-kit chest on the last morning when Moira drove up beside me.

'Good morning! Any flying to-day?'

'I don't see why not,' I said.

'Where are the machines?'

'They've been ferried over to the new drome. Would you like to drive me over and we can fly from there?' She nodded and I got in beside her.

'It must have been a lot of work,' she said as we went down the main road.

'It's all been a bit of a sweat, but it's finished now. What worries us is that it's not so accessible, so we probably won't do so well.'

'Why did you have to move?'

I told her of the trouble.

'But do you think that will stop them?'

'No, but I'm hanged if I can see their next move. This farmer owns his land and is at loggerheads with the local landowners, so we should be all right there.'

'They'll get you somehow.'

'I'm sure they'll try,' I said.

'The new field was small and had a bad surface at one end, necessitating cross-wind landings when the wind was southerly. I wondered, as we drove over to the aircraft, which of us would be the first to rip off a tyre or buckle an undercarriage.

'There's to be no nonsense about paying to- day,' Moira said, 'because I invited myself.'

'All right,' I said, 'how long d'you want to be up?'

'About half an hour.'

'Acrobatics?'

'No ... just ordinary flying around.'

I went over and started 'EN'.

'It was awfully interesting the other day," she said, 'I haven't done much passenger flying before and I noticed all sorts of things, familiar things, looking different from the air. I suppose you know all about that?'

'Usually you're too high to notice much ... it's all very unreal. But if one flies very low ... sometimes things look very strange ... grave-stones and pigs in farmyards and steam rollers and the pattern of ploughing and harrowing.'

As I helped her into the cockpit I looked up at the weather. The clouds were ten tenths at two thousand feet, the wind light and westerly; later in the day it would probably rain.

I took off and climbed at the stall. Beneath her goggles the bridge of Moira's nose was slightly freckled. Watching her as I piloted I thought of the previous evening when, under the influence of a certain amount of alcohol, I had imagined myself in love with her. Now the idea was strange to me. Not again, I thought, the restlessness, the striving, the tenderness, the inevitable bewilderment, the familiar disillusion, the admission of another into one's own world in the mistaken belief that one could be ever really close to another human being. (For lovers are as two aircraft spanning the sky in tight formation which, seen from the ground, are as one: but in reality their very proximity, the one to the other, is a delusion, for should they touch, disaster is certain.)

The sky was empty and looking over miles of motionless

beautiful desolation, so short a journey from the world below, I considered again the marvel of the aeroplane which has brought a new thing into life, the separating of time and distance.

The sun, which I had missed all day, slapped into my eyes, caught the grim reflection of my face in the instruments, found a new shade of auburn in the curls which strayed from beneath Moira's helmet.

At the end of twenty minutes I throttled down and sank through the grey coldness into the actuality below. Coming out above our new field I smiled watching the efforts of the others to erect the bell tent.

'Is that Swanmouth?'

'The aerodrome's underneath.'

'How did you know where we were?'

'You allow for the wind and fly on a triangular course,' I said, 'but it's luck really.'

After we landed I stood with my foot on the running board of her car. She was flushed with excitement and the clear skin of her forehead bore the red mark of a helmet.

'I love flying … this record's going to be fun.'

'Are you sure?'

'Why not?'

'Oh, I don't know.'

'You think it rather silly!'

'If the fan keeps turning you'll be all right.'

'What don't you like about it?'

'It seems … rather useless … bringing melodrama into a job … risking one's neck for short-lived notoriety.'

'You're frank, aren't you?'

'You asked me,' I said.

'Yes, I did.' Her mouth widened in a smile that almost closed her eyes. 'Incidentally, I want some more dual, especially in compass and blind flying. Can I get it anywhere around here?'

'If we fit dual in 'EN' you can have some with me.'

'Are you an instructor?'

'I've dabbled in it.'

'I may give you a trial some day.'

'That's a promise!'

She glanced at her watch: 'I must rush.'

'Come again … soon.'

'I shall.'

I went back to my machine. Chuck wandered over.

'What are you going to call it?'

'You're a lewd sod,' I said.

He looked about the deserted field. 'Not much of a house?'

'What d'you expect?'

'Well, we've got the new bills out.'

'Muck that,' I said, 'they won't do much good.'

'Why don't you go up and do your stuff?'

'That's an idea. Come up with me?'

He laughed.

'Well, give me a swing, anyway.'

'Gas on,' he cried as I got in.

'Petrol on,' I said, 'switches off.' He laughed again.

'Contact!'

'Contact!' The motor stuttered into life. I felt suddenly browned off. What a life this was, taxi driving for long hours at the mercy of a set of snobbish visitors and local bigwigs. As soon as I had the harness on I pushed the throttle hard open.

There was only a short run to the fence and I had to bounce her off with fear cold inside me. Once in the air I went into a vertical and dived on Chuck who threw himself on the grass. Down the road I looked for Moira's car but failed to find it so flew inverted over the town and did a spin over the promenade. Then I climbed up through the clouds.

In the sunshine once more I did aerobatics to my heart's content. As I threw the machine about with sunshine and shadow flapping alternately on my face, hearing the pure note of the engine, sensing the perfect rigging, conscious that was flying well, my mood was forgotten and I began to sing into the noise and the wind that rushed by my face.

⁂

Chuck's new girlfriend was one of the most beautiful women I had ever seen and as dull as only a beautiful woman can be. I found her late that evening in the cocktail bar of the Grand, a vulgar affair of mirrors and chromium plating filled with the local élite, expensive whores, rich visitors and other vermin.

'I know,' she said, 'he's shooting his first his moose.'

'He's terribly sorry,' I said, 'but he couldn't make it, he's doing the log books by tomorrow as there's an Air Ministry inspector coming down.' I hoped fervently that he wouldn't stagger in with some woman on his arm and spoil the story.

'He might have let me know,' she gathered up her fur.

'Do try something before you go!'

'No, thank you,' she said quietly and went out. She was a nice girl and disapproved of me. I went over to the bar and was small-minded enough to be pleased when I was recognized by the barman.

'Was that you to-day, sir, throwing out a streamer and cutting it up by doing stunts through it?'

'It was, George.'

'You'll probably hear more about it.'

'Indeed.'

'Yes, the town council didn't like it.'

'Didn't they?'

'No, sir. You see bits of the streamer blew into the Town Hall garden and turned out to be bits of toilet roll.'

'It was good toilet roll,' I said, 'give me a double rye.'

A few minutes later I glanced round the bar and saw Moira smiling at me. She was wearing a white evening frock that swirled about her feet as she walked towards me. My heart kicked … I knew I was in love with her.

'You here?' I said.

'Yes, I'm staying here now.'

'A drink?'

'Gin and lime, please.' She sat on the stool next to mine.

'Do you come here often?'

'Occasionally … but we start night flying on Wednesday.'

'What! Up at the field?'

'No … from the local RAF drome for practice for searchlight crews.'

'I'd love to go up at night.'

'You shall.'

'That's a promise.'

'I think it can be worked all right … they're not Service aircraft.'

I tapped the edge of my glass on the brass-bound bar conscious of the sweetness of her, thinking of my fingers on her smooth white shoulders, of her red mouth warm on mine.

'What are you thinking of?'

'You.'

'And what about me?'

'How little I know …'

'Your imagination won't help you much actually … I'm disappointingly ordinary … an orphan nowadays, I was born if Matterley in Yorkshire … the sweetest little town in the East Riding … d'you know it?'

'Yes … I was in hospital there once.'

It was a long dreary winter, my leg caged, my arm pinned on a board. I grew accustomed to hospital noises, the gongs for meals that marked the passing of time, the echoing of voices down the clean corridors, the moaning of the sick, the insidious rattle of a trolley returning from the theatre. Then there was the smell, the hospital smell of steam cooking, of floor polish and antiseptic.

'Had you crashed?'

'Yes.'

And the pain, the shape of it clear to me as the fog of morphia lifted, so that I lay at nights sweating with it, resolved that if only it would stop I should be happy for all the remainder of my life. (Sometimes the boys flew over, throttling back their motors to let me know that they remembered. Then I longed to fly as never before, thinking of the freedom of it, wondering if I should ever work my toes on to a rudder again, feel a stick smooth in my hand.)

Now and again they operated, chloroform and ether killing my body, filling my mind with bizarre dreaming. And after each trip there was the slow journey back to life, to the positiveness of being trapped abed.

'Since the convent I've just flitted around ... rather wasting my time I suppose. That's one reason why I'm so keen to do this trip ... there's something definite about a show like that. Don't you think so?'

'It's definite all right,' I said.

※

After they closed we went back to the Blue Boar. I was a little drunk and very happy, driving Moira's car with full brakes and throttle so that the tyres squealed on corners. It was quiet at the inn, with everyone in bed and a heavy stale smell of tobacco, beer, and human breath floating in the bar and corridor. She smoothed back my hair as I kissed her.

'I'm crazy about you ... you silly line shooter!'

'I love you, too,' I said.

※

It was grey with dawn and rain smoothed the small panes of the casement window and darkened a semicircular patch on the carpet.

'You're a lovely girl,' I said.

'Am I … like you expected?'

'You're wonderful.'

'Are you happy now?'

'I don't know what you mean.'

'Are you always happy now?"

'No … never before.'

'Then why now?'

'I was never in love … before.'

We listened to the world waking to yet an- other day, to common sounds breaking into the crust of night; we watched the stars fade and the coming of light.

'Are you happy?' I asked.

'Yes … Oh, yes. Now I think I've got everything in the world that I want.'

'Me, too.'

'Then what are you thinking of?'

'Nothing.'

'Paul?'

'Yes, sweet.'

'Why d'you always worry?'

'I'm not worrying.'

'What is it?'

'I've got everything too: everything in the world that I want … I was wondering how long it would last … we being like this, I mean.'

'Why can't you live in the moment?'

'I don't know,' I said.

Chapter 9

'I'd like to know,' said Chuck for the fifth time, 'who put that bull on to us.'

We were sitting in the tent a few evenings later, lazing as we watched the sunset before returning to supper.

'What's he talking about?' asked Eve who had just come in.

'We had a visit from a policeman,' Jack answered, 'who came to see all our tickets and log books and things.'

'Were they all right?'

'Yes ... only Paul had to go back and get them ... then he forgot to bring mine ... I'm taking it along in the morning.'

'What time was this?'

'Oh, about six. Just the busiest time of the day of course; didn't you see him?'

She looked quickly at me, saw me watching her, colour flooding her face.

'N'no ... no, I didn't see him.'

'Funny,' Jack said.

Now we watched the spearpoints of the stars pricking the vast curtain of the sky. I lay back gazing up into the hugeness of it, remembering a childish idea of time, mind untrammelled by adolescence, understanding not walled by the relative conception of one's own span of years, believing it to be a concrete thing with the lives of men sticking to it as barnacles to a hull.

Then I heard Chuck's voice out of the meaningless jumble of the others' conversation. 'Paul's doing a pretty good line with that Barratt woman, isn't he?'

'I can't think how he does it,' Jack flecked himself with foam as he opened a bottle of beer.

'Trust Paul to go for a red head,' Chuck said.

'She seems a good type to me,' Jack put in.

'I really don't know much about her,' Chuck went on. 'Paul's careful to keep me in the background in case I should check up on some of his special line shootin'.'

'You're not doing so badly yourself,' Jack said, 'judging from the way that little brunette follows you around.'

'Isn't she sweet?' Chuck said. 'She's a milliner you know, makes hats all day and love all night. The only trouble is she objects to my gettin' whistled.'

'It's nice to know she likes your refined sense of humour,' Eve murmured.

'You ought to hear me when I'm with nice people,' Chuck said.

I began to think of Moira, shaping her image in my mind, remembering the shades of her voice, her neat finished movements. Now almost every line of thought finished with her. I had been happy at the thought of being in love, prideful that someone should care whether I lived or died.

But once I'd been that way with Eve, lived for a change of mood in her, hoped to be with her always, doubted my ability to hold her love. I remembered, with shame now, dreams of a home and a fat kid, silly plans, whispered phrases, stupid little jokes that meant so much in our private world.

'I'd still like to know', Chuck repeated, 'who tried to fix us with the bulls.'

'Oh, some of the odds and sods in Swanmouth,' Jack said.

'Why worry about it?' I asked. 'We're doing, very nicely and the Robert couldn't do anything.'

'We're doing all right till we get a gale,' Jack's voice was quiet, 'then the aircraft blow away and we go on the wagon and look for work.'

'It's this country,' Chuck said, 'they've only got one thing and that's – '

'*No ruddy idea!*' roared Jack and I together.

'You've got things wrong about this country,' I said, 'like a lot of other people. You've only seen the life in Service Messes, in cocktail bars, the West End, and the retired gentry of places like Swanmouth. That's not the real England. The real England's dull and respectable and honest and kind. It's hard-working decent people who don't get much out of life. They slog all their lives bound up in a system they don't understand, working from childhood in factory and shop and pit, blunting their intellect before they begin to use it. Only once is a man free of the social system and that's when he dies and his family spend a month's wages on his funeral.

'That's the greatness of this land, in mean streets and men kicked out because they're too old to keep up, in collier boys, arms twitching under falls. And in their snobbery too, their meek acceptance of whatever they get out of life.'

'What you want,' Jack said after a pause, 'is a tub in Hyde Park.'

'No,' Chuck was sitting cross-legged, playing idle chords on his guitar. 'I think I see what Paul means. You remember in the Service, what grand types the men were. And sometimes when an airman got himself bumped off and his folks were poor, they'd auction his effects and his pals would bid, three bucks for a bootlace, six for a pair of socks, two for a razor he'd bought in the local five and ten.

'Now and then you'd have to see relatives and kind of fix the funeral. They were always so quiet in stiff Sunday clothes and didn't gas much. There was a sort of dignity about them, I can't put it in crap like Paul does, but I can sure see what he means.'

No one spoke and he picked up his guitar and began to play, singing quietly, silhouetted against the moonlit world.

※

The next evening we started night flying and when I landed at one o'clock Moira was waiting with her car in the shadow of the duty pilot's hut.

She smiled at my protests. I was happy and very tired. The engines still pounded in my ears and my eyes were sore with the strain of peering through the darkness. We drove through the camp and down the road. Chuck droned overhead, his navigation lights floating smoothly through the stillness. Moira looked upwards. There was high cloud, hard in the moonlight. The last of the searchlights to the south swung stiffly over the sky.

'Isn't it lonely up there?'

'Sometimes.'

'I don't like being lonely ... it frightens me and I hate being frightened.'

I smiled at her and touched her arm.

'What have you to be frightened of?'

'Oh, lots of things.'

'Such as?'

'Oh, being ill ... and things. And, of course, women's fear ... of growing old.'

'I'm afraid of growing old, too,' I said.

'You?'

'Yes.'

'But I never thought – '

'That men ...?'

'Your lives aren't in your bodies ... you've jobs and comradeship and things ...'

'Think of children,' I said, 'and the common delusion that they have ideal lives. But as you know, it's a time of frustration, of physical disadvantage, a period of uncontrolled emotion, intolerance, thoughtlessness and untried confidence. As you grow into a man you lose all these things, gain a wider, better life. But when age comes, you begin to die and live in the past, you get careful, your body begins to let you down, you can't drink and fight and make love like you used to … you're on the way back again. I hate the thought of it.'

'You love life … don't you, Paul?'

'I think it's grand,' I said.

'And you don't fear death?'

'Not really, I suppose.'

'At one time I used to despise your sort of life … now I'm not at all sure.'

I was beginning to get warm again and thinking of the party that would be beginning soon at the Blue Boar, how we would laugh and drink through the night.

'You haven't forgotten about your promise?'

'Which one, darling?'

'To take me up at night!'

'I you really want to go?'

'I do.'

'Then Friday?'

'That'll be lovely." She began to hum, beating time on the wheel with a small gloved hand.

※

Friday was a bad flying day, grey and cold with heavy cumulus building up to great heights. I rang up Moira's hotel after tea but she had already left and as I did my last joy-ride I saw her car creeping over the rough ground at the edge of the flying field.

'I didn't know you read much?' I heard her say to Jack as I came into the tent.

'I don't as a rule. This is a book that Jerry lent my missus. It's about flying so I thought I'd try it.'

'And you like it?'

'It's all right. But like all these aviation novels the bloke keeps describing what he sees when he's up in the air. Now I can't say that I ever see anything, except things you're looking for, I mean. Do you feel that way?'

'I haven't really had enough experience to say …' She turned sensing my presence. 'Oh, there you are, Paul.'

'I tried to get you on the phone,' I said, 'it's not going to be much good for flying to-night.'

'Are they going to cancel it?'

'You don't catch 'em washing it out if they can get off the ground,' Jack said, 'not when they're paid well by the hour.'

'Well, what's the trouble?' Moira asked.

'Everything's on the top line,' I said, 'but I'd rather take you up some time when you could see a bit more.'

'You're going up to-night, aren't you?'

'Yes.'

'Then I'd like to go too.'

We got into the car and drove through the quiet evening, rain splattering on the windscreen. We passed cyclists heading into the weather and groups of visitors in bedraggled holiday clothes, waiting for buses, and buses themselves, their windows steamed with breath. As we went by a favourite pub of mine Moira looked at me, her mouth twisting into a smile.

'If you'd like a drink, I'll wait.'

'I don't drink before night shows.'

'Really?'

'Yes. My father was the same and his father before him.'

Stopping before we reached the Royal Air Force station we used as a base Moira pulled a white flying-suit over her beach clothes and covered her hair with an old flying helmet.

'You're quite an aviator,' I said and kissed her.

'Darling! Won't there be dreadful trouble if I'm caught?'

'You worry too much,' I said, 'who's going to catch us?'

The sentry knew me and I drove through the camp, cheerless and windswept, to the hangar we used to house our aircraft.

I helped Moira into my machine and sent a mechanic off for an indemnity form.

'You must sign this, just put your initials and your surname.'

'What is it?'

'A blood chit … means your people can't claim if I kill you tonight.'

'Then the firm know I'm flying?'

'Yes … they've got your sex wrong … that's all.'

I went out to the flare path to find the Chief Pilot as the programme had been altered. How familiar it all was! The airmen grouped about the first flare, silhouetted against the brazier as medieval soldiers about a camp fire, the gay navigation lights of the aircraft circling the aerodrome as goldfish a bowl.

And when a machine came in to land, the lights growing brighter as they sank quietly towards one, the muttered conversation would die away and one would hear only the thrash of the airscrews, the rattle of throttled motors, the rhythmic click of the signalling lamp, the wind whispering over the short grass, the hoot of an owl, the patient chimes of the church clock. Again the old magic recaptured one, the acrid smell of a coke brazier and paraffin flares, the laconic speech of riggers and fitters, laced with obscenity, floating over from the hangars.

Suddenly the plane, seeming to accelerate violently and to grow to gargantuan proportions, bumps to rest up the flare path with a hollow rumbling, the engine cowlings gleaming in the malleable light.

Receiving my instructions I returned to my machine and started the engines. As I waited for them to warm up I tested the wireless, plugging Moira's telephones into the circuit. When the oil was warm enough I pushed each throttle open in turn, testing the dual ignition system on each engine, watching maximum revolutions and boost pressure. To my companion, who sat with head bowed and hands gripping the edge of the seat, it was simply a huge wave of sound, enveloping her mind, beating upon her ears.

She would find terror in the mighty power of the engine as it strained at the bearers and rocked the whole machine, while the slipstream beat across the tarmac and swirled dust and oddments into the hangar. But to me, mind hungry with anticipation, emotion brittle with experience, it was something more, the sheer noise subordinate to the idea that dominated my consciousness.

As I taxied out I saw the signaller at the first flare test his Aldis lamp by flashing it on the ground and a little later a green 'M' splashed over the machine. I came up to the bottom of the path, checking switches and petrol cocks in the darkness, each detail pigeon-holed in my mind. I thought of nothing, custom and dexterity were carrying me with them. Another green fell across my tail and I let off the brakes and opened up my engines.

Bumping down the flare path I was hard on the rudder as the aircraft had a pronounced swerve. The wheel too was heavy in my hands after hundreds of hours on light aeroplanes.

Gradually she became airborne and then the last flare disappeared and I was flying in blackness, seeing nothing. I bent back my head and looked through the roof at the stars. But they were only partly visible and no guide as to whether I was flying level. I throttled down and changed the airscrews into coarse, climbing on the airspeed till the gyro began to work. Then it was easy and I went up through three thousand feet of cloud, heading for my first run.

⨯

When we came out of the clouds it was clear below. I could hear Chuck on the wireless, reporting his position, and as

I watched the searchlights got him like a moth caught by a flashlamp on the ceiling, a tiny white plane thousands of feet above.

Below the world was stifled with darkness, all life stilled by the blanket of night which enveloped the earth. Occasionally a light, growing out of the blackness, would float towards us till it dipped beneath a wing and was lost. I used to wonder about these islands in a quiet world, think of them as quiet homes and happy crowds in pubs (as a lonely youth seeing man and woman walking together, thinks of them as lovers, imagines a strange intimacy to exist between them).

We turned over the town which formed the western limit of my run. Climbing still I looked down, watching cars pushing little cylinders of light along the roads, and the town itself, a thing of beauty, with regular illuminations of many colours.

At ten thousand feet I turned off my navigation lights and started on my first run, reporting to base as I ruddered red on red. Chuck, hearing me, chipped in.

'Hullo, Paul, you old so and so.'

'Hello Chuck … what's the weather like you?'

'Nothin' striking … there's some goosh coming from the south.'

'Where are you?'

'Twelve zero zero zero, flying a little west of north from Swanmouth.'

'What could you do to a drink?'

'I hope they leave enough for us.'

The operator at base ticked us off for talking and I flew on in silence. Cloud was forming far below and I had been up for three quarters of an hour before the searchlights got me, filling the cabin with blinding purple light. I half-closed my eyes and flew on the gyro. Then the clouds intervened, sucking up the strong light as blotting ink and leaving me in loneliness once more.

In a little while the cloud had completely covered the ground and lay as snow, peaceful and motionless, in the moonlight. Base ordered me to return and turning on the navigation lights I started to glide down, flying on dead reckoning.

The clouds came slowly up to meet us. Moira pointed down delightedly. I opened up both motors to warm them. Without warning the port engine coughed and cut. I pulled out the tiny flashlamp I carried stuck under my tie and checked the cocks. They were correctly set and there was plenty of petrol. I leaned over and pulled out my companion's telephones, then called up base, telling them what had happened, asking for rockets so that I could find the aerodrome quickly when I got down through the thick stuff.

I closed the starboard engine and dived into the clouds. In a flash the calm beauty vanished. It was bumpy and hailing, and I fought to keep her on her course. The cloud gleamed white in the light of the small headlight I had turned on while rain and hail swished rhythmically in the starboard airscrew. Ice began to build up on the windscreen, slapping across the glass as a wet floor cloth on stone flags.

Now I watched the starboard airscrew in the light of the top identification light to see if it was icing up. The next time I glanced at the airspeed the needle had flickered back to zero as the pivot head was now frozen up.

I glanced at Moira, but she seemed unperturbed. The gyro, on which I was now flying, was venturi operated. The venturi tube was almost certainly ice-coated and in a few minutes the instrument would be useless.

I rocked the stick laterally watching for lag on the gyro. There was enormous depth to this violent self-contained storm and a Whippet, having a flat glide, took a long time to get through. Gradually the tiny horizon, which was now my sole guide, moved more and more slowly, till it dropped away from the small replica of an aircraft. The gyro was no longer working.

Now I was powerless, having no indication of what the machine was doing. She began to dive steeply, the wind whistling in the half-opened window. I hauled back on the stick and lurched over on to Moira who was white with terror.

Grinning I shoved on opposite bank. I became conscious that the machine was standing on its tail, the controls losing effect. The altimeter needle was down to the two thousand mark. I began to get frightened. It was the old familiar sensation, as a dream well known, half fanciful, shadowing the mind as one lies half awake.

First my mouth grew dry and there was a cold empty feeling in my guts. I was conscious of the palms of my hands sticky with sweat, of my shirt clinging to my back. My teeth were chattering. Let me get out this time, I thought, let me get out this time with this woman I love. Let me get out this time and I'll stop drinking, I'll behave my bloody self. Let me get out this time and I'll never be unhappy again … it'll be enough just to be alive.

Again it was clear to me that the object of life was to continue living and my mind, quickened by fear, began to notice insignificant things, a loose screw in the corner of the dashboard, the pattern of shadow thrown by the top identification light on to my companion's flying-suit.

✳

At a thousand feet we came out of the clouds. I saw some lights above my left shoulder and wrenched the machine over, putting the starboard airscrew into fine and opening up the engine. The controls were very stiff, but whether from ice or speed I could not tell. Despite the override we were losing height so I decided to land and pulled off a parachute reconnaissance flare.

The blinding light lit up the countryside and shielding my eyes with a wing I searched for a field. In a little while I saw what looked like a pasture, with approaches free of trees. I throttled back and did an approach, pulling up the nose to lose height. At the critical moment the flare went out. I tried to hold the shape of what lay underneath in my mind and switched on the landing lamp, shouting to Moira to walk aft. But she no attention, sitting still by my side. Then I saw the dark line of the fence and knew that I was much too high. The Whippet was a low-wing monoplane and was popularly supposed to be impossible to sideslip.

'You bastard!' I said and put on fifty degrees of bank, kicking up the nose with top rudder. I was very scared.

The machine fell sideways, the slipstream screaming in the open window at my ear. As I pulled out I saw the hedge in front. My heart jumped inside me for I had already switched off. I pulled the stick back hard and then let it forward as we cleared the obstacle. We hit the ground with a bang that sent my head hard against the roof. Then we bounced and I waited for the crunch as we came down again but she bumped and swerved up the field to a standstill.

Moira was sobbing and holding my arm.

'Is your head all right?' I asked.

'My head's all right,' she said, 'my head's all right,' and went on repeating the phrase till it became meaningless. I got out and inspected the damage which amounted to torn fabric, broken tail wheel, burst tyre, and buckled oleo leg. When I climbed back into the cabin Moira was quiet. She clung to my arm again. Her hands were trembling.

'I was so sure … so sure … I knew your world … but dear God … I didn't know it was this.'

Far away to the north-west a rocket went up, turning slowly earthwards as it reached the clouds, like a burnt match in the sky.

Chapter 10

Rain whimpered against the glass sides of the telephone box. The ear-piece was sticky with condensation. Chuck answered the call.

'Paul here.'

'You OK?'

'Yes … the kite's in a field off a lane that leads from Little Bangley village to Broadacre farm.'

'What happened?'

'Iced up … port engine packed up.'

'Damaged?'

I told him.

'You clumsy monkey. I guess they'll have to crate it out.'

'How did you get on?'

'Came in with a swell load of ice. I wasn't scared –'

'Only piddling pink ribbon.'

'You've said it.' He turned from the mouthpiece and shouted to the Chief Pilot that the machine was all right. 'How's Moira?'

'Bit shaken. I've got her to a pub nearby.'

'Are you coming up to the Mess for a session?'

'I've got to see her home.'

'Of course … we'll have a couple at the Boar.'

On the next morning 'EN' developed carburettor trouble and I had to fly up to the Midlands for a new part. An east wind had cleared the sky and hard sunlight lit the ground so that the villages and little towns were clear in detail, the houses clean-lined as toys in the green surroundings. When I returned I was late for supper and as I hung my white sidcot in the hall I hear Jerry's voice in the bar. Going in I found him arguing with a youngster at the bar. He was a little drunk, his words worn, and he leaned with elbows on the counter, his face red, his shoulders hunched.

'I know I'm out of a ruddy job,' he was speaking very loudly, "but that's no excuse for the way you talk to me. When you're at your rotten work, it's "Sir" this and "Sir" that, but just because you're in here with the price of a drink in your pocket, you think you own half the country.'

Some of the hearers, and no one made a sound, were embarrassed, burying their faces in their pint pots. Others watched fascinated at what they hoped might quickly become a piece of village history. All showed unusual interest in the happening, which to them was another scene in the Lilliputian play of their lives.

The young man opened his mouth, then closed it again. He was slim with a red complexion. A cheap knitted tie was knotted loosely to hang beneath his stud and his hands were hard and misshapen with work. He looked at me as I stood behind Jerry, waiting eagerly for the suspicion of a smile to encourage him to ridicule the other, or a word to help him produce the witty reply that would otherwise writhe in his mind all his waking hours that night.

'I'm sick of it,' he went on and he was shouting now. 'I won't stand for it anymore. I'm entitled to respect and I mean to have it. If you'd been in my crowd in the old days you'd have known all about it. Let me hear you "Jerry" me again and I'll strafe you … d'you understand?'

'Yes … sir,' the youngster said.

As he was about to reply I touched him on the arm and he turned sharply towards me. 'Oh, hullo, Paul?' he said quietly and stared down at the counter, not knowing what to do. I knew how he hoped that he had impressed the drinkers in that bar, done a little to restore his former dignity: I realized how he anticipated their laughter the moment his back was turned, and fearing their contempt, was thinking with self-pity of long empty days ahead.

'Have a drink?' he said unexpectedly.

'Thanks ... no.'

'Come on, try something!'

'I'm on the job again to-night,' I said.

'I hear you crashed last night?'

'I force-landed.'

'Much damage?'

'Not as much as we thought. One of the pilots flew it out to-night.'

'Now our day was the time for forced landings,' he went on and I nodded, wondering how I could stop him shooting a line of bull about the German War. He began a long and involved account of an encounter in which he had, not altogether unexpectedly it was implied, been the decided victor. I contributed the correct number of grunts and nods and followed a game of darts which was being played in the corner.

The blacksmith's son, who usually played with me, wanted sixty-six to win a three hundred and one. He paused on tip-toe, his foot sideways to the line and threw quickly, a nineteen and a seven. He waited till the uproar and banging of mugs died away and sighted his last dart, muttering something about a double top to win. As the dart went home he turned and grinned in triumph.

I told the barmaid to give him a drink. She was a pretty little brunette with firm breasts and beguiling giggle. 'Your supper's ready, sir.'

'I'm going up now,' I said.

'I think I've mentioned Jim before,' Jerry continued, "he's an old war pal of mine, still in the Service, a Wing Commander. He comes down to Swanmouth every summer and I see quite a lot of him. Then occasionally I go and stay with him. He's well off besides his pay and I have a wizard time ... quite like the old days you know.'

'I want to see you,' I said, 'but not in here. Can you spare me a moment?'

'Surely, old man.'

We went up to the lounge. 'Did you hear me roaring that local up?' he went on. I made an affirmative noise. 'You have to keep 'em to it,' he said, 'it's no good being kind or they take advantage in a second. You have to keep 'em to it. By the way, what did you want to see me about?'

'Cigarette?'

'Oh, thanks.'

'It's about Eve,' I said.

He stopped in the act of striking a match and looked hard at my waist line, moving the tip of his tongue from one side of his mouth to the other.

'You know what I'm talking about?' I added.

He made an enormous effort to appear dignified, seeming as an actor who, finding a part too much for him, becomes self-conscious and so increasingly gauche. 'I haven't the slightest idea what you mean.'

'Well, you're having an affair with her, aren't you?'

'And what exactly do you mean by that?'

'To put it vaguely,' I answered, 'you're sleeping with her.'

'I resent that.'

'You can do what you like about it.'

'And what can you prove?'

'I'm not trying to prove anything.'

'Then it's pure guesswork?'

'Not the evening I came back to get the licences for the police.'

'What the hell's it got to do with you?'

'Jack's a good friend of mine.'

'And I'm in love with Eve and want to marry her.'

'For Christ's sake,' I said, 'stick to facts.'

'And what d'you mean by that?'

'Love's like everything else,' I answered, 'you buy it. It's like a house and a car. When you can afford it; you buy it. When you can afford a woman's body, you buy it. It's called getting married.'

'Meaning I'm a failure?'

'Yes.'

'I suppose you despise me?'

'I do.'

'I've done my best. I've tried hard. It's not my fault that I'm out of work. You don't realize what a rut you get into. And I've no experience of anything. Now when I was in the War – '

'Muck the War,' I said. 'I was a kid in arms then … I've got to die in the next one. I'm tired of hearing about it.'

'That's all the thanks one gets for serving one's country …' I made no reply and he continued in petulant tones: 'I don't see what all this has to do with Eve, anyway.'

'It's got everything to do with her … because it means that you're going to leave her alone.'

'I like the way you're on the high horse … one would think you led a moral life.'

I didn't say anything. I was watching the side of his jaw, the spot where I was going to sock him. He was tough and worked a lot in the garden. I would have to hold my hands high and let him have it quickly.

'You never wanted to marry Eve!'

I hit him with a right hook that took him by surprise and he went down easily, cracking his head on the fender. I slopped some of his beer into his face and he came round slowly.

For a few seconds he was bewildered, then anger fired his eyes. He struggled to gain his feet. My knuckles hurt.

'You took advantage – '

'Take it easy,' I said and smiled. I knew that he could have thrashed me with one hand; I also knew that he would never dare to try.

'I'm sorry, Jerry, but she's not for you. She's Jack's wife.' Some years ago I would have pitied him, tried reasoning, but now I felt, not proud of my own superiority, but contemptuous that a man should be weaker than I was myself.

He slumped into a chair, beat a closed fist upon his forehead. 'You don't understand … you don't understand – '

'I understand.'

'But you don't … you can't. It's all very well for you with a good job – '

'The world owes me a living,' I said.

'With me it was different. I had nothing … nothing … only the worry of what would happen to me if my father died … and she brought it all back … the feeling that someone cared about you … the feeling that you mattered … that you were somebody … like it used to be when we went up to town and shot up Murrys.'

I said nothing, for there was nothing I could say and in a few minutes he got to his feet, rubbing his jaw with the palm of his hand, and went out, leaving the door open behind him.

※

Chuck was off duty that evening and he came in with a pint in each hand as I was having my supper.

'Are you getting whistled to-night?' I asked.

'Hell, no. I've still got a mouth like the bot-tom of a baby's pram from last night.'

'You should have.'

'Has Jerry been up here?'

'Yes … why?'

'I thought he looked as if someone had socked him one.'

'Yes.'

'Was it you?'

'It was.'

'What did you do that for ... he's not such a bad head!'

'Eve.'

'Oh!' Chuck said. He drank half a pint in a gulp. 'D'you think he'll be all right now?'

'He should be.'

The villagers were playing quoits in the yard outside and every now and then a musical clink would flash in the quiet. It was almost dusk with the rich sunlight shining vertically into my eyes.

'Did you have a good flip north to-day?' Chuck asked.

'It was grand ... took rather a long time though.'

'Yes ... you missed some fun. Cookson brought Moira's record plane down for Jack to OK.'

'So I heard ... what's it like?'

'Very pansy with flaps and a de-icer and variable-pitch airscrews. With luck she and Blasket ought to do it. The thing about the ship that appealed to me was an aluminium jerry ... never seen anything like it before.'

'That'll be something to tell your people at home,' I said, 'when you get there.'

'If the Transcontinental Air Lines would only open up ... I'd be back like a dose of salts ... before I die of this stuff,' he added meditatively tapping one of the mugs against the mantelshelf. 'But there's nothin' doin' out there yet.' He thought for a few seconds. 'Gee! I'd like to get back home again after eight years and see the folks and get a good flying job and get hitched and raise a couple of kids.' For a minute or so he walked about the room. "You must come and stay with me, Paul, when I get back home. Come up in the fall and we'll go up to the cottage. It's on the lake. You'll love it up there with everybody happy and the girls tanned brown and the boys laughing all day and everything free and easy.

There's huntin', the real thing not horse-back riders chasin' foxes, and swimming and canoes and in the evenings you gather round the old camp fire and get the guitar out.

'And if you don't feel energetic … you just laze around and talk and make love and drink and watch the millionaires from the States who have little Union Jacks on their houseboats … hell … you'll love it.'

'It'll be a grand show,' I said, knowing as I spoke that I should never go. 'You'd better be careful', I went on, 'about going back in a hacking jacket with a Public School accent.'

'You're telling me! I guess I'll have to cable my sister to hide the Old Man's gun I'm getting such a God damn English way of talkin'.'

Chapter 11

All day now I took up joy-riders, for there were many visitors and crowds gathered each morning to watch us as we worked, many of them buying tickets for flights. Every night I went up to the Royal Air Force Station and, if the weather allowed, flew for a couple of hours for the searchlight crews in the neighbourhood.

And weary at the end of a day, stiff with long hours at the controls, I would at last return to the aerodrome, the camp lights and the big-mouthed hangars standing out in the obscurity below. I would reach up to the Morse key and send out my recognition letter, to be answered in green from the ground.

As I watched the flare path, judging my line of approach, I would glance at the leeward side of the duty pilot's hut where Moira, knowing my letter, would be signalling by switching her headlights on and off. Sometimes I was late, which worried her, and one night I had to sit above the clouds for a weather report to be sent up, and landing found her grey with anxiety.

Turning in, I would throttle down, put the airscrews into fine and motor in to the aerodrome, cheek against the edge of the open window, watching the flare path, judging my height from the merging of the yellow flares, looking intently for clumps of trees and the dark outline of road, railway, and hedge beneath.

Clearing the boundary by a few feet, for the glide was flat, I would float on to the flare path, the wind hissing in the open windows, sobbing in the lazily turning airscrews. I would now be looking at the men standing at the first flare, judging my height by their size, pulling my throttles hard back and letting her go down on the wheels when I thought I was a few feet off the ground,

'I know you so well, my dear,' Moira said one evening when I tried to laugh away her fears, 'I know what you're like and what you think about, and the funny habits you've got and what you believe in and where you think you go to when you die. But after the other night, as soon as you get into an aeroplane, you're a stranger in a strange land.'

'Don't worry about that … now,' I said. 'I've been thinking about you all day and it's grand to see you.'

'You're very sweet to-night … do you want to go round to the Officers' Mess for a drink?'

'No … let's go home … I'm tired.'

'I'm tired too … had about six calls from Tony about the trip.'

'Tony?'

'Yes … Tony Blasket.'

'Oh, that bastard.'

'Darling!'

'Oh, I'm sorry … but I know him so well. He's a line-shooter if ever there was one.'

'He's very sweet.'

'He's a reason to be.'

'Now darling, don't be bearish. I'm determined to do this trip so there's no need to be jealous.'

'Jealous?'

'Yes, of Blasket, you silly.'

'Don't talk such utter rubbish,' I said, knowing she was right.

'He'll get me there … Jack says so and he ought to know … besides I didn't know you and Jack … not well that is … when I decided to go with him.'

We drove through the camp. The barrack blocks were quiet, Service police prowled about the hangars and the shadow of the sentry's bayonet fell across the car as we passed.

'You loved the Royal Air Force, didn't you?'

'Yes, it's a fine Service. I had a cracking time. The lads were a wonderful crowd too.'

'Why didn't you stay in? … You and Chuck … and Jack too?'

'You only go in for a few years.'

'And then?'

'If you're lucky … jobs like this … otherwise door-to-door canvassing, motor salesmanship, jobs in big firms in the Midlands.'

'I think it's rather sad … breaking fine boys like that.'

'That's all right … you're pretty tough by the time they've finished with you.'

'Are you tough, darling?'

'You should know,' I said.

'I think you're grand … but I'm biased.'

'Biased?'

'Yes … I'm in love with you.'

'I'm in love with you too,' I said. 'I wish you weren't lousy with money.'

'Why?'

'Because then I'd marry you.'

'Darling … are you proposing?'

'I'm after a good test pilot's job at the end of the summer … then I'll propose.'

'And I'll accept.'

'Of course you will.'

'I'll always said you were conceited.'

'I'm young,' I said, "and perpetually financially embarrassed. I'm sound in wind and limb and I drink too much. I'm the answered maiden's prayer . . . a man to reform.'

We drove up a long gentle gradient, disturbing an owl, its wings flashing white in the moonlight. A sports car ripped by, swaying with speed, its headlights bobbing as an old man's head. A girl who crouched beside the driver, her hair covered by a handkerchief, threw a finished cigarette into the road where it bounced with little showers of sparks. Torn clouds, silver-tipped, hung as tattered curtains before the moon and a light breeze passed almost unheeded over the standing corn.

Moira slowed down and then stopped. I turned to her and, lifting her chin to kiss her, saw that her eyes were shining with tears.

'My dear,' she said in a whisper, 'you'll always be sweet to me?'

I nodded, looking far up the deserted road with its fringe of telegraph poles that stretched away into the distance.

※

A few days later as I was having supper (it was early for I had to test two Whippets before night flying) Moira rang up.

'Hullo darling!'

'Hullo,' I said.

'Night flying?'

'Yes.'

'When are you down?'

'Half one.'

'I'll fetch you.'

'That's sweet of you.'

'Done a lot of flying to-day?'

'Not so much … been fitting dual control into 'EN'.'

'My dear!'

'So we're all set … come up tomorrow?'

'I shall.'

'Where are you?'

'Cocktail party at Mabel's … Tony's here … he's going up to town on the eleven … can you come round for a rapid one?'

'Sorry … I've got to work for a living.'

'Now darling, don't be jealous.'

'I'm not jealous of that – '

'Darling!'

'I'm sorry ... don't know what's the matter these days.'

'Tired?'

'No ... actually I'm in rude health.'

'And how are things?'

'Not too bad ... we've had an official raspberry each for doing too much flying.'

'Does it mean anything?'

'Not really.'

'I must rush.'

'Bye, darling.'

'Bye.'

As I went back to my meal I felt suddenly angry and swore lustily at the hotel puppy who had stolen my ham and looked up guiltily from the shadow of the radio gramophone, showing the whites of his eyes.

✳

We finished fitting dual into 'EN' next morning and I went up on test before lunch with Matthews in the front cockpit. The ground engineer was one of the few men I had ever met who had no objection to being flown, and nothing I could do in an aircraft would ruffle him, no aerobatic disturb the stolid expression on his wizened face.

Coming in to land I saw Moira's car by the tent and began to show off, doing a half-roll off the top of a loop and kicking the machine out of a spin much too low over the trees.

'Nice,' she said as I came up to the car.

'Are you all set?' She nodded.

'Then let's crack off!' I said.

'I've been thinking,' the buttercups were thick as we walked across to the aircraft, staining our shoes with yellow, 'you'll be losing over this. The installation's cost quite a bit, and there's the time I'll be taking when you might be giving flights.'

'That's all right,' I said.

She stopped as we reached my machine and looked up. Her voice was pensive. 'It must be wonderful ... to aerobat like you do. I've just done enough to realize ...' Then seeing me smile: 'Don't tell me you get no kick out of it.' I stroked the sun-warmed frame of the cockpit windscreen, thinking how hard work took the glamour out of it, familiarity blunted the wonder, experience hooded the thrill of dexterity.

'Before I began to fly,' I said, 'I saw a Fury single-seat fighter rocket looping. I'll never forget it, the kite climbing vertically for hundreds and hundreds of feet, the noise filling my mind. Then I knew that there was one thing in the world for me ... to become a pilot.'

Chuck did a tarmac landing by the tent, helped his passenger out, and grabbing her by the arm prevented her from walking into the airscrew of Jack's machine which was being run up.

'I used to think a lot about it in the next few years,' I went on, "I lived to be really able to throw a plane about. But when the time came that I could ... it wasn't the same. There was the speed, there was the power, the ease of control and fear tugging at its chain inside ... but the wonder had gone ... there was only a sense of justification.'

'But it's all so marvellous!'

'Now, especially. You'll never get so much out of it again. The newness of it captures your imagination, the strange world that runs parallel to your own life. You've done so little flying that you remember each flight; your future holds its object.'

'You've got some grim views,' she said smiling and climbed into the rear cockpit. As she took off I followed her automatically on the controls, the patter coming easily to my lips.

She climbed to two thousand feet and I showed her how to fly a compass course, shouting till she learnt to keep red on red. There was broken cloud at twenty-five hundred feet and sometimes local rainstorms drifted towards us, hanging down from the cumulus in angry columns.

On the return journey Moira began to feel the strain and wandered to east and west of the track so that I had to give continual corrections to bring us out on Swanmouth.

'It's rather a thrill … getting there, isn't it?'

'Yes, that's about the only thrill there is in navigation. On your record trip you'll be using a gyro compass, they've got no errors and are much easier.'

'It's nice to know that.'

'Now try a landing … will you?'

'I've never landed this type!'

'It's just the same … nice steady glide and hold off at about twenty feet.'

She came in much too high and the feeling of slight impatience while I waited for her to realize it (which is the anathema of instructing) brought many memories to my mind.

'Put your engine on and go round again.'

This time she approached a little cross-wind, undershooting and easing up the nose to lengthen the glide.

'You know you're going to crash?' I said. She pushed the nose hard down. 'I've got her,' I said and started another circuit. I pulled up the green rubber mouthpiece. 'You must take things smoothly in the air. Polish is the secret of all good flying. That time you found yourself out of wind because you didn't do a proper gliding turn, but stuck a bit of rudder on now and then. It won't do … it's sloppy.'

'You're terribly grim as an instructor, darling … did you frighten all the people you taught to fly?'

'You don't teach people to fly,' I said, 'you try to stop 'em breaking their necks.'

'I suppose there's something in that.'

'Well, you teach a kid to walk, but not to run.'

'M'm.'

'Dabble with a landing, will you?'

She came in on a nice steady glide about twenty feet over the hedge. 'Ease it back,' I said, 'keep the wheels off the deck as long as you can,' and the machine went down for a three-pointer.

'I don't think I've ever flown so badly in my life.'

'You're all right, you just want a spot of dual. Remember that there are many ways of shortening a glide, but none of lengthening it.'

As we walked across to the tent she asked if I had taught any women to fly.

'Did you have affairs with them?'

'No.'

'You're not telling the truth, of course?'

'No.'

'Were they pretty?'

'Some of 'em – '

'Did you go to bed with the ugly ones?'

'I didn't go to bed with any of them.'

'You must have been a good instructor.'

'Why?'

'To be able to pick and choose.'

'You've got me wrong – '

'I know ... you're a simple sort of person.'

'Exactly,' I said.

Matthews came out to meet us with a telegram envelope for Moira. As she read it she turned down her red mouth at one corner.

'Oh, damn.'

'What's the trouble?'

'Tony's let me down!'

'How?'

'He's just not coming ... that's all.'

'He can't let you down like that,' Chuck had joined us unnoticed. 'Haven't you got a contract with him?'

'N'no.'

I said: 'You must have a verbal one.'

'Law means expense and delay,' Moira replied.

'Why isn't he going?' Jack asked when he learnt the cause of the commotion.

'He's got some job flying for the films.'

'Nice type,' Jack said. 'I hope he breaks his neck.'

'I'll have to get someone else, that's all.'

'That shouldn't be hard, Miss,' Matthews said as we went into the tent.

'You'd love to go, wouldn't you?' Chuck said to Jack. The latter nodded as he poured out a glass of beer. 'Remember last time,' the Canadian went on, 'when you were in hospital? You surely weren't going to climb into a record- breaker's cockpit any more.'

'Oh, one always talks that way after a record flip ... it's a good thing to do one occasionally ... keeps one awake.'

'Eve'll never let you go – '

'I know,' Jack said. 'D'you see ... I promised. It was so easy at the time.' He raised his glass. 'Anyway, here's the most astounding luck to all of us.'

'I look towards you,' Chuck answered, 'but I avoid your breath.'

A man and woman approached the tent diffidently. They wore open-necked shirts and khaki shorts, creased till they seemed like corduroy. They were red with sunburn.

'Customers!' Chuck said. 'Whose turn is it to go up and juggle with Jesus?'

We tossed up solemnly for odd man out. I groaned and went to work.

Chapter 12

Moira went up to London on the following morning to see if she could persuade Blasket to change his mind. Chuck had a Canadian friend down to stay with him and they talked for long hours of the peculiar ways of the English, of apple-pie, corn-'n-the-cob, flapjacks, hamburgers and the advisability of marrying someone one's own age, while Eve learnt to shoot crap and the meaning of snake eyes and box cars and could be heard calling upon an unknown deity to help her 'buy the baby shoes'.

A sea fog came up in the afternoon and Chuck took his friend to see the latest flying film which was having a pre-release run in Swanmouth. It took them some time to get back as the fog was thicker than ever and night flying obviously impossible.

'What was it like?' Jack asked.

'The usual bull,' Chuck said. 'Good shots of actual piloting, but an awful story ... and kites being taken off without warmin' their motors or running up, or testing the dual ignition. Then one guy was standin' up in the slipstream and waving his arms about. The hero was dramatic, of course, with a life full of thrills and dames, shouting and line-shooting and never doing a decent job of work. He didn't drink enough either.' As he spoke he put his pint on the mantelshelf and getting his guitar out of the case began to tune it. 'I wonder if we'll ever have a real film or book about flying?' he went on. 'All about the boys, what grand types they are, and the way they really talk and behave and drink.'

'No one would believe it,' Jack said.

'But I'd like to read it,' Chuck added. He began to play, singing sentimental songs such as Canadians love, so that some of the villagers gathered in the passage and stood silently with their drinks in their hands. In a little while the barmaid announced that supper was ready and I found myself alone with Eve. We chatted for some minutes but I knew well what was on her mind and it was no surprise when she snapped out: 'What have you been saying to Jerry?'

'Why?'

'Someone's hurt him very much, he doesn't come around to see us any more.' As I made no reply she went on: 'I don't like people interfering between me and my friends.'

'What makes you think it's me?'

'Whoever it was made some pretty nasty cracks about his war record … and I know your views on nationalism and war.'

'I'm dying in the next one,' I said, 'what d'you want me to do … shed a tear for England?'

'Oh, don't be smart … I hate you when you're trying to be smart … why can't you mind your own business?'

'It's finished, and that's all there is to it.'

'It's not finished … how would you like someone interfering between you and that red-haired adventuress you've got in tow?'

'She's nothing to do with it.'

'I suppose you've asked her to marry you?'

'Look here, Eve,' I said, 'we've had all this out before … a long time ago when you were going to marry Jack.'

'Are you still hero worshipping?'

'Don't be stupid.'

'Then you're trying to be smart.'

'For God's sake … isn't it a game we play … our attitude towards life … to our fellow men? We act all our lives, living in a sham existence of our own and trying so hard to mesh it into the world we know.'

'My dear,' she said and how well I knew the tone, 'this sort of thing doesn't suit you.'

'You'll die, Eve, in a few years … and me too, and everyone

now living in the world. There'll be other people around here. They'll be making love, hoping and fearing, saying the things we say, thinking the things we think, and believing themselves to be immortal. Now you know this game you're playing, and I know it too. I like Jack, he's a good pal of mine and I'll stop this monkey business if I can for his sake ... you understand?'

'You've always been a prig, Paul ... but just how much of one I've never realized till now.'

'I see,' I said and walked over to the window. Outside the country was still dead with thick mist, the only sound the hollow lowing of ships' foghorns. When I turned round she was gone.

※

Moira returned from town on the following day, having failed to find Blasket who, it was rumoured, was abroad dodging a writ. When she came down to fetch me after night flying I was already on the ground as fog was creeping up from the Channel.

The visibility was deteriorating as we drove through the camp and on the road that bordered the aerodrome we found a solid wall of fog, hard and impenetrable in the headlights. As I slowed down I heard a machine overhead.

'God!' Moira cried, "is that one of ours?'

'No, we're all down. It's a Service kite.'

'What's he been doing?'

'Probably practising landings in a big night bomber ... did one circuit too many and got caught up.'

'What's he going to do?'

'I don't know,' I said.

I switched off the engine and we sat in silence, the fog damp and cold in our faces. Then the pilot throttled back. I could hear voices and the rattle of a train and the sound of the ambulance and fire tender being started up, imagine him gliding into a flat sea of fog, unbelievably calm in the moonlight, trying, with fear shrouding his mind, to judge his approach till he could see the first flare. I heard him bounce. He put his motors on again and shot over us, a huge dark roaring shape that made us duck our heads.

'He came in between the hangars that time,' I said.

'I used to think I'd like to see something like this,' Moira answered.

'I know, my dear.'

'The pilot made two further attempts at landing, the first time undershooting so that he must have flown within a few feet of the trees at the southern boundary, and the next touching down at the last flare so that full throttles just dragged him over the fence. Then he began to circle the aerodrome, the drone of his coarse-pitched airscrews a constant reminder of his predicament.

'Why doesn't he try some other station?'

'Doesn't know the weather conditions, hasn't the maps and might have to change his tanks ... that means leaving the controls and running aft along the cat-walk.'

'Oh, I see.'

I heard an NCO ordering a man to fetch more paraffin for the flares. In a little while the latter could be heard bewailing the fact that, owing to the thickness of the fog, he was lost on the aerodrome.

'*You're* ruddy lost!' came the answer, 'what about *him*?' In a few minutes I heard the clatter of engines being started.

'He's all right now,' I said.

'How d'you know?'

'They've found a clear aerodrome by radio. A volunteer crew will take off blind on a pump-driven gyro and lead him there.'

'There were years of your life in that sentence ... weren't there, darling?'

'I suppose there were.'

'What will that volunteer pilot get?'

'What d'you mean?'

'Will he get recommended or anything?'

I laughed.

'What's funny about it?'

'It's just part of his job,' I said, 'if he avoids a raspberry he's doing well.'

During the stillness which followed we heard the machine run up, taxi, and take off. After a few minutes both machines flew off so that even our straining ears could no longer hear their motors and airscrews.

'What about his tanks?'

'They've chosen a place within range.'

'That volunteer pilot's a brave man,' she said, 'how does he know that this other place will still be clear when he gets there?'

'He'll get away with it,' I said, 'he's probably a line-shooter, but most of 'em in the Service have got the stuff as well.'

'You people make me very angry sometimes,' Moira said suddenly, 'the way you drink and behave, but you're men. You're not nancy boys, or modern novelists or young men with souls. The very idea of flying may be the worst thing that's ever happened ... but, by God, you're men just the same.'

'You embarrass me,' I said. 'What about creeping back to the Boar for a quiet noggin?'

※

'Had a good day?' Moira asked a few minutes later.

'It wasn't so good for flying but we had a visitor.'

'Oh!'

'Yes, one of the king pins of civil aviation ... heard we were making money … wanted to lend us an aircraft and come in with us.'

'Wouldn't that be a good thing?'

'Yes if the aircraft was serviceable … but Matthews is up to his little game. Having signed up the machine would arrive and we'd find that it was due for a yearly Government supervised overhaul called a C of A which costs a lot of money and takes a lot of time. Then we'd have to do it.'

'What did you tell him?'

'Where to put it, and it wasn't in the hangar.'

'It wasn't a very straight offer, was it?'

'That's nothing for civil aviation, some of it's the biggest ramp in this country. There's very little in it unless you get some form of subsidy. A lot of internal air lines go bust so quickly that a pilot's flying for a different concern practically every time you meet him. Then there's the municipal airport business.'

'Darling?'

'Yes,' I said.

'I'm not really a bit interested in civil aviation … I'm just happy to see you again.'

'I'm happy too … you're a grand girl.'

※

The fog, if anything, was worse, and at times I had to walk ahead while Moira drove. When we eventually got back we found Chuck in the lounge. He seemed tired.

'Hullo, you two! Have you heard about Eve? She hasn't been feeling up to much all day. Now they've taken her to a nursing home.'

'What for?' Moira's voice was hardly audible.

'They've just operated for appendicitis. She isn't doing so hot.'

Chapter 13

A few nights later it was foggy again and I went into a bar in Swanmouth to wait for Chuck who was up at the nursing home. The barmaid, who had worked at the Blue Boar until a few weeks before, asked about Eve. I said she wasn't so well, septic pneumonia having set in through a clot of blood on the lung. She lifted my tankard and mopped up the beer on the counter, clicking her tongue against the roof of her mouth. 'Then, Mrs Graves never did look strong,' she said and turned brightly to serve an old man who caught her arm as he ordered a drink.

I remembered how she had greeted the news of Eve's admission to the nursing home with a remark that an operation for appendicitis nowadays was like having a tooth out. To her, I thought, life was ordered by proverbs, governed by the observations of politicians. Her aim in existence was inherent in the latest catch phrase, her hope of immortality lay in some little understood texts from the New Testament. A panacea for all troubles and trials was provided by some stock stupidity prefaced with the words 'people say that'. Living for her was indeed a simple affair.

Chuck came in. I judged from his expression that there was something wrong. He took the pint I held out and drank half of it in a gulp.

'Well?' I said.

'She's had her last drink.'

I heard a man's voice through the lounge hatch. 'I haven't ridden a bicycle for twenty years.'

Once, I thought, I had loved Eve, thought of marrying her. Her presence had made a day worth while, her memory lighted the past, hope of seeing her made me eager for the future. But now the thought of her death hardly disturbed me, would as the years went by become collateral to the time when I first realized that she no longer loved me. For the dying of love, when jealous apprehension is rewarded, the acute observation of every action justified, the sounding of each remark compensated, is surely as great, love being rare, as the rotting of the body which is inevitable.

'How's Jack?' I asked.

'He's in a bad way, crying like a child. It sure tears your heart to see him.' He finished his drink and ordered two more. 'She was delirious all to-day, talked a lot about you, so the nurse said.'

I blasphemed quietly.

'No ... neither he nor Moira heard anything that mattered.'

'What about Jerry?'

'She didn't mention him at all, not so far as I know.' He pushed a pint over.

'Cheers,' I said.

'God bless.'

'This is going to affect us all right, with Jack broken up and her capital in the show!'

'You're telling me,' Chuck said. He suddenly put his drink down and turned to me. 'Am I browned off with hospitals and nursing homes? Ever since I've been over here it's been the same. Everyone I meet seems to finish up there. It's getting me down. I'm beginning to be afraid of the sight of the places. I hope that when I'm ripe for the bone bin I'll go with my boots on.'

'You want to settle down to some quiet drinking,' I suggested.

'I guess you're right.'

※

I met Moira later. She had been all day at the nursing home and caught my hands saying: 'Don't let's talk, let's go somewhere.' We went to the pictures. It was a British film with the leading characters in evening dress, concerning involved intrigue in night clubs, cabarets, and the homes of the rich. A young actor was wonderfully made up as an old man with the hands of a youth. The whole was noteworthy for bad camera work and appalling dialogue.

Before the end we came out into the solid world again and went to a café.

'I can't help thinking of Jack …' Moira said as she pulled off her gloves.

'You shouldn't think too much, darling, it's a bad thing.'

'It sounds dreadfully premature and all that and hardly decent really … but I wonder if he'll come on that trip with me now?'

'My dear! Why don't you throw up the whole idea?'

'Darling, I can't … not now. I've bought the plane and done a terrible lot of spade work … oh, it's simply got to go on!'

'I'd rather you didn't.'

'Why?'

'Oh, I don't know.'

'There must be some reason,' she spoke quickly.

The café was nearly empty and the fog dulled the traffic in the streets. A few holiday makers, incongruous with raincoats over shorts and beach clothes sat speechless at their tables. I ordered some supper. There was no licence and they had to send out for the beer.

'To you now,' I said, 'flying is an adventure. You see an aircraft land and the pilot is a superior being, calm-faced and confident, someone who has made a journey through the clouds. In a record bid you find not only an epic of human courage, not only a manifestation of skill and daring, but a pioneer spirit helping in the conquest of a new world. Do you agree?'

'Bit high-flown, my dear, that's all.'

'To me it's not the same. I love to fly as you know, but as I've said before it's the thrill of craftsmanship, with danger to reinforce the mind. If the fans keep turning you'll make the trip all right and gain fame that will last a month or so until another flyer wrests it from you. Against that you risk your neck, risk death by fire, by unattended injuries, by starvation, force brave men to search dangerous country if you're forced down. Don't you see that it doesn't justify itself? Isn't there enough pain and trouble and disillusionment in the world already? Will the results of this venture outweigh the risks you propose to take?'

'You haven't got this quite right, Paul. It's not only the glamour aspect, though I'm terribly keen on that. There's another side to it. To be honest, darling, flying frightens me … it just scares me stiff – '

'Bless you … I know.'

'But how?' Her voice was sharp.

'I'm an instructor and I've taken you up.'

'I'd forgotten that.'

'Besides a lot of good pilots are highly strung.'

'I thought they were dumb and tough.'

'They're tough enough but the dumb ones don't last long unless they get a good fright occasionally.'

'I'm learning a lot. But to go back to what I was saying … when something really scares me, I've just *got* to go through with it. That's the real reason why I'm such a keen horsewoman. Now this trip terrifies me more than anything I've heard about in my life … it follows that I must go on it.'

'I see,' I said softly. 'But I've got another point of view … how will I feel when you're out on the job and liable to buy it at any minute? I'm getting set now, tired of what Chuck calls "bumming around". I'm getting a little tired too of living in cheap digs and frowsty pubs and of amorous shop girls and incessant pub-crawling and getting to bed whistled every night. At least that's the way I've felt since I met you. I like to think I've learnt a bit of sense. This flip belongs to that game if you understand what I mean?'

'I understand.' She tapped her plate with slim fingers. 'Another thing,' she smiled as she spoke, 'I've got a surprise for you!'

'For me?'

'M'm. I was talking to Jack about the flight a couple of days ago – '

'Jack's a good friend of mine,' I said, 'and he's a wizard pilot, but he's not the only pilot in the world!'

'Now, darling, go on being jealous.'

'It's nothing to do with jealousy.'

She laughed wisely.

'You do talk the most utter rubbish at times,' I said and then began to laugh with her, knowing she was right. 'What did Jack say, in any case?' I continued.

'First, we've decided on the route. It's to be an attack on the Australia run. The first hop'll be to India.'

'That ought to be all right.'

'Yes, and this means we've room for an extra pilot, preferably a trained navigator.'

'Who're you thinking of getting?'

'You … if you'll come.'

I looked round the stuffy room at little men bored with their trivial lives.

'I'll come,' I said.

✳

We picked up Chuck at closing time and returned to the Blue Boar. The fog was lifting now; a sea breeze pushing it mournfully through the narrow streets. Moira told our companion of the new arrangements and we all talked enthusiastically of the flight which Chuck said was now certain to be a success. When we went into the lounge, Brian was waiting for us. He was flushed and the fog had condensed on his hair. He greeted us nervously and asked if we had seen anything of his brother. Chuck replied that he hadn't seen him around for days.

'I'm worried about him," the other continued, 'he's been in a terrible state ever since ... well, since he heard about Mrs Graves.' He sat down slowly and rubbed his lower lip with the backs of his fingers. 'That's been a shocking business.'

'He's probably drinking some place,' Chuck suggested. 'Have a drink and stick around awhile. He'll turn up any time now.'

'I hope nothing's happened to him,' Brian said shaking his head at a drink. 'I feel responsible.'

'He'll be all right,' Chuck said.

Moira sat very still in the window seat, her head and shoulders like a vignette against the mist-laden dusk. 'Can you fly me up to the factory tomorrow, Paul? I want to see how they're getting on with the modified petrol system on *Marie Lou*.'

'*Marie Lou*?' Brian asked.

'My record-breaker,' Moira said.

'When d'you think of going?' his interest was pure politeness.

'As soon as we can now, but there are tons of things to fix up, and we're trying to get some backing from various firms. The organization side of it is terrific but luckily Jack's had a lot of experience.'

'Oh, he's going?'

'Almost certainly now. It'll be a good thing to take his mind off ... this terrible business. Paul here's coming too.'

'Were you there,' Brian asked, 'all the time?'

'Yes.'

'Did you see my brother?'

'He was in the waiting-room, I think, for some time, but they only allowed Jack and myself to go up.'

'That flip'll be OK,' I said, 'we'll go in 'EN'.'

'*Marie Lou* should be ready, then you can fly her round.'

'That'll be grand,' I said.

We heard a car in the yard and were silent till Jack came in. He looked very tired and greeted us quietly, taking the stiff drink that Chuck held out, We began to talk about the cricket, and how the rain would affect the wicket. Then I heard Jerry's voice downstairs saying that he could find his own way up. When he came in it was obvious he was the worse for alcohol.

'Oh, here you all are!' No one spoke.

'I've been looking for you for hours,' he went on. 'But I thought you'd be back here eventually.' He went over to the table and, stooping, gripped the edge, leaning his weight on his arms, his face rugged in the lamplight.

'It's been an awful day,' he said.

The only 'Yes' came from Moira.

'It just shows one never knows what's coming to one, that's what I say.'

'Must you talk about it?' Jack's voice was cool and level.

'Sorry, old man, I didn't realize.'

'That's all right,' Jack said.

'You see,' Jerry spoke with grave deliberation, 'I was in love with her … so I know how you feel.'

Jack put his glass carefully on the windowsill. His voice was very quiet with a tone learnt and practised to perfection in the Service.

'What did you say?'

Jerry twisted his head and looked at his antagonist.

'I said I was in love with her.'

As he spoke I went over and touched Jack's sleeve, saying

quietly: 'Don't take a poor view, old boy, he's drunk and talking tripe.' As Jerry heard my remark he swung towards us, pulling himself to his full height. 'You stay out of this … you've interfered before in this matter. Besides Chuck knows it's true … don't you?'

The latter looked up from the illustrated newspaper he was pretending to read. 'You're talkin' hooey, old boy. You wanna go home and hit the snore pad. You'll feel fine in the morning.' In desperation the elder of the parson's sons turned to Moira: '*You* know it's true? We were in love … she and I. Paul tried to stop it, but it wouldn't work. There was something in my life again.'

'I'm afraid I don't know what you're talking about,' Moira said.

Brian went over and caught the sleeve of his brother's war-stained Burberry. 'Come on, Jerry, let's go home.'

'Oh, damn your eyes, let me alone for once. Anyone would think you're my nurse.'

'I think I'm turning in,' Jack said. 'Good night, chaps. Good night Moira and thanks for everything.'

'You're all against me,' Jerry shouted, 'and what are you anyway? Only a few pilots who can't get better jobs. You can look down your noses as much as you please, I can fly as well as the best of you even if I can't get rich women to back me – '

Chuck caught him by the slack of his raincoat and half-carried him to the door. 'It's time you went to bed, pal,' he said and pushed him on to the landing.

'I'm awfully sorry – ' Brian began.

'That's OK,' the Canadian replied, 'just tuck him up, we understand.'

When Jack had gone to bed the three of us sat about the fire, for the evening was chilly, chatting idly while Chuck played his guitar. As I watched an arch of glowing coal I thought of Jack now at the beginning of his lonely journey, how each trivial aspect of everyday living, how familiar belongings and surroundings would bring heart-rending memories, how even the escape of sleep would be belied by instant realization when waking; and the atrophy of her in his consciousness slowed down by dreams and their mocking of the order of time.

'What's the matter, darling?' Moira asked.

'Oh, nothing.'

'Thinking about Jack?'

'No,' I said.

'I was too.'

'It's a damn shame,' Chuck said.

'Perhaps it's as well,' I said. 'He really loved her, you know, she'd have let him down hard soon. Now he can at least remember her with longing.'

'Maybe,' Chuck said gazing into the fire. He picked up his guitar and began to play 'They Cut Down The Old Pine Tree'. We joined softly in the chorus, for it was late, tapping the time with our toes on the fender.

Chapter 14

We flew to the factory on the following morning. It was a lovely day with clumps of white cloud setting off the vivid blue sky. Moira did the piloting and I sat back with a map on my knee, resting my elbows on the sides of the cockpit, happy to be away from the everlasting circuits that joy-riding entailed. The *Marie Lou* was ready and I flew her for an hour, a sweet aircraft with every modern device but bad visibility from the pilot's seat making it difficult to land. The Chief Test Pilot entertained us to lunch, telling us the story of his initial testing of the last of a bunch of Service types, how he had put on a special show, being forced to climb above a layer of cloud to do his tests. After three quarters of an hour he looked down at his compass to find his way home to find that it hadn't been fitted.

'By the by, how's Chuck?' he asked.

'He's fine.'

'What about that first moose he shot?'

'He hasn't lived that down yet,' I said.

'Is he going on this trip?'

'No, Jack Graves, Miss Barratt, and myself.'

'I thought his missus – '

'She died yesterday … he's coming now.'

'I'm terribly sorry … poor old Jack,' he pulled the lobe of his ear, 'she used to be Eve Heathly, didn't she? I remember her. Actually it was you that introduced us … years ago.'

'Well,' I said. 'I certainly like the kite.'

'It's about the best in the world for the job. The whole thing's pretty well in the bag. All you'll have to do will be just to sit there and watch the fans going round.'

'What about the trifling matter of navigation?'

'These things fly so fast you can fly on your track over that distance,' the test pilot said, 'though of course you, being a navigation king, won't admit that.'

'I don't.'

He laughed. 'All you navigators are the same. Your aim in life is to take back bearings, shoot the sun, work out running fixes, come down through clouds on your ETA and fly into a hillside.'

'You on the other hand belong to the Old School – '

'No see … no fly!'

'Not a bad idea, either,' Moira said.

'It's been my guiding rule these twenty years,' the test pilot said. (In reality he was famous for foolhardy recklessness in bad weather.) 'When are you thinking of starting?' he went on.

'We want to do some consumption tests,' I said, 'and there are still lots of things to be fixed up. Besides we've a joy-riding show on our hands on the South Coast.'

'Machines picketed?'

'Yes … one or other of us is out every bad night turnin' em into wind.'

'Who's doing the maintenance?'

'GE, myself, and a boy.'

'You must be working!'

'We are, but personally I'm trying test piloting in the autumn.'

'Now that's a thing you should never do. Who for?" he added quietly.

'Maxwells.'

'I heard they wanted a man. Good show.'

When I taxied out to take off for home the acrodrome was deserted and I decided to do some low aerobatics, telling Moira to pull up her seat against the Sutton harness.

'Paul?'

'Yes.' I was turning into wind as I answered.

'How did you know Eve years ago?'

'I just knew her.'

'But I thought Jack only met her last summer?'

'That's right.'

'Then you knew her before?'

'Yes.'

'Were you just friends?'

'Yes.'

'Why didn't you tell me you knew her before?'

'Oh, I suppose I never thought about it.'

Coming down between the sheds with slip-stream worrying my goggles, ear subconsciously attentive to the sweet note of the engine, wind screeching in the wires, I was back again in the circus at the beginning of my act. When the ground grew horribly near I pulled back hard on the stick, rolling off the top of the resultant loop. I remembered how each day I had lived for this initial aerobatic when I was still a little frightened, not having warmed up properly. And in this manoeuvre, amid all the noise with brain and body harnessed to concentration, conscious of a huge crowd by no means adverse to my crashing, I had found a certain peace in spirit, an objective sought and gained.

But I suddenly thought of Moira in the front cockpit, remembering her presence with a great wave of tenderness. At once I hated myself for risking a life dear to me in an exhibition of self- conceit and flying over the aerodrome, ruddered red on red.

'Hold her on two hundred and two magnetic,' I said, 'and map read and watch the wind, you've got to do your own corrections.'

'Have we finished aerobatics?'

'Yes.'

✕

'Tired?' I asked. We were having late tea at the Blue Boar.

'N'no … just sleepy.'

'You've had quite a session.'

'I wish I hadn't got so hopelessly lost!'

'Got to make mistakes to learn.'

'If only you'd told me when the wind changed, darling.'

'You'll be flying without me, sometimes.'

'It's the way you noticed every little thing and knew what I was thinking about that maddened me, especially when you didn't tell me till I'd had to ask you to take it home.'

I laughed. 'My dear, you're going to be quite good, there's nothing to worry about, it's quite normal.'

'I'm glad you think that.' She caught my hand across the table. 'Darling!'

'Yes.'

'When are we going to be married?'

'Soon's we've got that record.'

'Can't it be sooner?'

"Fraid not.'

'Why?'

'This joy-riding isn't so good … the expenses are high … the weather counts for such a lot and we might lose an aircraft any time through a crash or a gale.'

'What's that got to do with it?'

'When we come back I'll have a good job with good money.'

'Darling! I've got money.'

'I don't want that.'

'So money comes between us?'

'Loss of respect would.'

'You're terribly proud.'

'It's not pride.'

'Still, I suppose you've got enough money to buy a ring?'

'A ring?'

'Yes, stupid … an engagement ring.'

'Bless you,' I said, 'I never thought of that.'

'You funny man, don't you ever think of anything except flying?'

'Yes.'

'I didn't mean that!'

I watched the sunlight in the down on her cheek, her eyelashes drooping over her eyes, the light burnishing her hair, the lovely precision in the movements of her hands. Now and then, I thought, unexpected as one daydreams, there comes a glimpse of place or person suddenly inexplicably beautiful, floating calm above the striving world. And reason, developed in the matrix of experience, tells one, not for the first time, that this wonder is but a delusion of the mind, hooding a mundane thing. Yet this transitory happening finds kin in the understanding so that one remembers glimpses, through the mists of early childhood, of cities still more beautiful, recollects meetings, on shores imaginary, with persons of infinite understanding.

'Penny for your thoughts?'

'They're not worth half that.'

'Paul!' there was a serious note in her voice, 'you think we'll always be like this … lovers and friends … laughing our way through … not growing bored and bickering and getting on each other's nerves?'

Youth being impatient, I thought, thinks the attitude of age unreasonable, cynical, and heartless, believes in the future with confidence untested, aspires the unattainable with hope untried. But age is wise, not in pure wisdom which is of the mind and does not come uncalled with the passing of the years, but wise with knowledge of living: and it looks upon those commencing life, not in the ruthless manner they imagine, but rather with a kind of pity. And yet may we not hope to achieve what others have achieved? Must our cry forever be a protest at our non-inclusion? The strong must sometimes triumph in battle and swiftness win its race.

'Darling! You're dreaming ... I asked you something.'

'We'll be alright,' I said.

※

'About Eve!' Moira said.

'Yes.'

'You were in love with her, weren't you?'

'Yes.'

'Why didn't you tell me?'

'It was dead long before I met you.'

'Did she love you?'

'As much as a selfish woman can love.'

'This explains a great deal.'

'No,' I answered, 'she was never jealous of you. It was seeing someone else happy she didn't like.'

'You must have loved her very much!'

'I did.'

'She must have hurt you badly?'

'She did hurt me.'

She got to her feet and began to pace the room slowly. 'That night you took me up and we force-landed!'

'Yes.'

'As I told you, I thought I knew you so well and then in the twinkling of an eye there was a whole new slab of your life. To-day again, a chance word and there's another piece of your past. I've thought so often how close we are and how well I know your funny ways and what you're going to say next ... but it's all a delusion ... we're really almost strangers.'

I laughed and kissed her, asking her to drive me down to the aerodrome as I had work to do.

Chapter 15

After Eve's funeral Jack began to drink. He would start before breakfast on spirits and lunch usually found him flushed, sitting before untouched food with a glass in his hand. He worked well, never complaining, showed an interest in our happenings, was up early each morning working out details of the record bid. Only after night flying when we sat drinking in the lounge and Chuck played his guitar, was emotion too much for him and he would get slowly to his feet, bid us good night and go to bed, carrying a bottle and glass to his room. If the wind rose in the night he would wake us and we would toss up for odd man out to go down and watch the aircraft which would be tugging at their ropes by the time one got there.

We were arranging for Chuck to take over the joy-riding while we did the record run, but found it difficult to get reliable pilots in our places as it was now the height of summer. As soon as it became known that we wanted a couple of men, numbers of youths in strange clothes made shocking landings in borrowed aircraft asking to be taken on. They generally had commercial licences on Moths, lived on their parents and talked impressively of their flying.

It was lovely English weather now, clear and fresh in the early mornings as I went down to do a daily inspection, the thick-leaved trees yielding to a cool breeze.

Then breakfast and the day's work which was long and arduous for we had become well known in the district. First we flew in tight formation over the town, did a little crazy flying over the sea, a few aerobatics, then returned to the aerodrome to sleep in deck-chairs till the first passengers arrived. From eleven o'clock till sunset visitors from Swanmouth would drift into the field and each day meant hours at a stretch in the cockpit when one was thankful for the cool slipstream on one's face which nevertheless did not prevent goggles sticking to one's cheeks with sweat. We flew the same circuit time after time, being familiar with the shape of every field in the neighbourhood. With every local clump of trees, every gap in near-by hedges.

Chuck and I finished early, except at the weekends, leaving Jack to do the last flips and after a hasty supper would motor across to the searchlight flight at the Service aerodrome. A little after dark I would take off and climb into the darkness, cruising high above the little groups of lights that were my only reminder of the world. Occasionally the searchlights would find me, sousing my little room twelve thousand feet above the earth, but for the most part I flew lonely in the night, thinking of Moira who would be waiting for me with the car, imagine her to leeward of the watch hut looking anxiously up into the blackness.

※

One morning I took up a farmer who, from two thousand feet, mistook sheep for mushrooms. Afterwards I was talking to him and watching Jack taking off. The machine wobbled slightly as it became airborne, then climbing dropped its port wheel on the aerodrome. My shout brought Chuck out of his deck-chair and as the aircraft turned he fired a red pyrotechnic while Matthews held up the spare wheel of the coupé. Then we tore Chuck's newspaper into strips and laid out the word 'PORT' before the tent.

Jack throttled down and flew low over our heads, waggling his wings to show that he understood. We loaded the fire extinguishers and a hacksaw into the coupé and drove to the middle of the field. Jack pulled his nose up and we watched him pass his cushion to his passenger, a girl blissfully ignorant of what was happening. He came in so that the machine would touch down a little short of us and at two hundred feet switched off his engine.

The Avro now approaching head on with slowly turning airscrew appeared to be travelling so slowly, for it was nearly stalled, that it required no small effort of imagination to think of it crashing. As we watched I thought of other shows I'd seen, remembered watching a wireless operator strolling into an airscrew. One second a man, curious, hands in pockets, the next a headless corpse whirling round in the airscrew like a suit of overalls. And then, as in all such scenes, I was conscious not so much of horror or pity as of a deep sense of the macabre, the sudden actuality of the occurrence breaking so brutally into everyday existence.

'Now!' Chuck whispered, sharing with me the impatience peculiar to this type of experience. Jack stalled on to his starboard wheel, ran some yards then slewed to a standstill on a crumpled undercarriage.

'Nice work,' Chuck said. 'I don't think longerons or spars have gone.'

We walked across. Jack grinned at us. The girl climbed out smiling brightly.

'Are you all right?' Jack asked.

'Of course,' her pencilled eyebrows, which were set above the white mark where her others had been plucked out, were raised in amazement.

Then she noticed the tilt of the main planes and getting out saw the broken undercart.

'Did we ... crash?'

'Hardly,' Jack said laughing.

'But ... it's broken!'

'A wheel fell off as you took off,' I was helping Matthews to strip the fabric as I spoke, 'and Captain Graves made a very skilful job of the landing.'

'Oh,' she said and fainted.

'What do we do now?' Matthews asked.

Chuck went over, looked at her and put a cushion under her head. 'Leave her alone,' he said, 'she'll make it OK herself.' We gathered round the aircraft trying to ascertain the damage and I looked round a little later to see the girl sitting up in the grass watching us with astonishment.

※

I flew up to London next morning for the usual commercial pilot's medical examination. It was past tea-time before the Air Ministry doctors at Clement's Inn were satisfied and then I rolled down the Strand, looking at the shops and watching pretty typists fighting their way on to buses. It was hot, the streets heavy with the stale breath of a summer afternoon. Shortly after six I met Jack, who had flown up with me, in the downstairs bar of the Captain's Cabin.

We talked to the barman for a while and then went over and sat by the miniature aquarium set over the fireplace. Jack had obviously been drinking all day and after several more gins his speech began to thicken.

Our conversation drifted to flying and we began to recall experiences, now so remote in time and setting.

'How did the medical go?' he asked suddenly.

'Oh, all right. Nearly burst myself holding up the mercury.'

'I only scraped my last one,' he muttered thoughtfully. 'I wonder how it'll go next time?'

'Look here, old boy,' I said looking very carefully at a lifebelt hanging in the corner of the stairs, 'it's none of my business or anything but don't you think you ought to pull the ladder up a bit on this booze?'

He went across to the bar getting me another lager and himself a double gin. Then he sat down again and passed a hand slowly over his face.

'Not for a while, Paul. I daren't stop for a while.'

'This flip of ours is going to take some handling!'

'Physically you mean?'

'Yes.'

'Oh, I'm all right ... I can pilot against any perfect specimen of humanity till he's mucked ... you know that?'

'Yes,' I said. 'I think you could.'

'I daren't stop now, Paul,' he continued speaking so quietly that I had to lean forward to hear him. 'I can't lay off for a while, it's just too deep. I'd never have believed that anything could tear your heart open like that. It's not so much the past but ... well, the thought of the future. I'm not sorry for Eve ... she's out of it now ... I'm trying to stop being sorry for myself.'

He drained his gin and tapped the bottom of the glass nervously on the edge of the table. 'I'm doing a lot of thinking as I fly these days. But when I'm flying I'm doing something so it's not so bad. It's when there's nothing to do that thinking's hell.'

I got two more drinks.

'God bless!'

'Suck in!'

'It's the little things that count,' he went on in the same tone, 'seeing her things about and expecting her to come in and waking up and talking to her and recollecting something that has to be done to the car, for instance, then remembering in a flash: "That doesn't matter now ... she's dead."'

He beat his hand on the table. 'Why did it have to happen to us? We didn't want so much, just a home and a flying job for me ... and in the evenings trickle down to the local or go to the flicks or have some people in.

'In a way I'm glad it's all over ... I mean that it ended with her dying ... rather than letting me down ... not that she'd have ever done that of course. But it would have been worse ... if you know what I mean ... to think of her being about and the two of us not in love any more.'

'This trip will be a good thing to take your mind off.'

'Yes, I think you're probably right about that.' He was more than a little drunk now. 'Christ … I won't be sorry … silly to see a big man in plus fours crying like a kid when he goes to the cemetery.'

'It's time to go, old boy,' I said and we returned to the aerodrome through the heated streets, afterwards flying homewards with the setting sun on our starboard bow, southern England mellow with haze below.

Chapter 16

The flight was scheduled to start on a Monday but bad meteorological conditions in southern Europe and trouble with a petrol pump delayed us for several days. We lived at an hotel near the factory aerodrome and were objects of some interest to the other guests.

Jack drank steadily and said little, while Chuck, who had come up to see us off and was by far the most nervous of the party, played his guitar for hours on end and tried, without much success, to keep the conversation away from aviation. Moira was very much on edge, chain smoking and rushing about in her car or cadging flights at the aerodrome. I went about with her, sometimes impatiently eager to start but on other occasions conscious of a feeling of relief when it was finally decided that another day must be spent hanging about on the ground. I was dreaming whenever I slept, recurring ever-fearful dreams of crossed elevator controls, fire in the air, structural failure and crashing; the sky dark overhead.

One of the firms who were backing the flight was pressing us to risk the weather as they wanted the advertisement of our success by the end of the week and their representative strolled about the tarmac all day and most of the night haranguing any of us he could find.

At last a knock at my door brought me swimming upwards out of a dream and Jack in shabby leather jerkin came in with a weather report in his hand.

'The weather's all right except for the odd storm, I think we should get off in an hour. You're all set aren't you?'

'Yes, old boy, everything's on the top line. I'll be there in twenty minutes,' I said feeling cold in my guts. It was still dark and I shivered a little as I dressed though the night was warm. In the distance a church clock was striking and

I began to count the strokes thinking as I used to at school: 'If it's three it'll be all right, if it's three it'll be all right, if it's three I won't be flogged for Greek prose in the morning, if it's three it'll be all right. Oh God! Let it be three!'

Moira was already downstairs sipping hot coffee, warming her hands on the cup. I kissed her and we ate the sandwiches in silence. When we had finished the barman came in. He was an ex-artilleryman with a repertoire of improper stories extensive beyond his calling.

'Is there anything I can do, sir?'

'Thanks, no, Harry,' Moira said. 'It was sweet of you to get up for us.'

'You're really going?' he asked.

'Yes,' I said.

He felt in the pocket of his white jacket and produced a little Saint Christopher medal.

'Would Madam accept this with the best wishes of the Staff?'

'That's really a kind thought,' Moira said. 'Thank you so much.' She read the inscription. *Regarde St Christophe puis va t'en rassuré*. Now this will certainly bring us luck.'

We began to gather up our things.

'Good luck sir, to you, and to you, Madam!'

Moira thanked him again and slipped her hand under my elbow as we went out.

'Thrilled, darling?'

'Yes,' I said.

✕

The small crowd standing on the apron before the hangars included a few newspaper men and flashlights leapt out of the darkness as we walked to the machine. We started the engines and then waited for them to warm up. I went for a walk across the aerodrome with Chuck. It was beginning to get light and soon birds were singing in a coppice on the western boundary.

'Hark at 'em,' Chuck said, 'singing like bastards this time in the morning. It might be a good thing to be a bird sometimes.'

'With a little luck we'll be in India inside a day,' I said.

'When I first came over here', Chuck went on, 'I sure didn't like it.'

'We've got de-icers, variable pitch airscrews, retractable undercart, plenty of speed, full blind-flying equipment and all the navigational gubbins … it ought to be easy.'

'Everything was so tidy and old looking. Then there was the way you'd find kids playing in the main drag and everyone drove on the wrong side of the street and there were shoe shops everywhere and the public lavatories were a disgrace.'

'All there is to this business is to keep the fans turning.'

'Then there's this social racket you find over here,' Chuck continued, 'that surely gets me down still. But I've grown to like the rest of it, especially in the south where the trees meet over the roads. There's something restful about it too that kind of grows on you if you get me … the funny little cottages with smoke curlin' up from the chimneys and pretty little country pubs where you play darts with the locals … and hay wagons pushing back the hedges as they go down the lanes.'

'The navigation will be mostly DR. In a way I'd have liked wireless, especially if we have to force-land somewhere in the wilds.'

'Mind you,' Chuck said, 'I'm not crazy on this country. Gimme back home anytime. Maybe it's changed since I left but it sure was grand when I was a kid going down to Belle View park in the evenings in the fall and holdin' a girl's hand and watching the boats go by on the river.'

If we break our necks on this trip, I thought, the silly things we're saying will be remembered and our foolish actions recalled by those who knew us. And they, seeking to justify death, pandering to a theatrical and illogical desire to ring down a perfect curtain on a poor production, will give import to our words, dignity to our actions, even finding reason in the whole undertaking.

We walked slowly back and listened to Jack running up the engines. Then everything was ready, more photographs were taken, everyone was shaking hands, someone gave Jack a horse- shoe, I was kissed by a barmaid I'd known years before. Chuck squeezed into the cabin with us.

'Good luck you kids and happy landings … don't get bumped off … I don't like drinking on my own!'

Jack waved away the chocks, a mechanic put up his thumb and we started to taxi out accompanied by a ragged cheer and a waving of hats. I leaned over from the second pilot's seat and set the first course on the magnetic compass.

At the far end of the aerodrome Jack turned into wind, pumped on thirty degrees of flap, felt both airscrew controls to check that they were in fine, wound the tail incidence adjustment a quarter forward, tried the petrol cocks and magneto switches. Then he let off the brakes and pulling back the override levers opened both throttles.

Slowly we began to move and he brought the tail up. Half-way across we were bumping and then he brought her off and held her down to gain speed. Owing to the heavy load of petrol the *Marie Lou* climbed slowly. He pumped up his flaps and undercart, throttled down, changed both airscrews into coarse and turned slowly to bring us back over the aerodrome on our course.

I smiled at Moira who was gripping my arm. Through my side window I could see the aerodrome, an untidy field below, the shabby hangars pushed up into one corner of the apron that shone with recent rain.

✳

I had only time to take a back bearing and work out a wind before we were in the clouds. Jack continued to climb and at nine thousand feet we were in a hailstorm. He reached down and turned the gyros on to pump drive so that when the ASI dropped to zero there was no change in our rate of climb.

At twelve thousand we came suddenly into the sunshine, the white floor of cloud stretching for hundreds of miles before us. Jack levelled off, flying to an exact computed airspeed of two hundred and fifty five. Each detail was so known to us, anything that had to be done so perfectly understood, every manoeuvre and decision so often discussed and rehearsed that we were like automatons, our feelings a hindrance to us.

I thought as I watched Jack how fitted he was to be a pilot. Rigorous training and experience had given him confidence tempered with perfect judgement. He was a machine as he sat by my side poker-faced, holding the *Marie Lou* on her course, his eyes sweeping the instruments every few seconds, and could be trusted to fly like a machine, to utilize his skill, undeterred by fear, and his judgement, unaffected by fatigue, to the utmost limit of human endurance.

We flew on for hour after hour, seeing nothing of the earth but the peaks of mountains standing up through the clouds, the only other moving thing our shadow which raced silently beneath us, following every curve of the clouds with effortless grace. Above was the dome of heaven, a nightmare blue except for the blazing ball of the sun, no trace of cloud to break its pitiless emptiness. The one sound in our ears was the roar of the engines mingling with airscrew thrash.

We were alone, racing through a dead world.

※

After six hours Moira took over, at first enthusiastic over the piloting but quickly becoming bored so that she needed constant watching to prevent her from wandering a few degrees off her course.

Then we went into another storm, the *Marie Lou* bumping about the sky, pitching and rolling while hail and snow came in through the edges of the windows. Jack took the controls again and Moira crouched at my side as I worked over the navigation. Jack, altering his height, was juggling with his throttles when the port motor began to bang. I leapt to his side and we watched supercharger pressure and revolutions. The trouble only occurred at twenty-two hundred and he pulled back the flap of his helmet and shouted, asking me what I made of it.

'Can't be plugs,' I said, 'must be automatic boost control piston sticking.'

He thought for a few seconds then held up a thumb and turned his attention to piloting once more, the engine running normally as he opened the throttle. I offered Moira a chicken sandwich. She shook her head.

'Try it, my dear, it'll do you good.'

'Don't feel like eating …' she shouted.

'It's the effect of altitude … try it!' But she smiled and refused again. Already she seemed tired.

When we came out into the clear weather it was beginning to get warm and I changed with Jack, sitting in my shirt sleeves leaning my face against the window-edge to try and get the most of the cool wind that sang in the narrow opening. Moira had lost interest in the countries over which we were passing and lay on the floor trying to sleep. The starboard engine began to run hot, the oil temperature rising to ninety-five and I had to throttle down, upsetting our scheduled average speed.

Hour after hour we sat there. Our clothes were wet with sweat, the wheel was sticky in my hands and my sun glasses slithered on the bridge of my nose. At one time it became very bumpy and Moira was sick. The oil pressure on the starboard engine had dropped a little and was worrying me. I told Jack that I'd have to inspect the pump when we landed.

'That'll shove our schedule back still further!'

'Can't be helped … we don't want the ruddy thing to pack up in the desert.'

We found our first refuelling point easily, being dead on our track. The oil pressure had crept up again and I began to feel better.

'Would you like to take her in?'

'No … you carry on.'

I throttled down, dropped the undercarriage, changed the airscrews into fine, pumped on twenty degrees of flap and put her down a little fast. A few officials greeted us and took Jack and Moira over to the aerodrome buildings for a rapid meal while I supervised refuelling and got the starboard covers off. I was a little deaf and my right leg hurt below the knee from the strain of holding on rudder. Handicapped by inadequate tools it took me some time to do my inspection. When I had finished Jack was standing by my side.

'I think it's all right,' I said, 'as far as I can see. What's the weather like?'

'The weather's grand.'

'Where's Moira?'

'That's the trouble … she's been sick again and doesn't want to go on.'

'I'll go and talk to her,' I said, 'just start up will you?'

In a sparsely furnished room in the airport buildings decorated with framed pictures from *The Tatler* I found her slumped into a ' wicker chair.

'Hullo, my dear,' I said quietly, 'd'you feel better now?'

'Yes.'

I drank a cup of coffee and ate a sandwich.

'If you're all set ... we'll get started.'

'Oh, Paul ... please don't think I haven't got the guts ... but I can't go on ... I just can't go on. You two go on and I'll follow you by Dominions.'

'I know how you feel.'

'It's being sick all the time. And there's no glamour in it ... you just go on and on and on. I'm tired of it ... tired of the inside of that aeroplane and the cramped conditions and the cabin full of petrol tanks and listening to the engines and the heat. I never thought it would be like this.'

'It's rotten for you, I know,' I said.

'And soon now it'll be dark ... hours of it alone up there ... if anything goes wrong we'll be ... just broken up out there in the desert hundreds of miles from anywhere. When I used to watch you night flying at home ... it was romantic ... even that night you took me up it was an adventure ... but now it's useless ... just a jeopardizing of our future happiness for nothing.'

'Come on, darling, you're in this, you and I and Jack, the three of us together.'

'I thought that too, once. But what use am I? I can only keep the gyro on "O". I can't fly on a magnetic compass, navigate, take off or land, or even trim the *Marie Lou*.'

'Yes, my dear,' I said softly, 'but we're going now ... Jack's got the motors going. Everyone feels like you do sometimes ... you'll be fine again soon.'

'That's the tragedy of it,' she stared straight before her, twisting her hands back to back and interlocking her fingers. 'You and Jack are just machines, but there must be many pilots broken by years of flying, by crashes, by war, who must feel as I do now ... then they've got to earn bread by the only way they know and they dull themselves with drink and drive themselves into the sky with superhuman effort.' She looked up at me. 'In a few years what courage the aeroplane has taken out of the world!'

'Darling … it's time to go!'

Slowly she got to her feet and followed me across the sandy aerodrome to the sweltering cockpit of the *Marie Lou* in which we had still to speed over nearly half the earth.

Chapter 17

Soon after we took off it grew dark and we flew beneath high cloud seeing no light, navigating on dead reckoning. Jack decided to get some sleep and I did the piloting, singing and repeating verse to keep myself awake. Sometimes I became drowsy, trying to remember where we were heading and would dream, though half awake, and think of Moira objectively as being hundreds of miles away in England, suddenly realizing with a start that she was crouching behind me.

The engines ran perfectly as it became colder but it was still bumpy and Moira was sick several times.

'When's it going to get light?' she asked.

'Soon, darling.'

'It's awfully lonely.'

'You'll feel better when dawn comes.'

'Paul?'

'Yes?' I was straining to catch her words for I was now fairly deaf.

'I'm glad I came on.'

'Of course you are, darling,' I said watching the starboard oil temperature which was rising again.

'You don't despise me for not wanting to?'

'I admire you for admitting it.'

'You were sweet the way you made me stick ... I'm frightened now ... but I'd have been much more frightened if it had got about that I'd lacked the guts to go on.'

'That's the answer to a lot of bravery,' I said.

After two hours or so Jack woke automatically, blaspheming lustily when he saw that I had throttled down. He asked how late I thought we should be at our next refuelling point.

'Working on dead reckoning ... don't know the wind ... about an hour!'

He nodded and glanced over his shoulder at the little flames swirling from the starboard exhaust which were the only things to be seen from that window. My eyes were tired, my legs a little stiff. I wondered how I should feel on the following night.

Suddenly there was a terrific noise in the port engine. The boost needle shot up from minus one to zero, the revolution counter sagged out of sight as I slammed the throttle back, ramming on right rudder to hold the *Marie Lou* on her course.

'What the hell's the matter?' bawled Jack, his face red.

'The supercharger's blown up ... the whole motor's gone,' I said opening the other engine up to maintain height.

'How long is it till daylight?'

'Just an hour.'

'What about going back?'

'Better to go on, the river's only two hundred miles away.'

He shot a glance at the oil temperature, then looked at me and grinned, 'What's the least you can hold her up on?'

'She's doing 'em now.'

I followed several obscene words on his lips. Moira, white-faced, pushed in between us, asking what was the matter.

'It's all right,' Jack said, 'we're flying on one motor to cool the other.'

'You're skipper,' I said, 'would you like to take over?'

'I would, old boy.'

We changed places. Now I had nothing to do but watch the wretched oil temperature and imagine that I could see signs of the dawn. We were losing height very gradually and I could feel Moira trembling through her thin frock as she leaned against me.

'Darling?' she spoke so that Jack was out of earshot, 'is it really dangerous?'

'No, there's nothing to worry about,' I said. I was thinking how we had both lied to her, wondering at this childish subterfuge employed by the strong towards those they imagine weaker than themselves, in that far from serving to lull fear it adds dread to doubt, tempers wonder with vague fear.

⁂

Just after it was light on the ground the starboard engine burst an oil pipe, the brown liquid covering the underneath of the wing and coating my navigation window. Now we had to come down. We were flying at six thousand feet and all around was the desert, brown and empty for hundreds of miles. The silence as we glided fell strangely on our ears and we strained our eyes to distinguish the surface below.

Jack dropped his wheels, turned off his petrol cocks and sat there expressionless, his rugged face, its purposeful features enhanced by crash scars, clear against the early light.

Soon we saw that the ground was level and almost covered with large boulders throwing purple shadows. Jack picked what seemed to be a clear patch and, watching it over his shoulder, went into a gentle turn pumping on as much flap as he wanted just as if he was coming in to land at an aerodrome. I smiled to see him, from pure habit, glance about the sky for signs of other aircraft as he turned into a straight glide.

Now we were skimming boulders, seeming to be travelling so slowly that an impact would be of little consequence, a thought hardly endorsed by the ninety miles an hour that showed on the ASI. Then Jack put twenty pounds on the brakes and the *Marie Lou* went down for a good landing.

In the dead silence I thought I could hear the gyros still running, but it may have been imagination for my ears still rang with the roar of the engines. Jack took his hands off the wheel and wiped the sweat off his face with his sleeve.

'That's the end of the record,' he said.

The record, I thought. Of course, that's the end of the record.

✳

We climbed out and stood in the shade of the fuselage for it was already warm. After some seconds Moira asked where we were.

'About a hundred miles from a Royal Air Force Station,' I said.

'Will they search for us?'

'As soon as they know we're missing and what track we were on.'

'How long will that take?'

'They'll be on the job this evening,' I said.

'Do you think they'll find us?'

'Oh, yes. They use a scientific method of search.'

'Then there's nothing to do but wait?'

'That's all, my dear.'

Jack produced a small bag from the rear of the fuselage. It contained ground strips which we proceeded to lay out, surgical dressings and iron rations. The latter together with what we had in the cockpit would last us for about three days, while the liquid at our disposal could be eked out for a similar period. Jack suggested that I helped him to gather dried-up scrub to form a heap for firing should we sight an aircraft.

'D'you think they'll find us?' I asked when Moira could no longer hear.

'Not a hope. I was out here years ago flying nine acks. I know this country well.'

'That's cheerful!'

'Cheerful's the word.'

Later I took the starboard covers off and did a thorough inspection. Jack watched me saying nothing. The heat now was intense and I was plagued by flies. Moira slept uneasily under the fuselage. Now and again I fancied I could hear aircraft but the only objects in the sky were a species of vulture strange to me. About midday I lay down for a rest, taking a half-cigarette that my companion offered.

'D'you think she'll go?' he asked.

'I'll get the starboard going,' I said, 'but the port's mucked to blazers.'

He lit a match and watched it without lighting his cigarette till it burnt his fingers. 'The test pilot told me she'd take off on one motor,' he said. 'If we clear a few rocks away down to the south there, there'll be plenty of run.'

'It's taking the hell of a chance,' I said.

'Do you remember those blokes in Australia?'

'Yes.'

'After they'd drunk the alcohol out of the compass they walked round the kite till they died.'

'I remember,' I said.

'There's *her* to think of.'

'I'm willing to try.'

'We'll settle that later. How soon d'you think you can get her going?'

'Not before dusk. But we've two flashlamps and with luck she'll be ready by dawn tomorrow. I'll have to rob the port engine, that'll take the time.'

'Right ... I wish I could do more to help.'

'You've done plenty all ready,' I said, "leave this to me; it'll soon be finished.'

✕

But things went wrong. First my tools left much to be desired as a full fitter's kit would have been too heavy to carry. Then in order to reach parts of the engines I had to stand on Jack's shoulders. Towards evening I began to feel giddy from working long hours in the sun and once I fell, bringing Jack down with me and bruising my shoulder.

At last it grew dark and as the work was too intricate to be done by flashlamp, I gave up for the day and had my first meal lying by Moira's side. It was a lovely night, the sky filled with stars.

'I feel responsible for all this,' she said suddenly.

'For all what?' I asked.

'This being out here,' she said.

'Nonsense,' Jack put in.

'But I do ... I was the tough one ... I was the one who always wanted to go.' She laughed quietly and bitterly. 'Why, Paul even tried to stop me once and now I lie here all day and watch him working in the sun. You see I had the wrong idea of it ... I thought a lot about the crowds at the other end and used to rehearse little speeches to them ... but I never thought of being out here ... just sitting in the desert waiting for someone to rescue us.'

'In three months time', Jack said, 'you'll be starting out again, probably on this same run. This game gets into your system.' He thought for a few seconds. 'On my last trip I got smashed up. When I promised Eve I'd give it up and live a normal sort of life I really meant it. But it wasn't long before I was itching to be off again.'

No one spoke for some time and when it grew colder we got into the cabin and I lay awake with a splitting headache listening to the regular breathing of my companions, my mind filled with the technicalities of aero engine oil systems.

The next morning was worse. I fell twice before midday and Jack was beginning to feel the strain of holding me. The second time I hit my head and regained consciousness in Moira's lap. Then I had a meal of iron rations and went to work again. My head was swimming and I had to keep one arm round a blade of the airscrew to keep myself upright on Jack's shoulders. The flies seemed worse and forgetting Moira's presence I began to curse and blaspheme till Jack twitched my trouser leg.

'I'm sorry, Moira … it's this pump housing.'

'That's all right,' she answered.

I had lost all sense of time, the only thing in my mind being the determination to get the engine running with full oil pressure.

At last it was done and it only remained to transfer the oil from port to starboard engine. For this we used a thermos flask and I grew unspeakably weary, counting each trip and saying 'ten more', 'ten more', 'ten more', 'do ten more', till the engine was full. Then I tried to start up but for some reason the engine was obstinate, refusing to catch, and soon she was rich and I had to wait. This went on until the battery ran out.

'What now?' Moira asked.

'One of us will have to stand on the other's shoulders again and turn her over with the handle,' I said.

'Not to-night,' Jack said, 'it's too late now.'

So we walked out into the desert and began to roll away boulders, clearing a runway. Moira's hands were soon bleeding and I was dazed, imagining that Chuck was with us. Finally we reached two large rocks, firmly embedded.

'That's all we can do,' Jack said.

'It isn't very long,' Moira said.

'It's long enough,' the other answered.

We went back and lay in the shade of the aircraft. The food and drink were nearly finished and Jack put us on half rations. Moira had been asking all day when the Royal Air Force were going to find us, but now she was silent realizing how slender the chances were. Jack was quiet too, walking slowly round the *Marie Lou*.

'Paul, darling, you look terribly ill!'

'I'm fine,' I said. 'How d'you feel?'

'I'm fine, too. Does your head hurt?'

'No,' I said.

She put a damp bandage across my forehead. 'Is that better?'

'That's grand,' I said, 'but you're wasting water.'

'Do you remember the first time we met?'

'I remember.'

'Regrets?'

'No regrets.'

'Whatever happens?'

'Whatever happens,' I said.

'At first I thought you only wanted to seduce me!'

'Didn't I?'

'Darling, I love being seduced by you.'

'You're going to marry me, as soon as – '

'We get out of this.'

I rolled on to my bad shoulder, the pain stabbing my consciousness so that I quickly rolled back again.

'We don't know each other very well, do we?' I said.

'What do you mean?'

'You never fool me when you're pretending to be dull.'

'This game we play of keeping up our spirits and hoping?'

'We don't have to. We'll get out of this if we have to walk it.'

'Now you're playing it.'

'I'm sure we'll get out,' I said. 'I'm just a bit browned off now and then, that's all.'

✳

I slept a little that night dreaming that I was in England in the autumn, the apples red on the trees in the Rectory garden at home and my people alive and the smell of leaves burning and horse chestnuts dropping on the lawn and the sky very blue and my father walking over from church after changing the colours, his thumb holding his spectacles on the cover of a black leather Bible.

When I awoke I felt better and after some rancid coffee I primed the carburettors and started to turn the heavy engine over, Moira sitting at the controls. Suddenly she kicked and started. Dead beat I nearly fell into the airscrew as I pulled the handle out but Jack bent his knees and pulled me clear.

As soon as she was warm I tested her to full revolutions, the *Marie Lou* straining at the stones we used as chocks. Then I throttled down again and switched off.

'Pressure's OK,' I said. 'She's fine.'

'Grand!' Jack said, 'but what did you cut the switch for?'

'We've forgotten to jettison the long-range tank!'

'Hell! I never thought of it … let it go now … it'll soon evaporate in this heat.'

I turned the cock as he spoke and hundreds of gallons of petrol poured out into the desert, washing about the wheels. Some time later when we judged the risk of fire from a flash to be negligible, I climbed on Jack's shoulders for the last time and started up once more.

Again I got into the pilot's seat and tried her up to full revolutions.

'You did a good job there,' Jack said. 'Just hop out of that seat and I'll be in civilization in an hour.'

'Don't talk tripe,' I said. 'You stay here with Moira while I have a stab at it. I weigh less than you and she'll be off the deck sooner.'

'I'm skipper,' Jack said, 'and I'm going.'

'Toss you for it!' I said. My voice sounded very far away.

'You two have got each other,' Jack said. 'I've only my job left and this is part of it.'

'I've got the navigation buttoned,' I said.

'Navigation my foot,' Jack answered. 'I can smell my way in from here.'

'I think Jack ought to go,' Moira said. 'You're not very well you know, darling.'

'All right,' I said. Without warning I felt very weary. 'Now this is our approximate position marked here,' I showed him the map. 'Fly on this course, I'm allowing you four degrees for drift, and you'll be dead on your track when you hit the river. At midday Moira and I will have a ruddy great fire going ... they can't miss us.'

'I'll lead 'em in,' Jack said.

I felt awkward.

'Good luck,' Moira said and kissed him. Her eyes were filled with tears.

'Good luck, you old monkey,' I said, 'take it easy if she doesn't seem to be coming off.'

He nodded and I touched his shoulder and followed Moira out of the cabin. Then I levered the stones from before the wheels and held up my thumb. He flashed a grin through a healthy growth of beard, pumped on flap, opened the engine till the aircraft began to strain. Then he let off the brakes and the *Marie Lou* began to move.

The Last Chapter

Slowly, so slowly the machine moved down the runway and I stood my hand on Moira's arm, urging speed, more speed, with all my strength, trying with useless effort of mind to force the *Marie Lou* into the air. It took Jack hundreds of yards to get the tail up and I could see by the elevators that he was making desperate attempts to bounce the aircraft off.

'He'll never do it!' Unconsciously I spoke aloud. 'Maybe we didn't jettison enough juice.'

Moira's mouth was twisted with anguish. I was looking almost up sun which hurt my eyes. The machine still showed no signs of becoming airborne. 'Throttle back, you fool!' I shouted. As he travelled faster he found it difficult to hold her straight. My companion gave a little cry and turned her face into my shoulder.

The *Marie Lou* hit a large boulder with her starboard motor, swirling into a cloud of dust out of which the port wing tip could be seen as a rock tip standing out of the sea.

In a few seconds the roar of the crash, the crackling and splintering, the anguish of intricate machinery rent asunder, broke upon us, then rumbled away over the desert, leaving horrible silence and a cloud of settling dust and the vultures wheeling and swaying on their broad wings overhead.

I began to run.

✳

As I ran I thought I was at school again, doubling round the big field before early school, a little sick with running on an empty stomach, my breath rasping in my throat, wondering how far behind the whipper-in was, dreading the inevitable blow with a buckled belt if I should lag, my mind busy with the day's work, hoping I could keep out of trouble with my Greek syntax for another day.

It seemed that as I ran the wreckage was receding and I wondered, as I had done several times in the past few hours, if I was going mad, or whether the whole affair was but a nightmare and I should wake, perspiring, into the grey tranquillity of an English dawn and, hearing the singing of the birds, be happy to be alive and well.

I was above all conscious of a great loneliness, feeling that an audience, shocked with interest, would have comforted me, and in some small way have compensated for the tragedy.

Then I saw the first of the flames and stopped in my tracks, the sweat gathering in my eyebrows, hopeless fear welling in my guts. Moira caught me up. Her hair hung over her face, she gulped her breath, leaning forward and holding her side. One of her high heels was missing. She was oil-stained.

The fire grew in intensity, sending a great cloud of smoke over the sunburnt landscape and as we approached we could hear the crackling, feel the heat brushing our faces.

I stopped and held her arm.

'It's no good,' I said.

'Isn't there anything … we can … do?'

'Nothing,' I said.

'Is he … alive … in there?'

'No,' I said.

'You needn't lie now, darling.' Her voice was quiet.

'I'm not lying, my dear. He must have been dead before the fire started.'

'Why?'

'You could hear him scream from here,' I said.

'I hadn't thought of that.'

She suddenly began to cry.

'Paul, darling! What's going to happen to us? What's going to happen to us? I'm terrified!'

I started to reassure her, marvelling that the stupid stock phrases I uttered, the inarticulate illogical arguments I cited, could, as indeed they did, soothe her so that presently she sobbed softly in my arms.

※

It was Moira who first saw him.

He limped out of the smoke on the leeward side, bleeding from a cut on his cheek, his left arm swinging loosely, his flying-jacket cut to ribbons.

We stood speechless as he came towards us. Then my companion rushed up and caught his arm. He smiled at us.

'So they take off on one engine!' he said. 'Wait till I see that bloody test pilot.'

He put his arm on my shoulder and we walked to the far end of the runway where we had left the first-aid kit.

'She didn't seem to be coming off!' I said.

'I couldn't do anything with her, though she was gaining speed all the time.'

'How did you get out?' Moira asked.

'Got a bang on the head … when I came round I could feel the heat … I wriggled through the window as quick as I damn well could.'

Moira did what she could with iodine and bandages, then left us for a while. Jack was very white.

'I don't like it,' he said.

'Have you broken your arm?'

'Don't know … quite probable.'

I divided a cigarette.

'We're up the creek this time.'

'And no paddle.'

He puffed his half till it glowed. When he spoke again his voice was slow with thought.

'I've seen a lot of blokes buy it, but I never thought much about dying ... not till now, that is.' He felt his shoulder tenderly. 'D'you think it helps to be religious or anything?'

'I don't know,' I said.

'Some of those religious types shoot a pretty line about it ... but they seem just as much afraid as anyone else ... in any case they're worrying about what happens afterwards. I don't care about that ... I'll take a chance on anything. It's sitting here on my arse waiting for a sticky end that doesn't appeal to me.'

'I feel that way, too,' I said.

He brushed cigarette ash from his sleeve absently.

'If there's another world and they don't fly," he continued, 'I don't want to go there. And if they do ... well ... I've done an awfully long time in cockpits already.'

'We took a chance,' I said.

'And had bad luck.'

'No, old boy, it's not a question of luck ... if you take a chance you must be prepared for this ... otherwise it wouldn't be a chance.'

'Perhaps you're right ... but just let me get out of this and luck or no luck, chance or no chance ... I'll break this mucking record if it takes me the rest of my life.'

We made a pathetic little tent out of the ground strips to keep off the sun. I grew delirious again, imagining that Chuck was coming to rescue us.

The next thing I knew I was in Moira's arms.

'Better, darling?" she rocked my head in her lap.

'Yes,' I said. 'How long have I been out?'

'Not long.'

'If only we could *do* something?'

'I know, Paul,' she said. 'I know.'

How we dramatize our lives, I thought, imagine we are secretly superior to our fellows, conjecture ourselves as masters of intricate situations, live, in our minds, gargantuan existences that can never be endorsed by the world. Even in this scene I felt, not so much despair at our predicament, as a sense of frustration, a lack of colour, an intense annoyance at the idea of a slow death in the depths of the desert exciting only the professional interest of the vultures.

'Don't worry, darling,' she went on. 'Jack says they'll see the smoke as they search and so find us. It's going to be all right, really darling, it's going to be all right.' I made no reply and she continued: 'Jack's been in tougher spots than this and so have you … there's really nothing to bother about. All we have to do is to wait.'

'When there was work to be done,' I said, 'It was I who comforted you. Now you've turned the tables on me and it's you who have the patience and the courage.'

She smiled, pushing her fingers in my hair.

'We seem to be the two halves that Plato spoke of … was it Plato?'

'I'm afraid I don't remember,' she said.

'It doesn't matter, now, anyway.'

'Darling?'

'Yes,' I said.

'You remember how, when I first took over the controls of the *Marie Lou*, I got tired so quickly?'

'Yes.'

'You were annoyed?'

'No.'

'Why were you annoyed?'

'I wasn't annoyed.'

'Because I was overcorrecting and because I really couldn't cope … because I was just a hindrance?'

'I was thinking of you as a man – '

'As a pilot?'

'If you like.'

'I knew … I was afraid … it seems stupid … I was afraid you wouldn't love me any more!'

I caught her hand and kissed it. 'That's over now.'

'I'm glad,' she said, 'especially about the love part.'

'When I say that's all that's left to me,' I answered. 'I'm not using a line out of a jazz song.'

✕

I grew drowsy and the voices of the others became senseless, losing all animation, and binding, thatched my mind so that I slept once more, pain forgotten in the merciful kin of death.

Then I saw Jack and Moira waving frantically and firing pyrotechnics while a Service aircraft circled overhead. God! I thought, another dream. For how many days now had I been seeing machines? Hearing fighters? The scream of the blower mingling with the wind in the wires, with airscrew noise and the engine's song? Or twins coming into land with the motors popping as the airscrews overran the throttle settings? Or light aeroplanes with the purr of their tiny hundred-horse-power engines?

This was worse in its actuality for I recognized the type, a Royal Air Force Moose fitted for desert flying, saw the pilot looking over his shoulder as he approached, noticed details of fuselage and empennage, heard the rumble as she went down for a three-point landing,

Then Moira came limping towards me, wringing her hands and laughing hysterically and I knew that it was no dream.

'You were lucky,' the pilot said as we ate the supplies he had brought. 'I'd finished my search detail and was going back to the aerodrome when my gunner saw your red light.'

'We thought you'd missed us,' Jack said.

'We had to find you.' The pilot was young and blue-eyed,

shy and tremendously pleased at having located us. 'I got a bearing from base on the long aerial before we landed. The lads will be here in a brace of shakes.'

'What an awful country this must be to fly in,' Moira looked up from a chicken sandwich.

'It's not bad actually Miss Barratt. We get plenty of hours in and there's usually active service round the corner. Some sheik or other is always starting trouble and believe you me, his troops are no cissies. Then we buy Arab ponies in the villages, break 'em ourselves and get some polo which is pretty wizard on a Flying Officer's pay ...'

There was something I wanted to ask him, I struggled to remember what it was, hearing a great roaring, conscious of a splitting headache. Then my knees wobbled and I fell, uninterested in the flight hurrying to our rescue which would soon appear as specks on the horizon.

I was in hospital for some time and it was autumn when the boat train carried us up to Waterloo through the blue mists of a perfect English evening.

'What are you thinking about?' Moira asked softly.

I was gazing at the little villages sliding by, thatched and tree-bound in settled peacefulness. It seemed that in this scene there was not only a joyful sense of homecoming, but also an answer to all the striving in my nature. I thought of how, as a child, there was this sudden magic in ordinary things, this wonder in a known scene; how for no reason a flood of experience, almost indefinable, widened the narrow path of one's life.

'What are you thinking about?' she repeated.

'I was thinking about us,' I said.

'How we'll always be in love?'

'Yes.'

'Even when we're old?'

'Even when we're old.'

Sitting beside me, her body warm by mine, her very youthfulness seemed to mock the content of her hackneyed words.

'And find happiness?'

'That too, my dear.'

✕

The sky behind the sheds was grey with dawn when we arrived and the metallic beginning of another day fell unkindly on the faces of the newspaper men, airport officials, photographers, and friends who were grouped about the monoplane, showing the strain in their tired faces. The wind that swept the acrodrome was cold so that Moira shuddered as she leaned against me and the electric lights in the offices appeared homely and unspeakably comforting.

'Where's Jack?' Moira asked.

'He'll be along right now.' As Chuck spoke I saw his fellow pilot leave the control tower and walk towards us across the tarmac, a swash-buckler in sheepskin-lined flying-coat (for it was winter, the country pitiless with streaks of dirty snow). Flashlights splashed in the darkness as he approached with microphone swinging beneath his chin and a little fat man and two girls running at his side.

'Remember, darling?'

'I remember,' I said.

'It was good of you to come down,' Jack began. 'I feel responsible, dragging staid married people out of bed at this hour.'

'All set?' Chuck asked.

'Yes, the weather's good. We'll be off as soon as the engines are warm.'

'Be careful, my dears,' Moira said and then added pensively: 'Now, I rather wish we were both coming with you!'

'You two don't want a record to make you happy.'

We shook hands and Moira kissed them.

'All the luck in the world,' I said. They smiled as they turned.

The roar of each motor cloaked all sound on the aerodrome, then Jack throttled down, waved away the chocks and taxied out, the noise now drowning the thin cries of the onlookers. The machine, heavy with petrol, rocked as it moved, seemingly ugly on the bristling legs of its undercarriage. But when it became airborne and the slowly rotating wheels tucked themselves into its belly, it turned into a silhouette of beauty, a slim and lovely thing tearing into the loneliness of the sunrise.

We stood arm in arm till the machine disappeared and the drone of its engines no longer fell upon our ears.

Merioneth
East Riding   *Mcmxxxviii*
Northumberland

Notes on the text

BY KATE MACDONALD

Many of the technical aviation terms in this volume are explained in the narrative. Specialist aviation resources are available if readers want to find out the meaning of terms not given here, which are those it was felt necessary to unpack for the better appreciation of plot and story.

England Is My Village

1 England Is My Village

Chinese game: mahjong, the Chinese tile-based game for four players which became popular in the West from the 1920s. 'Three Characters' is the name of a tile in the game.

The Field: popular monthly magazine for the hunting, shooting, fishing and sporting classes.

the show: RAF slang for a planned military action or situation.

erks: RAF slang for aircraftsman, the lowest rank in the service, usually serving as ground crew.

new twin fighters: twin-engined fighter planes.

fitter: the ground crew mechanic responsible for servicing and installation of the aircraft's equipment.

dope: dope was the slang name for a plasticized lacquer made from nitrocelluloid, a highly flammable coating that also stiffened the fabric of the plane's wings, increasing its aerodynamic capacity. Too much dope on the aircraft's fabric would reduce its speed efficiency.

hunkey-dorey: originally from the nineteenth century, slang for satisfactory, fine.

airscrews: the propellers and their blades.

cocks: valves in the pilot's dashboard to regulate the flow of fuel.

Archie: RAF slang for anti-aircraft fire from the ground.

ailerons: hinged control surfaces on the edges of the wings, which can be manipulated mechanically to let the plane turn by raising one wing higher than the other to bank.

tracer: intermittently glowing machine-gun fire, showing its direction to enable adjustments in direction to be made, but also revealing where it came from.

up on the beam: approached to fly parallel with the bomber.

got his: was killed.

2 The Man Who Was Dead

Meyrowitz goggles: the leading brand of protective eyewear worn by aviators between the wars.

shop: technical talk.

flight: a bomber squadron was divided into two flights, each consisting of up to eight planes with their crew.

bumps: pockets of air turbulence.

Irvin: the classic leather flying jacket lined with fleece.

shot up the camp: flown low as if to attack with machine-gun fire, to give the ground staff a fright.

dicky: a co-pilot with less experience.

wings: the uniform badge denoting a pilot.

Pip, Squeak and Wilfred: slang for the three medals awarded to most British servicemen who had served in the First World War from 1914: the 1914 (or 1914–15) Star, the British War Medal and the British Victory Medal. They denoted survival and experience.

stripes: the narrator has the stripes of a flight lieutenant or a higher officer's rank.

3 Too Young To Die

Zulu war medal: their joke is that that nurse is old enough to have served in the Anglo-Zulu War of 1879.

Guest Night: when a particularly energetic party would take place in honour of guests at the officers' mess.

Moose: the PZL.37, a Polish twin-engined bomber manufactured in 1938–39 and exported abroad, used by the RAF, among other air forces.

a lot of types: different variants of plane design.

his people: public-school slang for his family, parents and siblings.

4 Test Flight

longerons: part of the inner fuselage structure or frame, bearing load along the length of the aircraft.

Sutton harness: a safety harness with a quick release mechanism.

before a wing should stall: before that wing engine stalled and lost power.

put on full bank: tipped the plane so that it sloped steeply to the right, to begin the roll.

climbed to twelve thousand: the pilot has given himself enough height to be able to bail out and descend by parachute if the plane failed on this manoeuvre.

5 Night Exercise

logs: logbooks.

sidcot: an all-in-one flying suit worn over the service uniform.

Pitot head: the head of a device to measure air speed in a range of air pressures and temperatures.

7 You've Got to be Dumb to be Happy

ragged: public-school term for being teased, which can be on a scale ranging from light joshing to physical bullying.

batman: an officer's servant and valet, drawn from the non-commissioned ranks.

The World Owes Me A Living

Wilfred Owen: from Owen's poem 'Strange Meeting', written in 1918.

Chapter 1

raspberry: general RAF slang for a formal reprimand, fraternal derision or a aggressor's sneer.

pre-war kites: aeroplanes predating 1914.

piling up: crashing.

flannel: flannel was for casual daywear, whereas evening dress was required for dining.

Town: London.

DTs: *delirium tremens*, the shakes, and a sudden freezing brought on by hallucinations from drinking too much.

Sink that drink: in the original text this phrase is followed by 'and come down to dinner', which is an editorial slip since the characters are already at dinner.

Chapter 2

Waterloo: meeting at the station to get the train to the match in the south of England.

Camel: Camel cigarettes had been advertised for years as the RAF's cigarette of choice.

DR paper: examination on dead reckoning navigation, demonstrating competence at predicting the intended route, airspeed and time modified by wind speed and direction.

jen: early or alternate spelling of the more familiar 'gen', information.

barnstormers: stunt pilots giving demonstrations. The scheme Chuck is thinking of will take the public up for joy-rides, which requires a different calibre of pilot.

jerkwater: insignificant, too small to consider.

from the deck: from the ground.

full bank: a full turn of the plane along the nose to tail axis.

glebe: a field belonging to the parish for the vicar's use.

queer: odd, not quite right.

Chapter 3

front seat: the aeroplane seats were one in front of the other, with the pilot behind the passenger or trainee pilot, where an instructor could see the trainee's actions and take over the controls as needed.

phthisis: tuberculosis.

helping with the books: with the accounts.

London Gazette: still in existence, this is one of the statutory journals of record of the UK government and its departments, recording, among other matters, the commissions and transferrals of military staff.

Rabelaisian: François Rabelais was a sixteenth-century French author of grotesque satires and bawdy songs and jokes, his name now a metaphor for scatological and vulgar appetites.

In your flight: under Paul's command when he served in the RAF.

Kemble: RAF Kemble began operations as a flight training aerodrome in 1938. By not seeing the Service Casey means that the younger pilots have never flown in war.

lousy with money: having too much money.

tickets: flight certificates, which presumably Casey lacks.

browned-off: fed up, bored.

half shut, gassed: drunk.

pin: leg.

Chapter 4

leeward: away from the wind.

getting up stage: causing a commotion, the centre of attention.

Shire hoof: of a Shire horse, the largest and heaviest breed.

high stepper: expensive, demanding special treatment.

Chapter 5

one of our leading women writers: this may have been Rosamund Lehmann, whose *The Weather in the Streets* had been published in 1936, or Elizabeth Bowen, with *The Death of the Heart* in 1938.

mannequin show: a fashion show at a local department store to attract women buyers.

FTS: Flying Training School.

AOC: Air Officer Commanding, the senior officer in charge.

Chapter 6

listening to faint whisperings: hearing other voices on a phone line that should be silent could be caused by a phone cable inadvertently acting as a radio antenna, or when two lines connect by mistake.

five degrees of bank on: using the metaphor of aerobatics, acting showily to impress spectators.

antimacassar: a small cloth laid over the back of the chair to prevent hair oil staining the fabric. A Victorian invention, in tune with the over-furnished and fussy contents of the room.

Cook's tours: an early form of package holiday, for travellers too inexperienced or unenterprising to decide their own holidays.

ASI: airspeed indicator.

get a fix: work out your position on the map with the compass and/or the stars.

knock: a sound made when the petrol feed to the engine has a bubble of air in it, which might be a sign that the tank is empty.

jib: sailing term from the small sail at the front of a vessel, meaning to move restlessly, not stick to a fixed course, to respond adversely to stress.

Chapter 7

twins: twin engined.

muscular Christian: what we might now call an Evangelical, with an element of rugby-playing heartiness.

Klem Swallows and Leopard Moths: the Klemm Swallow and De Havilland Leopard Moths were recently designed monoplanes, first built in 1933. The Avro had been designed during the First World War.

Gosport tubes: speaking tubes fitted into the aircraft frame and connected to the helmets, with which the pilot and passenger could speak to each other.

Chapter 8

give me a swing: turn the propeller to make the engine catch.

Chapter 9

the Robert: an archaic slang name for a policeman, from Sir Robert Peel who established the force.

Hyde Park: Speaker's Corner in Hyde Park in London is the traditional location for *ex tempore* speakers informing the world of their views.

flare path: the lines of lights set on each side of the runway to guide night-flying aircraft in to land.

Aldis lamp: signalling lamp.

goosh: possibly slang for wet weather.

Chapter 10

stud: collars were attached to the neck and front of the shirt with detachable studs.

shot up Murrys: possibly Murray's Club, the long-established cabaret club in London's Soho, where the men would have had a good time.

jerry: a toilet.

Chapter 12

NCO: a corporal or sergeant, non-commissioned officer.

C of A: Certificate of Airworthiness.

ramp: a con.

Chapter 13

buy it: be killed.

Chapter 15

stalled: when an aeroplane wing is no longer able to generate enough lift for controlled flight (due to low speed or high angle-of-attack) and the plane subsequently drops towards the ground.

Chapter 17

acks: RAF slang for air mechanics.

The Last Chapter

up sun: straight into the sun.

empennage: the tail unit of the plane, including the rudder.